The Wrong Hands

Nigel Richardson

The Wrong Hands

OXFORD
UNIVERSITY PRESS

OXFORD
UNIVERSITY PRESS

Great Clarendon Street, Oxford OX2 6DP

Oxford University Press is a department of the University of Oxford.
It furthers the University's objective of excellence in research, scholarship,
and education by publishing worldwide in

Oxford New York

Auckland Cape Town Dar es Salaam Hong Kong Karachi
Kuala Lumpur Madrid Melbourne Mexico City Nairobi
New Delhi Shanghai Taipei Tokyo Toronto

With offices in

Argentina Austria Brazil Chile Czech Republic France Greece
Guatemala Hungary Italy Japan Poland Portugal Singapore
South Korea Switzerland Thailand Turkey Ukraine Vietnam

Oxford is a registered trade mark of Oxford University Press
in the UK and in certain other countries

British Library Cataloguing in Publication Data
Data available

ISBN-10: 0-19-271976-9
ISBN-13: 978-0-19-271976-8

1 3 5 7 9 10 8 6 4 2

Typeset in Sabon by Palimpsest Book Production Limited,
Polmont, Stirlingshire

Printed and bound by Mackays of Chatham plc, Chatham, Kent

Acknowledgements

I am indebted to Clare Alexander for her vision, Liz Cross for her belief, and Miren Lopategui for everything else.

To Miren

　　　　　must I be content with discontent
As larks and swallows are perhaps with wings?

Edward Thomas

Chapter 1

I was going to start with the plane crash because that's how come I met Jennifer. But you need to know about my hands first.

I was born with disaster areas for hands. My fingers had these folds of flesh between them that looked like the inside of an umbrella when it's closed up. They could get really clogged with dirt if I didn't scrub them properly every night with a scrubbing brush. It was Doc Morrison who told me I had to do that. Mum took me to see him when I was five. Not about my hands; I think I had mumps or something. But Doc Morrison noticed the hands. He picked them up as if they were CDs and turned them over and over. That moment, with this doc frowning and staring, staring and frowning, was when I first started to feel bad about them.

Mum said, 'Oh, we've been through that. No one can find anything wrong.' She meant, after I was born I'd been taken to see loads of doctors and hospitals about my hands and no one had a clue why they were like they were. But it didn't matter because they weren't doing any harm to anyone.

Doc Morrison said, 'I can't say I've seen anything

quite like it. On the other hand—ha! ha! no pun intended—if they function normally—'

Mum said, 'He doesn't seem to have any trouble.' And she smiled at me.

Doc Morrison said, 'There's a lot to be said for leaving well alone. Just make sure he keeps them clean. A good scrub between the fingers every night. Otherwise there could be a hygiene problem.'

This is how we thought of my hands, me and my mum and dad. As things to be scrubbed. The only time they were mentioned was when Mum reminded me each night to clean them properly. Dad never talked about them even once. But I would catch him staring at them; when I reached out to grab the marg, for instance.

Actually he did mention them once, or nearly mention them. I had this nervous habit of stretching my fingers apart. The skin in between would sort of rustle as it stretched. I can tell you what it sounded like because once I heard the almost identical sound. It sounded like dry leaves swirling around in a hallway when someone opens the front door. It was quite loud, and it used to drive Dad nuts. Usually, when I did it, he would just go still and stare at me until I had to look away. Once he exploded. 'For God's sake stop that.'

'Stop what?' I said.

He exploded again. He thought I was being a smart-arse but I wasn't. I just didn't know what else to say.

'You know what,' he said. 'Otherwise I'll make you wear gloves. If I can find a pair that's big enough.'

I stopped stretching my fingers apart when I was around Dad.

On my first day at school a big crowd gathered round me in the playground, trying to get a look at them. Because there were so many people, all jostling to clock them, someone said, 'Just hold 'em up high, you spakky,' so I lifted my arms and everyone laughed. They got a bit bored with my hands after a day or two but at least once a day, for my whole time at primary school, some kid would remember to shout, 'Oi, Spakky, hands,' and I would lift them up, and everyone would laugh. Including me, I wasn't stupid. And I wasn't being a wimp, not totally. I was quite strong, especially in my hands, even if I was weedy looking. But you don't stand a chance against five of them. And anyway, all I had to do was lift my hands, and after we'd all had our little laugh it shut them up, for a while anyway.

The name Spakky stuck right through primary school and on to secondary school. That first day at Sir Roger de Coverley comprehensive wasn't great. It was like walking out in front of a 67,000 crowd at Old Trafford, except they weren't cheering they were laughing. Plus, a lot of them had their phones out and they were taking pictures and zapping them off to mates, maybe even all over the world. All these kids I'd never seen before, from primary schools all over town, they all seemed to know. They all seemed to be waiting. They even chanted like a footie crowd. 'Spak-ky! Spak-ky!' A really bad thing was, girls were doing it, too. I liked girls, so that was sad. At primary school it had been mostly blokes.

Every day wasn't great. It was like waking up and looking in the mirror and finding a spot the size of a plate on your forehead. A volcano of a plook with red sides and a yellow hole where the lava's about to spurt out. No, it was worse than that. It was like having *two* volcanoes, fresh and smoking, every day. I liked it in winter when it was really cold. Then I could wear gloves. Once the heating in the classroom broke down and I could wear them indoors too. That was brilliant, to have my hands covered up all day for a proper reason. I wore this trackie top all the time, even in summer when it was hot. It had these big pockets in the front that were more like holes where I could bury my hands.

It's a funny thing about names. When I came down to London, they didn't call me anything except my real name, Graham (not counting the things Uncle George and Derek sometimes called me, like Junior Joe, or Joe Strummer, or Charlie Arse-Face). I'd never been to London before but the name thing made me feel at home straightaway. And my real home was the place where they called me bad names and pretty much hated me, even my own parents. Dad anyway. Mum was more complicated.

So here's the background, and then I'll get on to the terrible thing that happened. Me and my mum and dad lived on the outskirts of a medium-sized town in the flat, industrial part of Yorkshire. When I mentioned the place to people in London they either said they hadn't heard of it, or they thought it was in the Dales because that was the only bit of Yorkshire they knew. But there were no olde tea shoppes round our way. From my bedroom window I could see two coal pits and the cooling towers of a power station. These big towers looked like giant mugs of hot coffee, with great clouds of steam rising off them in slow motion. Between the house and the nearest of the coal pits was a motorway and a railway. The railway went to London. Trains screamed along it at night. When I heard them I would think of all-night gambling; fat, rich blokes stepping out of a giant hotel into Park Lane and not knowing what time of day it was, or even what day it was full stop.

Our house was a brick cube on an estate of about fifty or a hundred identical brick cubes. The people who lived in them all worked in things to do with railways or power stations or coal pits. They drove company cars like Vauxhall Vectras, and wore suits and carried clipboards and kept hard hats and wellies in the boot for site visits. My dad sold cement. His perk was getting free cement to build a rockery. A huge flatbed lorry turned up just to deliver one bag of cement.

We had a different front door from everyone else's. It was wood-coloured with panes of mock old-fashioned glass like the bottom of bottles. Then other houses got different things, like shutters that were only for show (too narrow to cover the windows and anyway they were nailed to the wall). And slowly the houses began to look a bit different from each other. But that didn't fool me. To me, they were always the same.

I remember being about seven and stepping out from the side gate of our house practically straight into open fields. I was quite happy then; I mean, waking up in the morning wasn't too bad and I could go for nearly a whole hour during the day without thinking about my hands. I tagged along with other kids on the estate. At school they were some of the major ones shouting Spakky etc., but in the holidays they were quite shy and hardly mentioned my hands. We skidded about on our bikes and went down to the railway crossing to watch the express trains scream by to London. Next to the railway crossing was a little stream where we fished for sticklebacks with bright green nets on the end of bamboo poles. We put the fish in old jam jars and took them home but they never lived more than a few days. I made a stickleback graveyard at the bottom of the garden. I was just floating through that summer like the dandelion clocks through the fields. But good things, even just OK things, never last. (Hey, pay attention! His name is Graham Sinclair. This is his wisdom.)

I was riding my bike down a lane between two fields when a man came out of the bushes and held his hand up. The way he did it reminded me of a traffic cop in a comedy film I once saw set in Italy (he got knocked down by a runaway Fiat). The man who came out of the bushes had grey stubble that looked like you could strike a match on it. He said he worked for the secret service and was on an undercover mission to spy on some criminals who were operating in the neighbourhood. He said I looked good secret service material. Would I like to join him? I didn't ask for his ID but he offered me a card anyway. It could have been anything. I was embarrassed to hold it for too long or read it properly in case he clocked my hands and made a comment. I handed it back and said I had to be going. Then he said, 'Before you join you'll have to have a medical. Just to make sure you're A1 health-wise.'

I wasn't daft, even then. I got back on my bike and rode home. I waited two days before telling Mum, I'm not sure why. The police came round. Dad exploded because I'd waited before telling them. The police never found anyone. After that I wasn't allowed to go out into the fields and play on my own.

Which wasn't such a big deal as it happened because the open ground and fields were disappearing anyway, so even if I'd been allowed to play in them, they wouldn't have been there because they were being covered by more houses. And roads. Even the little stream was covered over. The wood that protected the magical oak tree was cut down, including the magical oak tree obviously. These old blocks of stone that we said were the gateway to the centre of the Earth—carted off on a flatbed lorry.

It was like a dream that there had ever been anything around us but more houses. Each house had a spindly little tree in the front garden. The trees were strapped to poles by a piece of green rubber that went grey in the winter and then rotted off. Next to the trees were these manhole covers with big dimples in them that looked like the tray Mum made Yorkshire puddings in. We had roast beef and Yorkshire every Sunday. When it was raining the windows steamed up and I would be told off for making portholes in the steam to see out of. At night I listened to the trains going to London. All curled up in what is called the foetal position, with my hands between my knees.

* * *

When I was twelve, at the end of my first year at Sir Roger de Coverley, I made a friend called Brian. We weren't real friends. I knew that even then. But nobody else would have us so we just sort of joined up. Brian was big and clumsy and quite rude. Not just to me but to everyone, which is partly why no one liked him. I know we looked funny together because people used to laugh at us as we went by, even adults sometimes. I must have been ten centimetres shorter than Brian, plus I was thin and weedy-looking compared to him (except for the hands, of course). There was one thing I was grateful to him for. He never mentioned the hands. I don't think that was because he was kind, though. He just didn't want me mentioning anything to get my own back, like his gigantic feet or the way he walked on tiptoe, tipped forward on his huge feet, the way loonies do.

In the holidays I would cycle to Brian's house when his mum and dad and older brother were out. We would look at porn mags belonging to his brother. Silently, sitting side by side on his brother's bed with Brian turning the pages. One day he met me in the driveway with his bike. He'd been waiting for me. He said he'd found something secret. I followed him and he went down near the railway line. It was all built up now. Closes and Drives and Avenues and Boulevards. He took me through a gap in a hedge. 'See,' he said.

It was a ditch. Deep and dry. 'Let's make a den,' he said. He kicked at the sandy soil with his size 10 trainers.

'A den?' I said. Dens were for childhood, and childhood had gone, in case he hadn't noticed. We were reading porn mags now. 'We're not kids any more, Brian,' I said.

'Not kids, no,' Brian said, 'but you've got secrets, haven't you?' and for a split second I thought he knew. I felt myself blushing. Somehow he'd discovered my secret, and that was what all this was about. He didn't really want to be my friend, he just wanted to get close to me so he could find out more about my secret. But I was being paranoid. (Then I was, anyway. But as they say, just because you're paranoid it doesn't mean to say they're not out to get you. I told Jennifer that and she pretended she thought it was really funny. She pretended she hadn't heard it before. But I'm sure she was just being polite because it's quite a common saying and a woman her age would have known it.)

But Brian didn't know about my secret. He didn't even see me blush, he was so desperate to make out he had thrilling secrets of his own. He raised his eyebrows, he puffed out his cheeks and did a spooky thing with his eyes so that one looked up and the other looked down and his head looked like an old doll with those eyeballs that roll. 'OK,' I said.

We got on quite well when we were fixing the den. We waited until it got quite dark and then we lifted some planks from a building site where they were still building a house. We put the planks across the top of the ditch at its blocked-off end to make a roof. We put sacking on the planks and chucked some soil and weeds on it and then we had to go home because it was almost dark and soon my dad would get in his car and cruise the streets slowly like an American cop in a film, pretending to look for me and hoping it would take a long time so he could really lose his temper and stop me going out again for about a week. That's what he was like.

The next day we went back. We wondered if any of the workmen had spotted the planks but they hadn't. We collected ferns and grass and bits of old brick and stuff and put that on the sacking, too, until you really couldn't tell there were planks underneath, it just looked like a bit of scrubby old field. Then we stepped back and looked at it. Our den. The entrance was like a filled-in D lying on its curved side. We jumped into the ditch and crouched down. We shuffled along and looked right in. It was dark so your eyes couldn't see anything for about ten seconds, and it smelt of worms.

Brian had brought some gear with him, a bit of old carpet and other stuff in a placky bag. We crawled into the den and unrolled the carpet and pushed its edges up against the soft, soily sides of the den. Then we got right on the carpet. Brian rustled in the carrier bag and clicked on a torch which lit up the inside of the bag as he was bringing it out. He shone the torch back into the bag and brought out a candle and a box of matches. 'Just in case,' he said. We lay back side by side. Brian shone the torch against the roof planks. Little puffs of soil were falling from the roof, you could see them fall. Some landed in my eye and some more on my lip, which I coughed away. We didn't say anything.

Where they were building the new house, on the other side of the hedge, you could hear a cement mixer chugging. The workmen were listening to a radio

10

playing Elvis Presley. They were whistling and one of them barked like a dog. It sounded so close we held our breath. Brian shone the torch on my face and I started to giggle. Then he started to. It seemed funny, that the workmen were so close and didn't know we were here. Plus, we had nicked some of their stuff to make the den and they didn't know that either. We had to pinch our nostrils together to stop ourselves laughing.

Brian clicked off the torch. When I turned my head I could see the whites of his eyes, glowing in the dark. I didn't plan to do what I did next. I just had all this soil and general crap between my fingers and it was really itching. So I did that stretching thing with my hands. The rustling and crackling sounded extra-loud in the den. I could sense Brian's whole body go tense, like he was giving off static electricity. He clicked on the torch and said, 'Sshh, wassat?' The whites of his eyes were flashing at me.

I didn't say anything. I couldn't believe Brian couldn't hear my heart thumping. Because I was going to tell him, I really was. I was going to show him and I was going to tell him. He was my new friend, my first real friend. And I felt happy then, lying in that den with the workmen whistling outside and a little puff of soil falling on my bare knee, tickling my bare knee just enough so it felt good but not so I needed to itch it. I didn't know, until that moment, how much I needed to tell someone my secret. I opened my mouth to say it. Then I closed it. How would I put it? I thought of the sentence I would say. My heart was thumping away. But then it

11

stopped thumping quite so hard because I knew the moment had passed. I had chickened out.

Brian said, 'Oh no. It's chuffing rats.'

Brian said, 'I'm off.' He left behind the candle and matches. And the carpet. I asked him if he was coming back. He said he didn't know. I heard him tugging his bike through the hedge. Then there was silence. Not even the workmen making a noise. Friday. They must have knocked off early. I lay back in the almost dark and thought about what I almost did, i.e. tell Brian. I was glad now that I hadn't told him. I decided I didn't like him. But I still wanted to tell somebody. It was like going to the end of the diving board and looking down into the swimming pool. There would be a next time, and next time I would dive off the diving board.

I got the candle and made a hole in the soil to the side of the carpet for it to stand in. I was going to light it, then I heard a noise outside. I thought Brian had come back to get his bit of carpet. That would be typical Brian; I was surprised he hadn't taken it in the first place. The noise stopped, then started again. Somebody coming through the hedge. Walking about outside. But nobody came into the den. I said, 'Brian?' and the noise stopped. I crawled to the den's entrance and looked out.

I was surprised how dark it was. You could still see but everything was at that stage where it goes black and white, just shapes and sky. Right in front of the den was the silhouette of a person. I thought of the man who came out of the bushes. I had to stop myself making a noise. Then I saw it was a girl. She was looking away from the den, turning her head sideways like she was trying to catch a sound with her ears. She moved away from the den, walking slowly. Then she stopped and looked down. She pulled something up from the ground. It was my bike. I'd just dumped it there and chucked some grass and stuff over it. She pulled the bike right up and leant on the handlebars. Then she turned round and began to push the bike towards the hedge. I could hear the wheels ticking. I knew who the girl was. Kylie Blounce.

Kylie lived in the next street to mine. She'd been in my class at primary school and was at Sir Roger de Coverley but not in the same class. I was quite afraid of her because she was very sarcastic, especially about my hands. She didn't call me Spakky like everyone else. She called me Flipper and this was worse somehow. Like she was so grossed out by me she'd taken the trouble to work out her own insult rather than using the normal one. It wasn't just my hands that got her going, either. Whatever I did or said she was sarcastic.

Now here she was, Little Miss Sarky, pushing my bike towards the hedge. I didn't know what to do. I didn't want to say anything because she would just be sarcastic again. She would say something like, 'Dens are pathetic; don't you know anything, Flipper?' Plus, I would give away the den and we'd never be able to use it again. But she was nicking my bike. And even though I would know where it was, i.e. in Kylie's dad's garage, I wouldn't be able to get it back, because how would I explain how I knew it was there? I would have to wait until I saw Kylie riding it, which may be never.

I came out of the den. 'Kylie,' I said.

Kylie wasn't sarcastic at all. She didn't even call me Flipper. It was like I'd met a different Kylie. She came into the den and I lit the candle. We lay side by side and I looked at her. Something happened when I was looking at her. It was like my blood went heavy. Her skin in the candlelight was silky like it was out of focus a bit. I realized I'd never looked at her closely before. She had cheekbones that looked like the ends of Mum's padded coathangers, silky and hard at the same time. I didn't smell worms any more, I smelt apples. Kylie smelt of apples.

We didn't really say anything. We just kept looking at each other and grinning and once, out of nowhere, I gave this big laugh and I felt snot come out of my nose a bit and I had to wipe it away with the back of my hand. Which freaked me because I'd been keeping my hands out of view but I couldn't do anything else. But Kylie didn't seem to notice. She just said, 'What?' She didn't really say it actually, more just mouthed it.

Maybe we could have carried on like that for ages. Maybe we would have ended up being really close friends. But then I said what I said and everything changed. I didn't really know what I meant by it, it just came out. Sometimes you get days where it's really sunny and hot and then it just switches, the sky goes dark and it chucks it down. And then it goes sunny and hot again.

14

And when it's dark and raining you can't remember what it was like when it was hot and sunny, and vice versa.

It was like it was hot and sunny in that den (even though obviously it was really dark and we had a candle on the go) and then I said, 'I want to show you something', and it was instantly dark and rainy.

I thought it would switch back, like weather can. But it didn't. Kylie said she had to be going. She sat up on her shins. She had this very fine hair on her arms like the gold threads inside electric wires. Soil from the roof of the den had got caught in the hair and she was brushing it off. She wasn't looking at me now. I was sure she was going to say something sarcastic, call me Flipper. 'No,' I said, 'please don't go, Kylie.'

I reached out my hand and held her wrist. I stopped her brushing her arm. She was looking at my hand now. Really looking, like she was inspecting a plate of spaghetti for broken glass. And I felt like I was walking along that diving board again. I could feel the board shaking under my feet, and I knew that this time I was going to dive.

Chapter 2

All I wanted to do was show Kylie Blounce my hands weren't just ugly. I wanted her to know they could be beautiful. But that wasn't what happened. I just got myself a new name, an even worse one. I was going to say that Kylie betrayed me. But she didn't, not quite. It's complicated.

After what happened, she ran home yelling to the moon like a werewolf. I'd twisted my ankle so I didn't stand a chance of catching her up. For a few minutes I just stood there being a dork, my brain going round and round and not getting anywhere. The only idea I had was a stupid one: going down to the railway crossing and trying to hitch a ride on one of the trains that went to London. The kind of thing that unshaven blokes with serious blue eyes do in American movies. Solving a problem by leaving it behind. Moving on to the next life. But real life isn't like that (listen and learn here). You can't just run away from stuff, because stuff runs after you. And sooner or later it catches you up. Besides, the trains didn't stop at the railway crossing.

I set off home. I was scared shitless. I couldn't believe I'd been so stupid. Why had I thought I could trust

Kylie of all people? The whole idea seemed insane now. When I thought of what Mum would say, I could feel my neck start to sweat. Then the sweat dried and there was a breeze and it felt like a hand made out of ice was gripping my neck as I limped home through the almost-dark.

Even so, I wasn't expecting what was waiting for me. As I came round the corner of our street, I was hit by all this light coming the other way. It came from the headlights of the police car parked outside our house; it came from the house itself where the front door had been left open and Mum had forgotten to lower the kitchen blind; it came from the open doors of houses up and down the street. It was like that bit at the end of *Close Encounters of the Third Kind*, and not just because of the light. Because of the people, too. The silhouettes of silent people in doorways, behind windows. I didn't twig at first. I thought maybe a gas main had burst or something. But the way everyone turned and stared as I walked down the street, I knew Kylie Blounce must have landed me in it big-time.

Sometimes you dread things but when they happen they are not as bad as you thought they were going to be. In fact, if you make yourself think they're going to be terrible, you're relieved when they're not quite so bad. This time I thought things were going to be bad. And they were even worse. But they were also better in a way. That's what I mean about things being complicated.

* * *

17

From the corner of the street to our front door was the longest walk of my life. I was plodding from the condemned cell to the execution chamber, and I hadn't even had an anything-you-want final meal (mine would be Chicken Jalfrezi) to set me up. I'd never seen so many neighbours before. I felt their eyes going through me from both sides of the street, from bedrooms and kitchens and garden sheds. There'd be kids from Sir Roger de Coverley in there, standing behind their mums and dads, telling them what to think about old Spakky. Telling them to think the worst. Sometimes, when I was coming out of school, I'd see a kid who was a major Spakky-caller meeting his mum or dad. I'd catch his eye, like I was saying, 'Go on, call me names now, in front of your mum,' and he'd just look away like he'd never seen me before. There were at least four kids like that who lived on our street. Now their parents would be saying, 'Oh, we thought he was odd but harmless,' and the kids would be going, 'No, he's seriously weird.'

I didn't look left or right, I concentrated on getting to our house. A policeman was still in the police car, listening to the police radio. As I got nearer I could hear it crackling and squawking and a voice saying, '*Roger delta tango bla bla over.*' Another cop was stood half in and half out of our hallway. He had handcuffs hanging from his belt. I wondered if he'd try to use them on me. I wondered if they'd fit round my wrists. When I scrunched on the gravel in the drive, the cop looked round and said, 'Graham Sinclair? In here, son.'

The cop didn't get out of the way, he just lifted his

arm. I ducked under it, went along the hallway and into the lounge and it was like a footballer coming out of the players' tunnel. In the lounge were the crowd. It was a relief, not to feel the neighbours' eyes coming at me from all directions. But now there were eyes coming at me from the front, dead close, full on. Eyes that I could see, not just imagine. Eyes are weird things. Sometimes they're amazing, other times they look gross and squidgy, more like internal organs that you're never meant to see than things you should have right in your face. There must have been sixteen or twenty eyes in that room and every one of them looked like animal giblets. (I had my trackie top on, as per usual. My hands went straight in their holes and never came out till I was up in my bedroom half an hour later.)

Mum came towards me and said, 'Graham?' She meant, 'Is it true?' I didn't know the answer to that; I wasn't sure yet what Kylie had said. Mum tried to hold me but I pushed her off with my shoulder and she just stood there, next to the old brass standard lamp that they bought from a shop near Lulworth Cove, that time we went on holiday. I didn't look in Mum's eyes, I didn't look at any eyes. Not Dad's, not Kylie's—I just saw enough to see Kylie's were red—not Mr Blounce's or Kylie's mum's, not a neighbour's whose name I didn't know but he had sticky-up hair and somebody once told me he was an alcoholic, not the fat neighbour's, she was a nurse, I think, with huge arms that were bare that night. Not the other policeman's.

I didn't look at any eyes and I didn't blush or cry. I don't think I even said anything hardly. People didn't like that, they thought I didn't care. But it wasn't that. Perhaps I was in shock, because what I thought was, my secret was about to be exposed. Mum had said that just telling one person would be bad enough. But all these people? You couldn't trust all of this lot to keep shtum, could you? I imagined them rushing home and phoning friends in, say, Bromsgrove. Emailing someone from Wyoming they had met once in Disneyland. Stepcousins in Singapore, etc. It would be all over the place in no time.

That's what I was thinking as I stared ahead, notlooking at all the eyes. Panic in my head. But I was also dead calm. Part of my brain was like a camera. My eyes stayed a bit out of focus but I was still noticing things. I'd never seen so many people in our lounge before and the whole place looked funny. The policeman had his helmet under his right arm and he was trying to write in his notebook with his right hand and he dropped the pencil and I thought, why don't you just put your helmet under your left arm? Kylie didn't just have red eyes, she was sniffling. She had marks on her arms, a cut on her leg, and a bruise on her cheekbone.

People talked at once and then shut up. Dad and Mr Blounce had a go at each other, which surprised me, Dad defending me. And Kylie suddenly had this full-on crying fit. Mrs Blounce hugged her and the fat nurse-lady said, 'Why don't we put the kettle on?', and Mum got angry at that and said, 'Why don't you mind your own business, *I'll* put the kettle on,' but she didn't move from where she was, next to the brass lamp. She didn't move because everything went quiet. The policeman was asking Kylie to say what happened.

The copper tried to sound all soft and concerned but it just came out like he had loads of phlegm in his throat. He said to Kylie, 'Kylie, tell us what happened. What Graham did to you. Just so we can hear it out of your mouth.'

Kylie was sobbing. You could hardly hear what she was saying. It was like listening to a mobile that keeps cutting out. We were all standing there, trying to listen to a Nokia with a dodgy signal. As she spoke, Mr Blounce was standing behind her, playing with her hair, saying stuff like, 'That's it, sweetheart', and 'Good girl'. The fat nurse was making the sort of noises you do to a dog that's just caught a bollock in the catflap. I could just make out, outside, the sound of the police walkie-talkie. I wasn't looking at Kylie; I still wasn't focusing on anyone or anything. I knew some people were looking at her, but most people were looking at me. Or they were going between me and Kylie with their eyes, I could sense it. They were waiting for me to show something. Just something. A blush or a tear or doing something with my feet.

Kylie said she went for a walk and found this bike. It turned out it was Graham Sinclair's bike. Graham came out of this ditch that he said was his den. Kylie went in the den and it was all OK. Was there anybody else in the den? No, there wasn't. Just Graham. What did they do in the den? Nothing, they just lay there. And then Kylie said she had to be getting back, it was getting dark. And that was when it all happened.

21

The sobs were getting worse. The eyes were all on me now. You could hardly make out what Kylie was saying. But this was it. I did react at this point. I screwed up my eyes. I knew when I opened them nothing would ever be the same again. That's what Mum told me. Why didn't she say something to stop what was going on? The world was about to flip over and go splat like a badly tossed pancake, and there was nothing I could do to catch it. When I opened my eyes, there it would be, all over the floor. And my life with it, all smashed.

But things were not happening as they should. My heart gave a back-flip of joy. The world was not changing because, guess what? Kylie was not telling the truth. She was not saying what really happened down by the den. I couldn't believe it but it was true. Kylie was lying. She was saying something completely different happened.

She was saying I hit her. I knocked her over. Hence the marks on her arms, etc. It was more than just hitting her, though. It was more than she had words for. Twice she opened her mouth to say what it was, and nothing came out, she was just standing there gasping for air. People shuffled in closer and bent their heads down to listen but still nothing came out. It was like they were all gathered round a really deep hole, trying to see the bottom. But there was no bottom, the hole just went on and on and the air got stuffier and stuffier till it smelt like rotten eggs and you couldn't breathe. And somewhere in there was the terrible thing I had done. For ever after, when people saw me, they saw that bottomless hole smelling of rotten eggs and containing that unspeakable thing.

Still, I was chuffed, considering. What they didn't know was the thing in the hole was my secret. And it wasn't terrible, it didn't smell of day-old farts. Quite the opposite. I know I shouldn't have grinned. Big mistake but I couldn't help it. I was just relieved. It was like I was waiting to receive a lethal injection and all they did in the end was slap me with a fish. But everyone saw me grinning and suddenly all these people were saying shocked things to me, including Dad. The copper said, 'What have you got to say, Graham? Is it true what Kylie says? Is that what happened?'

What could I say? I said nothing. Which meant GUILTY in big fluorescent letters, all jiggling about like an internet pop-up.

Mum grabbed the standard lamp and the shade went wonky and for a split second people took their eyes off me and looked at her.

Mum sent me to bed. She didn't kiss me, which normally didn't bother me. I could hear voices downstairs, then shouts, then it went quiet. I stood at my bedroom window with the lights off and watched everyone leaving. Alcoholic and Fat Nurse walked off down the middle of the road rather than on the pavement, like what had just happened was so important that normal rules didn't apply. Kylie took ages to walk down to her dad's car. Her dad had to take tiny little steps to go as slow as her. One of the cops gobbed on the lawn after my mum had closed the front door. Along the street, lights were being switched off but people weren't going off to watch the end of *The Bill*, they were rushing through to back rooms where they had their PCs set up. They were all giving their versions of what was in the bottomless hole, that's what I reckoned. And not one of them had a clue.

I watched the lights of a couple of trains go by on their way to London. I saw Dad going down to the shed. He had a bald patch and the streetlight shining off it made it look perfectly round and silver. If I'd been in a different mood I'd have laughed at how bright it looked. I heard Mum coming upstairs to bed.

I went out on to the landing. I whispered, 'I didn't hit Kylie. She's lying.' Mum stopped but she didn't say anything. She was holding a glass of water. I said it again. 'I didn't hit Kylie. All I did was—'

Mum said, 'I can't hear you.'

I started to say it again. To say it louder. But she stopped me. She held her hand with the glass of water in it up between her and me. She said, 'No, I mean . . . I won't take notice of you, Graham. Kylie won't either. Don't you see? No one will ever hear you, Graham, and that's the best way.' She started to whisper. 'Remember what we talked about, that time in Lulworth Cove?' I nodded. 'It's the best way, believe me.' And she ruffled my hair, which half made up for no kiss earlier.

Chapter 3

After the incident between me and Kylie, Mum developed this weird thing where she would hardly go out of the house. It wasn't because she didn't like going out, it was because she didn't like being clocked by all the nebby bastards on our street. As soon as she was away from the street she was OK as long as she didn't bump into a neighbour, which she did a few times at Morrison's (which is why she switched to Asda). So if she had to go shopping at Asda, for instance, she'd make Dad drive the car into the garage so she could get in it without being seen. Then she'd lie flat along the back seat till they'd got on the main road. Same thing on the way back, he'd have to drive the car into the garage so Mum could get out of the car and straight into the house without the neighbours clocking her. She was generally weird then. At tea, when I had to reach for the marg or chocolate spread, it wasn't just Dad who pretended not to stare at my hands.

I reckoned she needed help, but it was me who got it. Not that it *was* much help. The police and social workers made me go to see a psychiatrist in a hospital in Sheffield. There was a doll's house on the table in front of me and the doc said, 'Pretend this is your house.'

He picked up these little figures and said, this is your mum, this is your dad, this is you, now put yourself and your mum and dad in your house, where you would normally be. I put me in a bedroom, my mum in the garage, and my dad in the garden. 'What's your dad doing? Is he mowing the lawn?' said the doc and I said no, he's in his shed drinking whisky but there's no model shed so I just have to dump him in the garden. 'And your mum?' he said. She's off shopping in Asda, I said. The doc looked at me over the top of his glasses and made a note in his notebook.

Then he said, don't you ever get together? To eat for instance, or to watch television? It's true, Mum used to really like us watching this one programme in particular. She would call Dad out of the shed to watch it. It was about antiques and was incredibly boring but Mum said it was the kind of programme there should be more of on telly. She said it didn't harm anyone, which was true except if you count boring someone to death.

The doc said, take the figures and show me how you all get together in one room. So I picked up the figures and tried to stuff them into the lounge, where there was a little telly in the corner that looked like a matchbox painted silver. But the figures were too big to fit properly. They were as big as the entire length of the lounge which meant me and Mum and Dad would have been about three metres tall. I slotted them inside sideways, so we looked like sticklebacks in a grave. Then the doc said, 'Is that what it feels like in your house? All hemmed in, not enough room?'

* * *

26

I was called Perv by then. Brian never spoke to me again, except to call me Perv with all the rest. They used to deadleg me in the dinner queue and kick my shins under the table when we sat down to eat. Poke my hands with these light-sabre things we all had, force armpit spray down my throat in the changing rooms, and set fire to my hair. I can still smell the smell it made, my burning hair (halfway between bonfires and dust on a lightbulb). I didn't feel too bad about it though because I still had the secret. I even thought about letting it out. I had this fantasy where I'd do it in front of the whole school. I'd get all these people into the assembly hall and I'd go for it. Mum was usually there, somewhere near the front. Dad would be there, too, but he would be dressed like a caretaker, in grey overalls. He would be so busy adjusting the hydraulic mechanism on the doors he wouldn't even look at the stage.

The worst thing about that time was that no girls would talk to me. I'd always liked girls and I had a bit of a crush on this girl who was in *Coronation Street*. I got a shock when I saw her being interviewed as herself, a real person. She looked completely different and she spoke different. Much posher. Plus she didn't live in Coronation Street country at all, she lived in London. I made some comment and Mum said, 'What did you expect, she's an actress. They put things on, that's their job. That's probably not the real person anyway. They're still acting, even when they pretend not to be. Best get interested in a *real* girl, Graham.' And then she looked away.

She looked away because she'd said something stupid. The thing was, because of what I'd done to Kylie Blounce—because of what they *said* I'd done to her—girls weren't allowed to see me. Or even talk to me. And I wasn't allowed out because I might get up to something, in inverted commas. I did see one girl a few times. I know why she agreed to see me. Because she had eczema. Not just a bit on her hand or her leg or whatever, but all over. Like her whole body was made of sandpaper. I didn't mention her eczema and she didn't mention my hands. We never spoke it out loud but we both knew that was the deal, and it worked for a while, we got on really well. But then her mum found out and phoned my mum and that was the end of that.

Then a terrible thing happened. That loony who'd come out of the bushes at me when I was a little kid must have come back. That's what me and Mum reckoned, even though the police never solved the case. What happened was, that down near the railway line, a man assaulted two little girls. Then he ran off.

The girls went home and reported it to their mums and their mums reported it to the police and the next thing was, the police were knocking on our door. I was being interviewed by them. Twice. Once in our house and once in the local police station which had one of those really old-fashioned blue lamps outside and was in the pit village that was next to the coal pit. The neighbours saw the police car parking outside our house and going away again. Coming back, going away, and bringing me back. Dad was furious about that. Furious

28

with me! I mean, I didn't drive the police car. (But I *could* have, as you'll find out.) Mum just cried. She said, 'Why can't they just come in an ordinary car? Because they like humiliating us, that's why.'

Mum and the social worker came with me. The social worker was one of the people who took me to the hospital in Sheffield. Mum lost her temper with the police. She said, 'He's fourteen going on seven. You said the girls said it was a man. Graham's not a man. Look at him.' The police kept going on at me. Where was I on the afternoon of bla bla? They spoke like cops in telly series. I did that thing where I went all quiet but inside I wasn't quiet. I could see they didn't like that. They called me a cool customer. The social worker touched my arm and said I should tell them what I knew, and Mum screamed at her and said I didn't know anything. I didn't know anything because I hadn't done anything.

I felt like saying, if I didn't do this cool customer act I'd explode, like a balloon full of phlegm. You'd have to pick bits of snot off the ceiling. There'd be snot every-where. (Hopefully all over the social worker's face.) But I didn't say anything. You don't say things like that because it makes you sound a bit mad. That's the thing. Everyone's a bit mad on the inside, but they don't want anyone to know it. So if you show your madness they jump on it. It's like they're saying, I'm not a loony like you, I'm sane. Which was the same reason they called me Spakky and Perv.

* * *

When I failed my exams, Dad was furious all over again. He said I'd done it deliberately, to spite him and Mum. To give Sir Roger de Coverley the finger (that's not what he said, but that's what he meant). He thought I'd deliberately sat down in that hall and written wrong answers to the questions even though I knew the right answers. He said it was the straw that broke the camel's back. I wondered if this was true, if I'd done it without realizing it. If it *was* true, I was cleverer than I thought. Because a major thing happened after that last straw broke the camel's back. I was offloaded to London for the summer so I could get my head together and give everyone some breathing space. Mum's brother, Uncle George, said I could stay in his flat in Putney and work in his piano showroom in Fulham and that was very cool.

Mum and Dad had a row about me going to stay with Uncle George. Funnily enough, it was Dad who was all in favour and Mum who was a bit iffy about her own brother. I heard them arguing in the kitchen when they didn't know I was listening. Mum said, 'I'm not happy with him going down there, Vince. The place is full of weirdies and God knows what, if you ask me.'

Dad said, 'Exactly.'

There was a big silence and I imagined them having an eyebrow fight. Then Mum said, 'I'll be generous. I'll forget you said that.' Then they must have put their eyebrows away and she was saying things like, 'He's still a child, for God's sake,' and Dad was saying spending the summer holidays in London would be good for me. 'But is George going to be good for

Graham?' Mum said and Dad said, 'Well, George seems very keen for him to go,' and Mum said, 'Exactly. What's that all about? He's never really taken to Graham, you know,' and Dad said, 'He needs to cool down and grow up. It'll be good for us too, to have him out of our hair for a few weeks.'

There was another silence. I imagined Mum pouring hot water into two mugs with teabags in them. Then she said, 'That's what it's really about, isn't it? You just want him away. Your own son is an embarrassment to you.' And Dad didn't say anything, but he might have wiggled an eyebrow.

I'd never been to London before. I'd never really been anywhere, except York for the day on a school trip and Dorset for a week in a caravan. When Mum and Dad waved me off, Mum was snuffling in her hanky. She pushed something in the top pocket of my jean jacket when Dad wasn't looking. As the train left I hardly even looked back. I checked my top pocket, though—there were three tenners in there. Five minutes after leaving the station, the train went past the estate where we lived. You could see my house as it whizzed by. I hurt my neck, staring back to watch the house before it disappeared. Then I looked forward. After the houses, there were fields, like the fields that were there before the houses. Like the fields I floated over like a dandelion clock. I felt as light as a dandelion clock as I sat in that train and got nearer and nearer to London.

When I got to King's Cross I walked really slowly

down the platform. The whole place echoed like there were pingpong balls of sound pinging around. I was so knocked out, I forgot to think about my hands, to check on where they were and if people could get a good look at them. I didn't look beyond the barrier. I didn't want to see Uncle George, who'd never really taken to me, before I had to. I stopped and looked at the buffers. These great big things like drawing pins made out of iron that stopped the trains just going straight on into Trafalgar Square or Park Lane.

I felt like I was in a film. In a minute I'd wander out of the front of the station and be swallowed by all this noise and red buses etc. like plankton getting hoovered by a whale. But, depending on the film, things would probably turn out all right. Better than all right. In about five minutes I'd be a photographer or a scientist with a classy girl in tow.

Chapter 4

When I got to London I had to register with the police because I was on a list of people who the police reckoned might do certain things. Uncle George knew about it because Mum had told him. He took me to the cop shop in Putney. HE DID NOT LIKE THAT. On the way there he kept pulling his collar up on his jacket and saying, 'Christ almighty, Strummer.' I got taken into this room to fill out forms and Uncle George didn't want to come with me but the copper said he had to. Next to 'Next of kin' on the form I started writing 'George Oxnard' but Uncle George saw it and said, 'Put your mother.'

The copper said, 'Who's looking out for him day to day?'

I said, 'Uncle George.'

The copper said, 'Right then.'

Uncle George said, 'Thanks a lot.'

Of course, Uncle George told Mum I was staying with him and he was looking after me, feeding me Sugar Puffs and ironing my underpants etc., but really he was

33

over at Sheen most of the time with what he called his
bird, when he wasn't up in Lancashire sorting out the
dentist's practice he'd bought earlier in the summer, as
a back-up in case the Piano Showroom didn't work out.
So I was on my own usually. 'Best not tell your mother,'
he said. 'You know how she flaps. And remember—you
won't meet any nutters and whatnot round here, but if
you do, show them your disappearing arse pronto. What
do you do?'

I said, 'Show them my disappearing arse pronto.'

I don't think I could have handled sharing his place
anyway because it was about the size of Dad's shed and
Uncle George was not of Kate Moss dimensions (not to
mention his permanently whiffy pits). The flat started
off quite cool with this big metal John Lennon head
facing you on a stand when you open the door. The
head was wearing real, wiry, round specs that Uncle
George told me about five years ago had really been
Lennon's. But when I said this when he was showing
me round he looked at me like I was a nutter and said,
'What you on about, Strummer?'

But after John Lennon the place went seriously down-
hill. There was stuff everywhere. Running gear he'd never
worn, you could tell that by his porkiness. A trampo-
line he'd never taken out of its box. A big silver and
black coffee-making machine with knobs on that he never
used because there was a World Bean Inc. right on the
corner.

On the toilet wall there was a picture of his hero,
Elvis Presley, looking even fatter than Uncle George. He
pointed at it and said, 'The king. The burger king as it

happens, by that stage. But he was still the sexiest bloke on the planet even then. Ask any bird.' The first night I spent there there was no toilet paper, just these bits of torn-up old *Moon* newspapers lying on the floor. I had to wipe my bum on Beckham's new haircut.

Still, things were cool because I was in London. What was brilliant about London was, it didn't know about the deep dark hole and the terrible thing in there, the thing I was supposed to have done to Kylie Blounce. Plus people weren't bothered about my hands. I got really relaxed about them, like I didn't even wear my trackie top every day. After two weeks of being here, London seemed like a weird, impressive bloke that you couldn't quite suss out. First of all I just reckoned London didn't even notice my hands because there was so much stuff going on that was more interesting. Then I decided it did notice but it didn't think it was worth commenting on. I mean, this was a city of serious weirdies. I'd even seen a bloke in Putney Exchange Shopping Centre with only half a face. Then I decided London didn't care. It didn't give a toss. Whatever, it was all cool. I was happy.

I really liked going to work. Not the work itself, which was just being Charlie Arse-Face in Uncle George's Piano Showroom, but the getting there. I'd walk over Putney Bridge, looking left along this major silver freeway of water that I'd seen on telly because the boat race went down it, to the trees leaning out opposite Fulham footie ground that made it look like a hundred years ago. I'd clock the planes flying in low towards Heathrow, coming down slow like a puppet's hands on its strings.

I'd clock the classy girls who floated along the pavements in floating clothes. Then I'd plug myself into the Discman I'd bought with the money Mum stuffed in my jean jacket pocket the day I left home and I'd listen to something loud and rude. There I'd be, trying not to react to the music, trying not to put an extra wiggle in my walk. It had to be a secret, what was going on in my head. I didn't want passers-by getting an idea of the silent noise that was me. Then I'd get to the showroom. All good things come to an end (that Charlie Arse-Face wisdom again).

I worked with Kate and Derek. 'Two South London operators,' Uncle George called them when he introduced me. 'Just don't let them operate on *you*.' With Kate, fair enough as things turned out. More than fair enough. But Derek? The only thing he ever operated was a train set.

We all preferred it when Mister Porky, as they called him, wasn't in the showroom; it was just so uptight with him around. Uncle George ruined the quiet atmosphere, i.e. he stopped me having vertical kips. Sometimes he farted really loudly because he thought it was clever/funny but not even I thought that and I was less than half his age. 'Lampard. One–nil,' he'd go, meaning Chelsea had scored. Or sometimes he'd get all serious. Once he said: 'Pianos are not an impulse buy.' Oh, thanks a lot. Like he was giving us brilliant info and training us up for a lifetime of piano selling.

Anyway, things pootled on for about three weeks with me chilling out in the Smoke and giving the entire North of England a major break from Spakkydom, and then it happened. The Fulham Plane Crash. One Tuesday, bright blue sky, Someone Up There cut the strings of Flight RF 3409 from Tashkent, the capital of Uzbekistan, and this giant silver fuselage, looking like the cigar tube that Dad kept his rawlplugs in in his shed, was practically sitting on my head. On thousands of other heads as well, but mine was the one that mattered to me. The Tupolev, which was ancient apparently and probably had rust marks around the rivets and Sellotape holding the joystick together, took out a tower block near the river. From what I saw on TV later—amateur video; why is it there's always someone videoing a postbox or a sleeping policeman who's lucky enough to swivel his camera and get the Big Shot?—it was a devastating hit, like an idiot at a wedding falling backwards into the cake. Then it ploughed a furrow a hundred metres wide and a half-kilometre long through half a dozen streets. One of those streets was just a few blocks from the piano showroom. Death had almost come calling (this is what a TV reporter said). In fact, for quite a few people, it had actually come calling.

The first I knew was the noise, which was like a newsflash of sound. I'd just popped out to get some coffees from the World Bean Inc. down the road. It usually came down to me to get the coffees, seeing as I was Charlie Arse-Face. I was plugged in, of course. I saw a gorgeous girl. My face was straight as I passed her, but inside I was hoovering her up with my eyes. More woman than girl, actually. She was quite old, about twenty-eight. She wouldn't have been interested in the likes of me, not in a million years. Not just because of the age difference, the fact that I was less than half her age. Or even to do with my hands, which were obviously a big problem.

It was because she was too classy. I'd never seen what I meant by classy till I came down to London. In the north, girls and women did what I called clodhopping when they walked. Their hips swayed around as if they were trying to dislodge flies. They clump-clump-clumped with their big heavy shoes. They wore white lipstick that made them look like ghosts. They swore.

The woman I saw in the street on the day of the crash was classy. From a perfect-looking world that I hadn't known existed a few weeks before. Her clothes floated about her and she floated in her clothes. There was no clodhopping. Her hair was black and glossy and cut fairly short with a kind of shaved bit around the back of the neck. I noticed that when I turned round after she walked past. Also, I smelt her as she passed. Her perfume, or perhaps just her soap. I slowed down to keep the smell with me. Like a little bubble of heaven. The woman didn't look at me. And I didn't think anything more of her.

It was because of being plugged in that I didn't realize sooner what was happening. The noise of the plane was just swallowed up by the noise in my head. And then I couldn't believe it. The knackered old Tupolev was passing the end of the street about a hundred metres away and it was lower than the chimney pots. It didn't seem in any hurry. Then there was the explosion. And the buildings and roads disappeared in great big clouds and I felt I was on a rackety travelator. The pavement shook, the ground under the pavement shook. I couldn't go anywhere. I couldn't move backwards or forwards. I just concentrated on staying on my feet. And all the time the music was going off in my head and I could taste a new taste. It wasn't just the clouds of dust. My mouth had something new and terrible in it. The taste of something terrible.

The clouds were tiny particles of buildings. They were red from the brick. They rose around me until it was like being inside a big red tent. There were suddenly no shadows, that was the weird thing. It was like a retractable roof had slid across the sky. I knew I had to move, to get out, but I didn't get out. I can't say why. Things would have been very different if I had. Instead, call it a major hit of madness, I ran down the street *towards* the crash. At the end of the street was a wall of rubble that a minute before had been a big old building. I couldn't go any further. I took off the head-phones. I pushed the Discman in my pocket and just stood there catching my breath and coughing from the brick dust. And trying to listen. For the first time, listening to the crash.

It was like going out to look at the stars on a clear night, which I did once in Lulworth Cove. At first I didn't see that many. Then they began to spring out of the blackness as if someone somewhere was flicking silent switches to make them come on. And the sky was full of stars, alive with light. At first I just heard a single short scream, like someone far away had seen a rat or caught their finger in a car door. And then another scream. Longer and louder. Like someone was being murdered. And then the sky was full of murder-screams.

One of them turned into a device hammering at my skull. The other screams faded into the background and all I could hear was this. It was the wailing of a baby. It came from directly above me but when I tried to look I couldn't see properly beyond the end of the arm I held above my head because of the dust cloud. All I knew was that somewhere above me, jutting from all that mashed up building, was a cot or a bed with a crying kid in it.

I looked at the wall of crap in front of me, looking for a way to climb up. Bricks were being coughed out, falling from the rubble in little puffs of dust and landing around me. No way was I going to risk climbing up there. I would have ended up with half a block of flats lying on top of me. Then I had an idea. I felt in my pocket for my mobile phone. I always carried the mobile. Mum and Dad had told me I had to have it with me at all times, just so they didn't feel too guilty at having sent me 350 kilometres away, so they could say to themselves, and to neighbours, Graham's always at the end of the phone. But I wasn't because I kept it switched off. But now I was going to use it. I was going to ring Mum and ask her if it was OK to do what I now planned to do. I flipped back the front and thumbed up the number. My thumb hovered over the little green handset icon.

I wondered what she'd say in answer to my question. There were various possibilities, e.g. 'It's your funeral.' Whatever, she'd almost certainly say No. And I realized I didn't want to hear No, which meant that I had already made up my mind without help from her. So I put the mobile back in my pocket. And then I got so nervous about what I was about to do that I started divving about. I checked my other pocket for the Discman, making sure the headphones weren't trailing from the pocket. I knelt down and made sure the laces on my trainers were tied tight. I wondered how many twenty p pieces I had on me.

Talk about dork. The baby was still wailing but less often now, as if he/she had batteries and they were running out. Now or never, do or die, as Dad would say. I cocked my ear to the sound, trying to work out exactly where it was coming from (even five metres up, visibility looked distinctly iffy). Then I closed my eyes and started taking the deep breaths.

Chapter 5

When I stood again on the broken pavement in front of the wall of rubble, coughing and spluttering with being knackered and with all the dust and crap in my mouth, making coo-cooing noises, when I wasn't half-barfing, at the tiny little dark brown face I held in my arms, I felt like I held the world in my arms. And the world was as light as polystyrene.

I nearly rang Mum but I didn't want to risk dropping the baby while I got the mobile out. I'd have said, 'I've done it, I've rescued this baby. End of story.' But that would have been dumb because the story hadn't even begun.

The baby was a boy, I found out later. He had really thick black hair that made him look like a miniature Elvis Presley (in his cheeseburger phase). I'd picked up a pink blanket from its cot and I held that around him. I rocked him while I got my breath back. Then my legs just went. I fell to my knees on the pavement. The baby woke up and opened his mouth that was all twisted and rubbery and a bit like a fish's and out of it came major amounts of screaming and crying. And I turned into an ambulance, weioouu-weioouuing all the way back to the showroom.

'Quick,' I said. 'Here, someone.' I held out the baby. Kate took him. Her face was something else. She couldn't believe it: Graham with a screaming baby. Then I burst into tears. And my legs turned back to jelly, followed by my arms, and my head, and I spent the next five hours being a human wreck.

I wanted to go home. Or rather I wanted to go back to Uncle George's flat. But Uncle George said to stay there in the showroom. He was in Lancashire that day, sorting out some problems with the new dentist's practice. After he heard about the crash he phoned in to check we were OK. Actually to check if the pianos were OK, that was what Kate said afterwards.

Derek phoned 999 while Kate took me to the toilet cubicle and put a plaster on a graze on my knee. It had made a bit of a hole in my combats. At some stage I must have taken off my shirt because, later that day, I suddenly realized I was wearing this seriously baggy sweatshirt with HONKERS GO GO GO written on the front of it. It was Uncle George's, who weighed about three times as much as me, so no wonder it was baggy. Then these paramedics turned up in a big vehicle that looked American and the baby was taken away.

Kate sat me down on the sofa that's usually reserved for clients and said, 'Just sit here and relax.' And she stood behind me and massaged my neck. Only I didn't relax, in fact that was when my head started to feel as if it would explode. I held my hands to my head and I moaned. Kate sort of hugged me from behind then and said, 'Ssshh, it's all right. You're in shock, that's all. It's OK.' And then Uncle George rang.

Kate told him everything that had happened. Then she said I should go to hospital; I was in shock. But George said I should stay there. He said the hospitals would be chaos and I would have to wait days to be seen. And if I went back to the flat I would be on my own and that wasn't a good idea. It was better to keep me there. As I watched Kate on the phone to Uncle George I thought about her. Was she clodhopping or classy? She was neither. She was just Kate.

There were the sounds of helicopters and sirens outside. Kate said I should try to sleep. Her mobile rang again. It was Uncle George. I could hear him shouting. Kate said, 'All right, all right.' When she came off the phone she said to me, 'Your uncle says you should switch your mobile on, your mother's been trying to call you.' I said I didn't want to talk to her. I gave Kate Mum and Dad's number and she went outside and called them. I saw her through the window, nodding, then I drifted off to sleep for a bit.

Derek found an old radio in the toilet cubicle with white paint splashed on it. There was a non-stop news programme about the crash. That's when I found out it had been Flight RF 3409 from Tashkent etc. They went over to a reporter outside a hospital. She told a story about a baby being rescued right in the crash zone, where no other survivors had been found so far. The rescuer had disappeared. He was a hero.

None of us realized they were talking about me at first. The reporter said it was a miracle in the nightmare.

Kate came over to the sofa and squeezed my shoulder and I realized the reporter meant me. That was the first moment I wondered about what I had done.

A policeman called in to the showroom and asked if we would stay there until he gave us the all-clear. The crash had happened about 9.30 a.m. By 3.30 p.m., shortly after the policeman called in, the dust clouds began to clear. At 4.30 p.m. the first TV news people began to set up on the street outside. I took a chair to the window and watched. People-carriers and 4WDs covered with satellite dishes and heavy duty aerials were parking up along the street, crunching their tyres right over the broken glass, riding the bricks and stones. Men in T-shirts set up cameras that were surprisingly small. They had rolls of silver tape which made a screeching-sucking noise as they tore bits off. They used it to tape cables to the pavement and the road, which surprised me because I didn't know you could tape things to roads.

You could spot the reporters. They had polythene-looking heads. They held clipboards or notepads and combed fingers through their hair. A police helicopter hovered down low. Newspapers and cardboard and drinks cans that you didn't even realize had been there started to circle about in the street. The sheets of paper on the clipboards blew about. The reporters clutched their hair as if they all had wigs on and they might blow away. Someone yelled: 'Get that chopper outta here.'

Kate came and stood by me at the window. Then she brought a piano stool and sat on that. She waggled her bare feet and said, 'It's like the end of the world.' Derek came up behind us. He said to Kate, 'I'll rub your neck if you like.' The way he said it, it was like he was really saying: You've massaged Graham's neck so now it's allowed if I massage yours. But Kate just said, 'No, it's fine.'

We just watched through the window. No one said anything. Then a woman in a sleeveless fleece and those yellowy Caterpillar boots was trotting down the street. She had a mobile phone in one hand and a megaphone in the other. Her boots were scrunching glass. She did a kind of dance on the spot. 'Listen, everybody.' Her megaphone voice echoed around. 'This is very important. Did anyone actually see the crash, did anyone see the plane coming down? We really want to hear from you if you did.'

And before I knew it, Kate was banging on the show-room window, and shouting. 'He did, here, missy, he did. He rescued the baby, he was the one!' Did I try to stop her? I would have done but she was so quick. She jumped up and she was out of the door, running after the gunslinger with the megaphone.

'Excuse me, Graham Sinclair,' she said to the gunslinger. I did follow Kate out on to the street, it's true. But it was to try and pull her back. Too late. She said, 'My colleague Graham Sinclair rescued that baby that was on the news. He's—oh, he's right here!'

There were quite a few people around the gunslinger. But she locked her eyes on to mine. She said: 'Graham? You rescued Baby Ade? That's great. Can we just get a few words from you?'

I said, 'Baby Ade?'

46

She said, 'That's what the nurses are calling him. He's doing fine. Can you tell us what happened?'

I really didn't mean it to happen but sometimes you just get carried along. They lined me up in front of the showroom window and when I watched myself on the box later I saw that behind my head you could see the arts and crafts Bechstein boudoir grand. (Uncle George said it was the best piano he had. The others were crap. His word. They were made in Korea or China even if they did have German names.)

The interviewer called me 'Shop assistant Graham Sinclair'. I thought of kids from Sir Roger de Coverley watching their tellies. I thought, Suck on this, you Spakky-callers. I kept my hands down by my sides so the camera couldn't see them. The interviewer said, 'The last moments of Flight 3409 were witnessed by shop assistant Graham Sinclair.' Then something about 'unimaginable tragedy'; 'heroic part he was to play in it'; and 'death coming to call'. And then he pushed the mike at me and I just started talking. I remember thinking that what I was saying sounded like rubbish but when I saw it on TV later it was OK, I didn't come across as a major moron (and at no point could you see my hands). I mentioned seeing the plane and hearing the baby—Baby Ade—and then I invented a drainpipe that I climbed up.

In the evening Kate and Derek and me went to the pub and I was on the television news. The first time I went in that pub the barman refused to serve me because I looked under age. Then Kate got me fake ID and he let me in after that but he still didn't like me being there. Now he was my new best mate. He loved having a bloke on his TV screen and standing at his bar at the same time. He gave us free drinks, which is how I got a bit drunk. Not falling down drunk but enough to make me feel what Dad calls ropy next morning. Kate dropped me at Uncle George's in a cab and gave me a bit of paper with her mobile and landline numbers on it in case I got freaked in the night and needed to talk to someone. But I was out like a light.

In the morning the phone rang in Uncle George's flat and it was Mum. She didn't mention seeing me on telly so I asked her if she had. She just said, 'It's your funeral, Graham.' Told you.

I went to work. There were police and fire engines everywhere. Also coaches with blacked-out windows and all these people milling about in white body-suits and face masks. The first bunches of flowers that people had left were just lying in the road, still in their placky wrappings. I thought maybe you wouldn't be able to get to the street where the showroom was, but there wasn't a problem.

I bought a couple of papers. The local World Bean Inc. was closed because its windows were smashed in and I had to scoot about a kilometre to find the next one. The coffees had cooled right off by the time I got to the showroom. I was first in for once. I didn't log on straightaway. I had a look at the papers.

I was in both of them. They had taken a videograb

from last night's news. I looked fine. Blurred, of course, but older than fourteen. You couldn't see how thin I was and you couldn't see the hands. There was a head-line above one of the pictures that said:

BOY HERO RISKS LIFE TO SAVE BABY

Underneath that it said:

Baby Ade 'will pull through': rescue from crash carnage is symbol of hope amid the despair.

I was quite proud but I was also scared. I felt like a million pairs of eyes were looking at me, which they probably were. At that very second, over their teas and bacon sarnies or Egg McMuffins. The article said Baby Ade was serious but stable in hospital. They reckoned his parents had probably died in the crash.

Then I logged on. Jennifer must have seen the papers, too, which is why she put 'To the boy hero!' in the subject field. My heart started really thumping when I saw it. I swigged about half the first coffee before I double-clicked on the email. I scrolled straight down to the end to see who it was from. I had this crazy idea it would be from Kylie Blounce. Kylie had seen me on telly and tracked me down. She just wanted me to know how proud she was of me, and that she'd never call me Flipper again. But it was from someone called Jennifer Slater. Who? I remember feeling disappointed, which is what you call ironic.

I was just scrolling up to the top when Kate came in.

I closed the email down. Kate had one of the papers I'd got. 'Hey,' she said. 'Boy hero.' And stuff along those lines. She asked me how I was and I said fine. She said I shouldn't have come to work, Mister Porky wouldn't have minded, but I said I didn't know what else to do. Then she said, 'Well, I'm glad you came, anyway.' Which I thought was a bit weird. And all the time I was wishing she'd go away, go to the toilet or something, so I could read this email from this person Jennifer Slater in peace.

Then she said, 'Want another coffee?' She didn't know I was on my second because I'd already drunk the first one and thrown the cup away. I told her the local World Bean Inc. wasn't open and where the next nearest one was. She was whistling as she went out of the door.

I went back to the email.

To the boy hero! it repeated at the top.

Congratulations on a brave act. I know how brave it was because I saw what you did. I saw everything that you did. Do you understand? I was walking along the street behind you when the crash happened. I followed you because for those few minutes I did not know where I was going or what I was doing. And then I watched you rescue the baby. I saw in detail what you did.

There can be no mistaking what I saw unless I am mad. Or unless I went mad for those few minutes. This is possible. The crash was a terrible occurrence and anyone who witnessed it will have been in a state of shock. In fact they will still be in shock. I certainly still feel very peculiar and shaky.

However, as my friends would tell you, I am a very down

to earth sort of person. I am not prone to flights of fantasy. I do not make up fantastical tales. Some of my friends might even say that I am the last person they know to get carried away on tides of feeling.

One way or the other I need to clear this up. I know where you work because I followed you after you rescued the baby. I followed you back to the piano shop. And then I saw you on TV later, outside the piano shop.

My apartment is less than half a mile away. You know how to contact me. You simply reply to this email. You may not want to. I can understand if you do not. But I'm afraid if you choose not to contact me I will be forced to come and find you in person.

Please understand that I do not wish you ill will. But I saw you do something that has unsettled me greatly. I need to understand what I saw. One way or the other.

Yours, Jennifer Slater

PS There was no drainpipe. Was there?

Chapter 6

Uncle George didn't get back down to London till three days after the plane crash, which was fine by us. I just hung out watching all the stuff going on in the street while Kate and Derek sorted out the sale of the Bechstein boudoir grand. It was Kate's favourite piano, she said it was like a beautiful vintage car and she didn't want to see it go but that was showbusiness (she said this sarcastically because it was what Uncle George said). She said it was a double-shame, because she'd been going to sit down and play it, when she found the right bit of music to play. (I had the idea she was talking crap, when she said this.) The way we sold the Bechstein was weird. It had been behind me on the telly when they interviewed me. Next day a bloke rang Kate up and said they were calling on behalf of an English bloke living in Switzerland who'd seen my interview and noticed the piano in the background and wanted it for his office.

After the crash we got more people in the showroom than I'd ever seen in there before but they weren't interested in buying starter pianos for their little Peregrines or Heidis (You got a lot of snooty kids round the showroom with snooty parents. The kids wore weird pink-and-grey uniforms and walked around in crocodiles. Their mums drove them about in 4WDs that looked like tanks).

No. They came in because they were interested in the crash. A lot had flowers to lay in the roads. They carried them in their placky wrappings. They were also interested in me; they recognized me off the telly. They wanted to know if it had been a miracle, what I did. The rescue of Baby Ade. They'd been reading the papers.

Two days after the crash there was an article in one of those big serious papers I never normally looked at that weighed about half a ton and had all these glossy advertising bits in them that dropped out when you picked them up. It was Kate who saw it. This was the headline:

Is Baby Ade a true child of God?

Underneath was a picture of the writer. 'Blimey, Mister Porky Mark Two,' Kate said when she saw it. 'If I looked like that I'd keep my picture out of the papers.' The article rabbited on for a bit and then it said:

Who may doubt, having examined the scene of the rescue of the so-called Baby Ade (a disobliging sole-cism for which our tabloid brethren must hold up their inky hands), that near-miraculous levels of skill and bravery must have attended Ade's safe deliverance? In short, was young master Graham Sinclair, who seems from all accounts to be that most English of heroes, a modest one, aided by a sort of celestial fireman's ladder? Amid the devil's work of last Tuesday morning, did God leave his calling card?

Etcetera etcetera. It went on for ages but, having read it about ten times, I worked out it was all basically saying the same thing, which was that my rescue of Ade was a miracle, like Jesus did. I was pretty freaked by this. I was going to get found out if this went on much longer.

Then the people started coming in and phoning up. A couple of papers. Some radio stations. What did I think of the idea that God may have worked a miracle through me? I said I reckoned it was more to do with me being a top-class mountaineer (a lie) and put the phone down.

That stuff was bad enough. But what really did my head in was when this bloke turned up in the show-room dressed as Jesus in a white sheet. He held up a big Bible at me and started yelling and Kate called the police. He was exactly the sort of bloke who would have had a gun under his cassock and thought I was the devil and needed sending to hell. After that Kate helped me out big time. She wrote a notice on her computer that said

CLOSED TO THE PUBLIC
BY APPOINTMENT ONLY

and stuck it in the window. When Uncle George saw it the next day he went ballistic.

* * *

54

So did I forget about Jennifer Slater in all this? Of course not. But I didn't have any time to think. My head was buzzing. I needed to wait for it to calm down so I could work out what to do but that never happened. Apart from anything, I'd got Mum giving me a hard time.

After she'd seen me on the telly she read the article in the paper and tried to call me on my mobile, but it was switched off so she called Uncle George, who called me, and I had to promise to call her that evening. So I called and she said, after she'd got all the crying over, I had to come home right now. She said she must have been mad to let me go to London. I'd only been there five minutes and God knows what I'd got up to.

I said that wasn't my fault, it was because of the crash. I started to explain but she didn't want to know. I told her I was happy down here and I never wanted to go home. She said she'd come and get me. She'd come down to London and drag me back if she had to. And that's when I said it. I didn't plan to, it just came out. And as soon as I'd said it I knew it had worked. I said, 'I wouldn't do that if I was you, Mum. I wouldn't come down here and try and take me back.'

'What do you mean?' she said.

I said, 'I might do something. You know what.'

There was silence. Then she put the phone down. Result.

My best chance to think was the third day after the crash. I'd got Mum off my back the night before and when I got into the showroom in the morning Kate said

Derek had called to say he was feeling a bit sick and he wouldn't be coming in. So it was just me and Kate. And then the bloke dressed as Jesus came in, and the police turned up and took him away, and Kate put the notice up saying we were closed. And it was back to square one, just me and Kate again.

I was just thinking, I've got to do something about Jennifer Slater, when Kate said, 'How's your knee?'

'Fine,' I said but she insisted on getting me to put my leg up on a piano stool and making me roll up my trouser leg so she could see it and then she started fussing about with it and there was no way I could think about Jennifer Slater with this going on, so I thought about Kate. Like, for instance, the parting in her hair was a zigzag. I hadn't noticed that before but with her bending over I couldn't help it. Also, it was dyed. You thought it was coppery like wire but really it was black, right in the zigzag was coal black. Also, her legs were quite bandy. They came out of her skirt like a chicken wishbone has been hiding up there, except darker.

I didn't know, then, how old she was. I thought, maybe twenty-five. She'd got me that ID for the pub no problem and you had to be quite old to do stuff like that. I knew she didn't have a dad and she had a brother but he was in a young offenders' institution for robbing someone and sometimes she went with her mum to see him. And her mum sang in a choir on Sundays. And she wanted to be a piano player. Or more like a pianist. Not in a band but classical. She said just being around pianos was good. Maybe she'd get vibes off them that'd make her play better. (If she could play at all.)

56

Now she said, 'Have you spoke to your mum?' It was like she was talking to my knee because she had this mug of warm water and she was dabbing cotton wool in it then dabbing it on the cut. I said yes then gave a little laugh, like I was also saying my mum gave me earache. ''Spect she wants you to go home,' said Kate. '*I* would.'

'I'm not going,' I said.

She looked up then. She had really big brown eyes that looked like glass and toffee mixed. 'Good,' she said. 'I'm glad.' I didn't say anything. She put a new plaster on my knee and rolled my trouser leg down and patted my knee through the trouser leg and said, 'Good as new.'

There were still people ringing me up about God and miracles etc. Kate said she'd take the calls. She was like a really efficient secretary in a film. She said things like, 'Please put your request in writing, Mr Sinclair is a very busy young man.' She'd be looking at my desk and holding her hand over her mouth, trying to stop the giggles coming out.

Now at last I had time to get my head round Jennifer. I checked to see if she'd emailed again. Nothing. I took out the print-out of her email, which I had in my back pocket, and looked at particular bits:

You know how to contact me. You simply reply to this email. You may not want to. I can understand if you do not. But I'm afraid if you choose not to contact me I will be forced to come and find you in person.

and

PS There was no drainpipe. Was there?

I'd been half-hoping if I did nothing the problem would go away. But that wasn't right. It wouldn't go away. This woman Jennifer Slater had me right there in her sights. She only lived half a mile away. She might have a brother who was a copper. I shivered, thinking about that. There was something about the ways coppers acted, about the way they looked. When I was a little kid I had an imitation Action Man, a cheapo version. He looked all solid but when you poked his cheek it just caved in. He was made of a glorified placky bag. That's what coppers reminded me of.

Jennifer might be watching me, right now. I looked through the showroom window at the comic-book shop across the street. There were two windows above the shopfront. One was half-open and there was a net curtain half-blowing out of it. There could be a bloke in there with a camera on a tripod.

I started deciding what I would write in my email to Jennifer Slater. First of all I thought it in my head, then I had to start writing it down in a proper email because I couldn't remember what I'd just thought. What would I call her, for a kick-off? I keyed in

Dear Jennifer

but that looked wrong. She might be in her sixties for all I knew. I tried

58

Dear Mrs Slater

but that wasn't right because she might not be married.
Then

Dear Ms Slater

But she might not be a feminist. I fussed about over this
for about ten minutes. I was just wasting time, putting
off when I would have to actually say something proper
to her. Then I knew I had it. I keyed in

Dear Jennifer Slater

and was about to put down this complete sentence when
Kate said, 'I'm doing the paperwork for the Bechstein.
You've got to fill out all these shipping forms.' I'd sort
of forgotten she was there. The phone hadn't rung for
a while and we'd both been dead quiet.

'Right,' I said. She'd made me forget what I was going
to say to Jennifer Slater. I put a comma after 'Slater'
while I waited for the sentence to come back.

Then Kate said, 'Graham? Can I ask you a question?'
She said aks instead of ask.

I said, 'Yes.' I hit the backward delete button and
wiped out the comma. I wasn't thinking about what
Kate was going to say. It was like she ambushed me.

She said, 'I was wondering about your hands. If you
don't mind me aksing.'

This freaked me quite badly. I didn't think people in

London gave a toss about my hands, but now here was Kate giving a major toss. I didn't know what to say so I just said, 'Yeah.'

She said, 'Sorry.' She was pretending to end the conversation but she was really waiting for me to say, No it's OK, what did you want to know? etc., so we could carry on. But I didn't say anything and after quite a few seconds she said sorry again.

And I said 'No problem' and then we didn't talk for about two hours.

I tell a lie. Kate did talk to me in those two hours but it was only to say Uncle George was on the line.

He said, 'Have you talked to your mother?'

I said, 'Yeah.'

He said, 'All right. OK. How's the flat? Still in one piece?' Which was a cheek because he was a bigger slob than me. Then he said, 'See you tomorrow, then. I'm back in first thing.'

While I was talking to Uncle George I was messing about with the keyboard and I pressed the Send & Receive button by mistake.

This did two things. The first was that it sent my unfinished email to Jennifer Slater. The email said:

Dear Jennifer Slater

and that was it. Which was pretty stupid but not the end of the world. And the second thing was that this new email came up. It said:

Hey there. Hero. Do I have to come round?

Nothing else. It was from her, from her address, which was jennifer.slater@slassoc.co.uk.

I didn't think. It was like I was on the diving board again. I hit Reply and typed really fast:

Dear Jennifger Slater
Sorry about the last email. I sentit by mistake. I will meet you.
Just say when and were.
Yours sincerley
Graham Sinclair

Then I sat there, fiddling about, waiting for the reply. Heart thumping. Noise in my head. I hit the Send & Receive button about twice every minute. Kate must have noticed. I could feel her looking at me. She thought I was still mad at her, like I was this angry guy in a movie that couldn't stop tapping or fiddling then suddenly he'd explode and kill someone. I didn't look at her. I was hoping she would go home, it was after five. Then I heard her chair scrape back. The click of her purse. On her way out she stopped at my desk. I could feel her looking at me close up. She said, 'Graham,' with a sigh. 'I've said sorry.'

'Not a problem,' I said.

'It looks like it is,' she said. 'Will you come for a drink with me at least? Make use of that ID.'

I said, 'I'm busy.'

She said, 'Oh yeah, I can see that.' I still didn't look at her. She clicked her heels and went to the door. She said, 'You'll lock up and set the alarm, yeah?'

I said, 'OK.' Then I felt a bit sorry for her. I said, 'Mister Porky says he'll be in first thing.'

She said, 'Oh, great.'

I waited another hour at least. Nothing back from Jennifer Slater. I decided to go back to the flat, get a takeaway pizza on the way. There was this place near Putney Bridge that was a mock-up of a proper Italian place. Walls painted like brick with flowers on it. There was even a lizard if you knew where to look. They'd got a big oven and this bloke put pizzas in it on a long shovel. Really good pizzas.

I set the alarm. Uncle George had used his sister's (my mum's) date of birth as the six-digit number and made me memorize it (070661). I went out the door. I locked the top and bottom locks and all the time I was fiddling in my pocket for my Discman so I could blast my earholes out on the way to the pizza place. Which is why I wasn't looking where I was going. I turned round and I walked straight into this woman. I mean literally. I went boinngg off her bosoms.

Chapter 7

It was the woman I saw just before the crash happened, the classy one that floated along the street. It took me a couple of seconds to work this out. I was just staring at her, trying to think where I'd seen her before. I even thought I might have known her from TV, she was that special. It was the perfume that made me realize. It whizzed me back like a time machine, back those few days to before the crash, and there I was, walking along all innocent, not knowing the crash was about to happen, and seeing this classy woman and feeling that painful happiness you feel when you see such a person on the street who you know will never talk to you or care about who you are. Except she did.

I came out of the showroom and bumped into her, right on her bosoms. I could feel them on my chest, the memory of how they felt sort of stayed in my blood for a few seconds after I'd stepped back. 'Graham,' she said. 'Jennifer Slater.' I was just staring at her and she crossed her hands over in front of my face like I was a patient in a coma and then she started laughing and she said, 'It *is* Graham, isn't it? Let me tell you something, Graham.'

Her eyes. Her eyes were brown like Kate's but even bigger. They were like the sun, I could only look at them for a split second, right into the middle of them, then I had to look away. Her voice was southern posh but it wasn't like the voices of the women who came into the showroom. Those women arrived in Range Rovers or 4WDs. You saw them parking outside the window. They didn't care if they got a ticket, they were rich. Sometimes their vehicles were the greeny-grey colour of tanks and that was what they reminded me of, these women—tank commanders. They barked at me poshly. They may as well have had helmets and headsets on and be reporting back to their command and control centre in a tent somewhere secret. Their voices were cold, that's what I mean. But Jennifer's was warm.

Mum taught me a trick, which is how to get honey out of the jar when the jar's been in the fridge. You hold the spoon under hot water, then you stick it in the honey and the honey melts and wraps itself round the spoon. The hot spoon makes it all so easy and the whole thing feels nice, like it was meant to be. That was Jennifer's voice, nice and easy, the spoon and the honey.

She said, 'I'm not easily amazed. I just want you to know that.' Now she was holding me by the shoulders. Quite tight. She felt strong but not as strong as me. I was much stronger than I looked, the hands being a help. I could see a bit down her top. Her bra was the colour of pistachio ice cream.

'OK,' I said. I shrugged and she took her hands off my shoulders. She thought I was trying to get rid of her hands there but I wasn't. I liked her touching me, I just didn't understand what she was saying.

'OK yourself,' she said.

She took my arm. I had my tracksuit top on. I didn't take my hand out of the pocket, I just let her push my arm open so she could put hers through mine. She leant on me a bit, as if to say, 'Let's walk' and we set off. Her heels clacked. People heard and looked and when they looked they did a double-take. Not at me, at Jennifer. At how great-looking she was. And maybe also a bit at both of us, what this weedy kid was doing with this stunner. We didn't say anything for a bit. We were walking towards where the crash happened. It took me a while to work this out. When I did she must have realized. I went a bit weird and Jennifer said, 'It's got to be done,' and continued to steer us towards the site.

Then she said, 'What sort of food do you like? I thought I'd take you to dinner sometime.'

I got really confused with this. I was still trying to remember what time dinner was down here and what sort of thing you ate. What food did I like? Pizza was all I could think of. 'Never mind,' she said. 'I'll let you know. Somewhere classy. You'll have to get used to classy.'

She used the word! I wanted to tell her how funny that was, her using the word classy. But it wouldn't have sounded right. Now we were walking along the street where I had first seen Jennifer. I told her I had noticed her and she said, 'Did you?' in a gooey way. She didn't say she had noticed me, which wasn't necessarily bad. I was sick of being noticed for the wrong reasons, i.e. for having the wrong hands. I wondered when we would stop walking.

Jennifer said, 'Do you read the papers? You should, you know. Not just one, get a few every day. Find out what you've been up to.' She looked at me and laughed then, which I didn't really like. She was taking the Michael out of me. There must have been a look on my face. 'Don't worry,' she said, 'I understand. I'll be a good back-up.'

I didn't really understand the things she said. But the way she said them it was like she just assumed I did, and I didn't want to disappoint her so I just nodded. We reached as far as we could go. Blue and white police tape formed a barrier across the street. We stood by the tape and looked. In front of us was a row of smashed buildings. The fronts had come off some of them. They looked like doll's houses. You could see an old fireplace hanging halfway up a wall, and a poster of a girl pop band. But we just glanced at all that. What we were really looking for was at the end of the street. The building that had once been the block of flats where Baby Ade lived. This building was the worst of the lot. It was just a pile of rubble. Taller than a tall house, with a mist of dust hanging over it. There was a budgie cage poking out, which made me think of a budgie I'd known called Eddie.

I hadn't been here since the crash. I suddenly felt peculiar. My legs began to shake like on the day it happened and I could feel the dust again at the back of my throat, and I tasted just a flash of that strange taste I had tasted that day, the taste of something terrible.

66

Jennifer squeezed my arm and half held me up. 'I was standing about here,' she said. 'I'd followed you because I thought you knew where you were going. And then I saw what you did. As I say, I'm not easily amazed.'

Jennifer's mobile rang. The ring tone was like the noise a lorry makes when it reverses. She let go of my arm and turned away from me. She didn't say hello when she switched the mobile on, she just listened. After about a minute she said, 'Absolutely. Do it,' and flipped the phone closed. Her voice sounded weird, not warm but cold. Then she spoke to me and it was warm again. 'I've got to go,' she said. 'I'm so glad we met. I'll let you know about dinner.'

She walked off and left me there, by the blue and white tape. I watched her go. The way she floated, and that triangle at the back of her neck where her hair was shaved that looked like black velvet.

The morning after that first meeting with Jennifer I was a bit late. I didn't even have time to pick up a latte at World Bean Inc. I was thinking about her all the way to the street where the showroom was, then I saw Uncle George's Merc and I couldn't think about Jennifer any more for the moment. Now I had to deal with Uncle George. When he was in your head he elbowed everybody else out.

Through the window I saw him pacing around the pianos, like he did when he was mad. He had a piece of paper in his hand. And then I noticed that the sign that Kate had put up in the door was missing. There was a little jingle that played when you opened the door. It was supposed to be a bit of piano music. The first time he took me to the showroom Uncle George pointed above his head and said, 'Geddit?' I said I thought I might have heard it on an advert on TV. 'For God's sake, Joe,' he said. 'Choppin. Choppin?' I shook my head.

Mr Choppin's job was to make it impossible for anyone to sneak into the showroom without the people inside realizing, but it was a bit pointless, I reckoned. No one was going to run off with a piano in their pocket.

I opened the door and the jingle went da-da da-da da da da-da *daaa*, and everyone was looking at me. Uncle George stopped what he was saying to them and said to me, 'Afternoon.' And Derek laughed. Uncle George waited while I sat down. Then he started walking between the pianos again. He'd got a new jacket on I'd not seen before. The jacket cheered me up. It was really light leather that was almost orange and it had loads of pointless pockets. I know my combats had lots of pockets but there were reasons for them. Mobiles and Discmans and CDs all went in there nicely. Uncle George's pockets were just for show, you could tell by how flat they were, and they looked crap. He was pretty big and the whole thing made him look like a chest of drawers. The reason it cheered me up was that I knew that George thought he looked classy.

There was another thing about Uncle George. He had weird ears. There was black hair growing out of them, and the lobe bits were very long so they looked like earrings made out of flesh. You'd never have known he was Mum's brother. Mum was quite small with dainty ears. Also, she was light-coloured, like me. She had a very faint moustache but you couldn't see it because the hairs were white. If her hair had been dark like Uncle George's, she'd have looked like a freak. Perhaps they were adopted, or one of them was. Perhaps Grandma and Gramps, they were both dead by this point, had had a secret. There were lots of secrets in families that you might never know, or only know when someone died in about fifty years and then it was too late for it to mean anything anyway. I used to wonder if *I* was adopted, for instance. I didn't look like Mum *or* Dad.

Uncle George ran his fingers over the top of one of the Rickenmullers, looking for dust. He inspected the ends of his fingers. 'So,' he said. He held up the notice. '"Closed to the public",' he read out. '"By appointment only." Brilliant, eh?' He stopped and looked at us, one after the other. 'I mean, let's open a shop but don't let anyone in all day. That way we can all ponce about and have a great time. Eh?' We didn't say anything so he said 'Eh?' again.

'It's been mad,' said Kate, 'with the crash and everything.' She shrugged.

George shook his finger at her and said, 'Who put the notice there?'

There was silence; it was like being back at school, and I thought I'd joined the grown-ups. Uncle George was looking from one to the other of us. Then Derek said, 'Junior Joe.'

I hated it when Derek called me that. How old was

69

Derek? No idea but in any case sometimes it didn't matter how old you were in years, you were always about seven in your head. Derek was about that. If he'd been my age, at my school, he'd have queued up to set light to my hair. If the Germans had won the Second World War, Derek would have worn their uniform and got special privileges for bossing about the English.

Kate said, 'Derek. For God's sake. You weren't even here. It was me, OK, George.'

Derek said, 'Yeah, but you did it for him. You must of.'

Kate said, 'It was mental OK? All these people coming in. I just thought it was the best thing.'

Derek said, 'They think he's Jesus or something. Talk about nutters.'

I said, 'It's not my fault, is it? I can't help it what people do.'

Uncle George said, 'Gentlemen. Ding ding. We got pianos to sell. Hey. Talking of which.' And he did this thing of switching. One second he was throwing a wobbly and the next he was all smiley and sweaty and rubbing his hands.

'We shifted the Bechstein, I'm hearing,' he said. 'The one in the window. Well done, Joe.' He punched my arm. Now he was like a stand-up comic and we were his audience. 'I've read some top things about my family relation here these last few days. Did you see this one?' and he held up his arm like he was writing a big headline in the sky:

JOE STRUMMER TOUCHES SOUL OF NATION

'Did you see it? Well, just so long as you don't touch its arsehole, Joe. That'll be the next one:

JUNIOR JOE TOUCHES ENGLAND'S ARSEHOLE—AND WISHES HE HADN'T

'Ha ha! Do us a favour, Joe. I'm parked on a double yellow.'

There were two good things about Uncle George. One, he never mentioned my hands, not once. And two, he let me drive his Merc. But these things don't mean he was a good bloke. (A prize bit of Graham Sinclair wisdom on its way: You can do good things for bad reasons.) With the hands, I reckon he didn't mention them because he was fat. The car was more complicated.

When Uncle George came up to visit us when I was twelve, he took me out in his new Merc to this old airfield that Dad told him about and he showed me how to drive. He had to put the seat right forward for me but basically it was a doddle once I'd sussed the automatic gear shift. I took to it dead easy, which is how I could drive when I came down to London even though I was only fourteen-ish and I'd never had a proper lesson.

He even let me drive on proper roads. If he was parked on the double yellow outside the showroom he'd chuck me the keys, or tell me to fetch the spare set from the toilet cubicle, and then I'd have to drive the Merc out towards Hammersmith and park it on a meter up there.

I used to think, what an amazing bloke, but then I

wasn't so sure. Do you think he would have admitted he'd asked me to drive the Merc if the police did me? No way. And the cops would have believed him, not me. And Kate and Derek would have been too scared to say anything even though they knew. Well, Kate might not have been but that was the risk Uncle George ran. He liked running risks because he didn't feel scared of them. Not because he was brave but because he didn't have feelings full stop. That's what I reckoned.

I had to slide the seat right forward so I could reach the pedals. There were some traffic lights on the way to where I usually parked. I prayed they'd be on green when I got there. I hated standing in a traffic jam because the other drivers looked at me. They'd do a double-take like you see in cartoons but they happen in real life too. All my life, people had done double-takes at my hands. It was like their brains were wired a bit slow. They looked then turned their heads away then turned their heads back because they'd only just realized they'd seen something weird; they were making sure they really did see what they thought they saw. This is what other drivers did if they saw me at that traffic light on the way to Hammersmith. Not because of my hands, they couldn't really clock them properly from their cars, but because I was a kid.

BOY DRIVES MERC!

is what they were thinking. This time I sailed through the lights, and I found a parking meter straight away. I decided I had enough time to go and have a coffee in this caff that I'd looked at from the outside but never been in. There were old blokes in there minding their own business and it smelt of cigs and cooking grease and the coffee was crap compared to World Bean Inc. but I still liked it because nobody looked at you. Everyone was weird in there. Not half-a-face-missing weird, but weird enough. Nobody did double-takes.

I bought a few papers in the paper shop next door. You had to keep up with what they were saying, that was what Jennifer told me. This is what I read:

FULHAM AIR DISASTER
'NOT TERRORISM'

The likely cause of Tuesday's plane crash in west London was catastrophic systems failure. That's the preliminary finding of impact site investigators . . .

And

DEATH TOLL RISES TO 47

I couldn't find anything at first in the *Moon*. The front-page story was about David Beckham being caught with painted toenails. They had a huge close-up of his toes in these sandals. Purple. But then inside I found a couple of mentions:

'WE LOVE ADE' SAY READERS

Our phone lines were jammed yesterday as
you pledged cash for the Baby Ade Appeal . . .

And

**SICK
SCUM
LOOT
CRASH
SITE**

Next to this was a CCTV picture of a really fat bloke
in a baseball cap carrying a piece of electrical equipment with wires coming out of the back. He'd just
nicked it from a Dixon's that had its windows smashed
in the crash. I wondered if it was the same Dixon's, near
the showroom, where I bought my Discman.

It's true, I was disappointed there was nothing about
me in the papers.

Chapter 8

When I got back to the showroom from the caff Uncle George sniffed me and said, 'You been smoking, son?'

I said, 'No.' I couldn't tell him I'd been skiving off in the caff.

He turned his eyes into slits. I could see Derek watching him, really interested. Then Uncle George said, 'Have you phoned your mother today?'

'Not yet,' I said.

'Well, I have,' he said. 'She's not brilliant.' He rolled his eyeballs up and looked at the ceiling. I didn't ask him what he meant, I could guess. Recently, Mum had been going to bed in the afternoon. She took pills and watched old black and white films on the TV. Dad brought this old portable Toshiba out of the spare room and rigged it up with an indoor aerial.

I thought of phoning her but I didn't really want to at that precise moment. 'I'll call her,' I said.

'When?' said Uncle George.

'Later,' I said.

'Just make sure you use your mobile,' he said, 'not my bloody phone in the flat.'

'OK,' I said.

'How is the bacteria factory anyway?' he said.

Ten minutes later when I was making a cup of tea Kate came up to me and whispered, 'Sorry to hear about your mum. What's up with her?'

'The usual,' I said. 'I expect.'

I spent the rest of the morning putting cardboard trousers on the Bechstein so it would be ready to ship off to Switzerland. I ran out of parcel tape on the last leg and had to nick some off the first leg, which meant the cardboard was sort of falling off two of the legs by the time I'd finished, but nobody noticed. To be honest, there wasn't a lot for me to do in the showroom, just dogsbody stuff like parking the Merc and doing a coffee run to World Bean Inc., and getting flowers in every other day from the flower stall down the road.

While I was sorting the cardboard trousers for the Bechstein I kept thinking I'd stop in a second to phone Mum but I kept putting it off. I couldn't really handle it. I knew we'd probably get in a row about her wanting me to come home, and then my good mood would be ruined. I preferred thinking about Jennifer. I wondered what that shaved bit on the back of her neck felt like when you ran your finger over it. I imagined it would be like the inside of Mum's jewellery boxes that I used to open up and feel when she was having a bath. I didn't really know Jennifer, it was true, but I just had a good feeling about her.

Like for instance, what would she think if I died out of the blue? She read about me dying in the papers, say, or came round to the showroom again to see me, to take me out to a posh restaurant, and somebody said, 'Oh, Graham died yesterday, didn't you know?' I reckoned she'd be shattered. I pictured her on the pavement outside the showroom, sobbing her guts out, not caring when her tears stained her Prada jacket or whatever it was. Me and Jennifer had some special connection, and the age difference didn't matter. I amazed her, she'd already told me that, and she didn't even know me.

My brain was really off on one now. I thought about what other people would think if I died. Uncle George, for instance. He didn't like me, Mum had said, so he wouldn't care. In fact he'd be pleased because he'd be able to get a proper rent for his flat instead of the pork scratchings (his words) he got from Mum and Dad for me staying there. Dad? I didn't know what he'd think, he never let on what he thought. Maybe he didn't think. With most people there was noise and voices and ideas and suddenly-remembering-things going on in their heads all the time, but maybe inside Dad's head there was nothing. Therefore the question didn't apply. But I knew what he'd do if I died: go down to his shed, which was the opposite of his head, i.e. full of things.

Derek would be pleased if I died because he was a creep and because it would give him an excuse to put his arms round Kate, at the funeral and after. Kate would care, she would definitely care but it would be in quite a soppy way. She would light scented candles, and make people hold hands in a circle while they thought good thoughts about me.

Which left Mum. I knew Mum would care. She would feel really bad because apart from anything, as she kept telling me, I was their only kid and I didn't reckon they were in a fit state to have another if I popped off. She was the opposite of Dad, there was too much going on in her head and if you weren't careful it all went pear-shaped in there.

Once when we were on holiday at Lulworth Cove she packed a coolbox to take down to the beach. The coolbox was square-ish with rounded corners, made of red plastic with white trim round the lid. There was too much to fit in and it was all spilling out over the top so she couldn't get the lid on. A bottle of lemonade poking out and a pork pie that she broke trying to push it down. And then she just lost it. She picked up the coolbox and emptied it all over the caravan floor. Her head was like that coolbox. You'd got to pack it carefully. Someone dying would be too much for her.

My secret was in that coolbox. More wisdom coming up.

I was seven when we went to Lulworth Cove. We had a caravan up on the cliffs.

At night the wind blew so hard the caravan would rock, which I liked. Mum was in a good mood on that holiday, up to a certain point anyway. She said the wind was the ghost of the sea, come to tell us who's boss. When it rained, which it did for quite a few days when we were there, it sounded like someone was pouring gravel on the roof.

To get to the beach you walked along the cliffs then down a steep path that had been cut in the side of the cliff. The last bit really hurt your legs. Because it was a long way we would pack loads of things in a coolbox, plus rugs and a windbreak, and go down there for the whole day. Except Dad would go down there twice. The first time would be early in the morning when we were still in bed. I think perhaps he was missing his shed. Going down to the beach on his own, when there was no one about, was the equivalent of going to his shed. He would collect shells.

He brought the shells back in this old khaki rucksack that Mum said had belonged to Dad's dad and he should throw it out because it smelt. He emptied the rucksack on the grass outside the caravan and got down on his hands and knees and arranged the shells in a pattern. The pattern was a bigger and bigger spiral that he just added to each day.

While he was doing this Mum would be cooking breakfast. We had eggs every day, which was unusual. The eggs were from a local farm and Mum said they were the freshest eggs we'd ever eaten and they were very good for us. But to me they tasted the same as the eggs we got from the supermarket and anyway they looked worse. There were black bits and a white whirly bit in each one that might have been the beginnings of a baby chicken. So we sat there eating those eggs and Dad would be looking out of the caravan window at the shells he'd laid out on the grass.

79

One night he woke me up and said, 'Come and look at the stars.' He took me outside in my pyjamas and bare feet. Mum said, 'Put something on his feet,' but Dad said, 'It's summer.' The grass was wet under my feet and cold and clean. Dad said, 'Look.' I looked up. I couldn't see anything at first. Then one by one I saw the stars until the sky was lit with them. While we were looking up Dad needed to put his hand on my shoulder for balance.

The caravan was clever, the way it all folded down and partitioned itself off to make a private shower/toilet and two private bedrooms. Luckily my bed was at the back so I could lie in while Mum got up and made her bed and got the breakfast going.

One morning it was really sunny. The sun woke me up. It came through a gap in the curtains. Mum had closed the middle section of the caravan to screen off the shower/toilet. I could hear her having a shower. Her feet squeaked on the plastic base and she snorted occasionally. I imagined the water running into her nose to make her snort. The sun was on my eyelids. I didn't open my eyes at first. I just looked at these two orange blobs of light that the sun made of my eyelids and I listened to Mum next door in the shower. Dad, I assumed, was down on the beach already, collecting more shells.

I still didn't open my eyes. I started thinking of the day before. On the way along the cliffs to the beach I had got a bit left behind. I did this deliberately. I got sick of being with Mum and Dad all the time. No disrespect, as Dad said, but sometimes I couldn't think the things I wanted to think when they were near me. Not bad things, just private ones. Mum had stopped and turned round and yelled at me to hurry up but Dad had touched her arm and said something I couldn't hear and she had shrugged and changed her mind. 'See you down there,' she said.

'Don't be too long and don't go near the edge.' They reached the steps down to the beach. I watched their heads bob downwards then disappear below the grassy edge of the cliff.

I was on my own. No one around. I stood there for a bit with my fishing net made of bamboo and green nylon. Then I sat down in the grass. It was springy and quite long. I lay back in it. I watched the white clouds moving across the blue sky. They seemed to move much faster when you lay on your back and watched them than they did when you were walking along. After a while I felt dizzy watching them. It felt like I was standing upright and watching the clouds on a cinema screen. The edge of the cliff was about ten metres away. I couldn't see over the edge, even when I sat up, but I could sense what was there. Nothing. Or rather just air. I could hear it. It sounded like a shell sounds when you put it to your ear.

There was another sound. The sea, far below. I could pick it out from the other sounds, the sound of wind, the sound of nothing. The sea sounded like traffic. Like cars and lorries, never stopping. Like the bypass I could hear at night, at home. I thought about this. It was the same sound but you would think differently about it depending on whether it came from the sea or from the bypass.

I remembered Mum had told me not to go near the edge of the cliff. But I thought if I crawled there, through the grass, it would be safe. That's what I did. When I reached the edge I discovered it wasn't a sharp right angle. It sloped down. The grass stopped and there was soil and then there was rock. Far below there was a bay that was a semi-circle. The beach looked like orange sand but I knew it was only orange because it was wet and it wasn't sand, it was small pebbles. The sea was sliding up it in thin sheets of white foam. I couldn't quite see how far the foam reached up the beach.

Sometimes I had superstitions. On that holiday at Lulworth Cove, whenever I had an ice cream I would blow the ice cream into the bottom of the cone. I would try to make sure the bottom of the cone was completely filled with ice cream. If I bit into the last bit of cone and it was empty I would think something bad was going to happen. I would be worried for a few minutes and then I would forget about it. Who knows, maybe something bad did happen after I had stopped thinking about it which was because I hadn't filled up all the cone with the ice cream, and I never realized. It's possible.

Now, looking at that sea, I knew I had to see how far up the beach it reached. It was just a superstition but it was important. I moved forward and down a bit, shuffling through these giant daisies, until my elbows were in the soily bit. Then I stuck my head right out. Quite near I could see a jutting bit of rock with a plant growing out of it. The plant was flapping madly backwards and forwards, which seemed strange because there wasn't that much wind that I could feel. I still couldn't see where the sea reached.

I looked behind me. The grass sloped up very steeply to the flat bit at the top of the cliff. The slope hadn't felt that steep when I slid down it. I could just see the green nylon fishing net I'd left in the grass. I decided to go a bit further forward.

I admit I was a bit scared, especially when I looked back and saw how steep it was behind me, but it seemed a shame, when I'd come so far, not to have a final try to see how high up the beach the sea was. I levered myself a couple of inches forward on my elbows. Then things all seemed to happen at once.

The soil gave way under my elbows and there was a mini-landslide of stones. Not just of stones. I was sliding too, I realized. Slower than the stones but going on on on and there was nothing to grab on to. Then there was the wind. It rushed up and slapped me in the face. It howled like a ghost in a film. It felt like it was sucking me forward and down. I remember sliding towards a jagged bit of rock and thinking I didn't have time to hold on to it or fend it off. That it would stick me right through the chest. Then, just as I was about to get impaled on it, something else happened.

There was a sort of swoop in my stomach like when you drive fast over a humpback bridge. I felt like I lost touch completely with the ground. I felt I was floating free. The sea was right below me, pale as fog and glittery like fairy lights. The wind was in my ears and my

83

nose. I felt light as a dandelion clock. I threw out my hands in front of me. And this was the weirdest thing of all. I stopped falling.

The next morning, this is what I was thinking about as I lay in bed in the caravan with the sun on my eyelids. I hadn't just stopped falling. I had sort of gone into reverse. I had gone back and up and landed in the long springy grass and the giant daisies up on the top of the cliff, near my fishing net. I didn't even have a bruise. I didn't think about it that much at the time. I was just grateful it had happened. I think I thought it was the wind. A freak gust of wind had lifted me up and flipped me back and saved my life.

I lay there looking at the sky, at the clouds whizzing across the sky, while I got my breath back. Then there was a seagull. I heard it before I saw it. Its wings creaked quietly, and then it was right over me, quick as tenpin bowling. It trembled on the wind and for about six seconds it stopped dead still in the air above me, just holding the wind. It was big as a cat with a tiny shiny black eye. I had this weird thought that it had come to tell me something. Then it dipped to one side and got swept away, like water down a plughole.

I carried on down to the beach with my fishing net. When I got to the bottom of the steps I couldn't see Mum and Dad. I could see our windbreak but there was no one there, just a big line of clothes in front of it. Then the clothes moved and I realized it was Mum and

Dad. Dad was lying on top of Mum. But not for long. They shot apart when they saw me.

How had I stopped falling? I thought about this properly for the first time. I tried to open my eyes but the sun was too strong. I moved my head on the pillow until I found some cool shadow then opened my eyes. I knew it was something to do with my hands. I put my hands on top of the bedclothes and looked at them. I lifted them into the sunlight and looked at them properly, really properly, for the first time. Next door, the shower had stopped. There was silence. I imagined Mum drying herself with a towel, or looking at her teeth if the mirror wasn't misted up. Once I had caught her looking at her teeth, with her top lip all curled back like a dog's when it's mad.

I flexed my fingers. I didn't do this very often now. Even when I was scrubbing them I would just scrub across the top of the fingers and hope for the best. They made that dry rustling sound. I looked at the skin between the fingers. I held my hands up to the light and the sun shone through the skin. My hands looked amazing, like giant oranges cut in half. I sat right up in bed. My heart was thumping. I wasn't thinking any more about what had happened on the cliff edge. I just had this feeling that there was even more in my hands if I only tried. If I knew how to try. I closed my eyes and concentrated.

I felt something give in my hands. I felt them get bigger. Even bigger. The sun was on my forehead now.

I was really hot and my heart was hammering away and I didn't dare open my eyes. My hands felt as big as beach towels. Then something was happening that I wasn't making happen, that seemed to have nothing to do with me. My hands were shaking, trembling, very fast, so fast that my whole arms ached but I could do nothing to stop it. I tried to close up my hands, to fold the flesh back up. To send time whizzing backwards to before this started to happen and my hands were just hands. Big and clumsy and weird looking, but just hands. Now they were—? What were they? I didn't dare open my eyes to look.

I felt myself lifting off the bed. That light feeling again. Dandelion clocks. Now I didn't want to open my eyes because I didn't want to break the spell. I didn't want to find a boy in a bed in a caravan. That seemed much too boring compared to what I was now feeling. The feeling of floating in air. It seemed so real, like a dream in which you smell real engine oil or sardines in tomato sauce and think this must be proof of real life. Even the bedclothes felt as if they were falling off me. And then bang! I hit the back of my head on the caravan roof. I opened my eyes.

My hands, they were the first things I looked at. They were out in front of me, moving in a blur like film of insects' wings I've seen on TV. They seemed huge in that caravan, like eagles in a budgie cage. The bedclothes had fallen off me. They had fallen off me because I was about a metre above the bed. I was in a sitting position. It reminded me of an advert I'd seen, with a man in pyjamas sitting in a car that was invisible except for the steering wheel. That's sort of the position I was in, in mid-air, with my hands out in front. My hands somehow making it happen though I had no control over them.

My head hit the roof again. And again. I could feel the caravan rocking like it did when the wind blew at night. I shot to one side and my shoulder hit the side of the caravan. Then right across the other way to hit the other side. Then there was someone calling. Mum calling out from behind the partition. 'Graham, what on earth are you doing?' she said. I wanted it to stop but I was afraid it would stop. Afraid it would never happen again. And besides I didn't know how to stop it. I tried to say something back to Mum, something normal sounding to make her go away. But I couldn't speak. The air seemed to get trapped in my throat when I tried.

I flew sideways and caught my eye on the corner of the window. I must have made a noise, yelled or screamed, because Mum rattled the door handle and shouted, 'Graham, what is it, who's in there?' And then the door opened and there she was, looking up at me. And me looking down at her. That seemed to go on for a long time, us just looking and everything else quiet, but the sort of quiet where you know there's a lot of sound just waiting to burst out. And then it did burst out. Mum screaming, what was I doing? Me screaming back. And then it all stopped again.

It was like somebody had flicked a switch to turn gravity back on. I just fell back on the bed. I lifted my hands to show Mum. We both stared at them, not saying anything. Now the sun wasn't shining through them they weren't like oranges sliced in half. They were more like a cross between a boxing glove and a flipper. Mum said, 'Hell's bells.'

She sat on the bed. She just had a white towel round her. There was water dripping from her eyebrows. She said, 'You've cut yourself. Hang on.' She went back into the bathroom/toilet bit. While she was gone I put my hands under the bedclothes. She came back with a bit of toilet paper. She dabbed my eye. She said, 'You'll live, love.' Then she said, 'How long?' She whispered it. It was funny but she didn't seem that surprised by what she'd seen.

'Just today. Just now,' I said.

She stood up and turned away a bit so she could readjust the towel round her. She reached over me and pulled open the curtains properly. The sun came flooding in. 'It's a lovely day,' she said. She turned round to open the curtains on the other side. I could see the backs of her calves. They were pink from the shower and they looked very young. They could have been a girl's. She carried on talking but she didn't turn back to face me. 'Is this the only time then?' she said.

'Yes,' I said.

'No one knows?'

'Knows what? Like who?'

'Dad'll be back soon,' she said. 'I wish he'd throw that damn rucksack away. The whole car smells of it. You won't say anything to him, will you? I think we just forget everything. It never happened. Nothing happened. Nothing ever will happen. Will it?'

'No,' I said.

'Ever again. And you won't mention it to anyone, will

you? Ever. Everyone has secrets. Everyone carries around one terrible thing that no one else knows. Do you understand me, Graham? I'll put the eggs on.'

Dad came back from the beach. I heard the shells in the rucksack shaking as he walked up to the caravan. It sounded like footsteps on the beach. The caravan shook as he stepped inside. He yelled to me, 'You not up yet, boy?'

When Mum served the eggs to me and Dad, she said, 'What a lovely morning.'

Half an hour later she tipped up the coolbox and the stuff inside went all over the caravan floor.

And that's about the size of it, as Dad would say.

The truck arrived to pick up the Bechstein about two. I had to take a clipboard down to the loading bay for the driver to sign. Uncle George didn't even let me finish my sarnie. After that Derek made me sort the piano brochures in the filing cabinet. They were filed alphabetically. I had to file the new brochures from a big stack next to the toilet cubicle, and chuck out the old ones, but only if there were new ones to replace them. In other words, I couldn't just bin the whole lot of old ones, then file the new ones, I had to go through them all one by one, which was a real pain. It took me about three hours. Derek kept watching me do it, I could feel his eyes on me. On my hands. Once he said, 'What are you chucking that one out for?'

I said, 'Because—'

He stopped me and said, 'All right, just checking, Joe, just checking.'

Uncle George was on and off the phone to some bloke about dentists' equipment. When Derek went to the toilet, Kate said, 'Don't worry about Derek, he's just sad.'

'I'm not bothered,' I said.

'How about that drink sometime?' she said. She whispered it so Uncle George wouldn't hear.

'OK,' I said.

'I got you that ID, you might as well use it,' she said.

I almost told her that soon I was going to go to a posh restaurant with a really classy woman and you didn't need ID for that, you just needed to know the right people, but I thought that would sound snotty so I just said 'OK' again.

I wondered how much Jennifer twigged. Because I knew I was going to choose her. It made my stomach go hot and liquid to think about it, but I couldn't help it, I was going to tell her my secret. I thought about where to start. Should I just show her? She'd half seen it already, although how much she'd taken on board I wasn't sure. At least she hadn't done a Kylie Blounce and completely freaked out. Or should I just tell her about it first off. Tell her what happened with Kylie, or even go right back to Lulworth Cove? Give her time to take it in, *then* show her. I decided I'd play it by ear.

I really wanted to see Jennifer. Fifteen minutes later, I did.

Chapter 9

By five thirty I'd had enough of brochure filing. I put my jean jacket on and plugged my headphones in and was opening the door before Uncle George noticed. He shouted something but I didn't hear it, what with Mr Choppin going off as well. Outside there was a brand new, metallic, sunburst-red Mini Cooper parked on the double yellow. It looked like a toy, like it had just come out of a giant box with neat flaps at the ends. I tried to clock who was sitting in there but the driver's side was away from me.

But then the passenger door swung open in front of me, I had to jump out of the way to stop it catching my knee. I saw a slim hand with a bracelet and painted nails. I caught the scent before I clocked the eyes. Her mouth was moving, she was saying something that I couldn't hear because of the headphones. I took them off and Jennifer said, 'I said, "Get in".'

It was low, in the Mini Cooper, and the seat was half reclined, so I was laid back like at the dentist's. There were lots of circles on the dash. The speedo and revometer and air vents were all round like the eyeholes of binoculars. The surfaces of the dials were dull silver and the Jennifer-Mini Cooper smell was peachy. Imagine there's a brand new plastic box, giving off that clean plastic smell, and then you flip off the lid and in it there's a rose oozing out these heavy waves of scent. I said, 'Are the seats real leather?'

She had on jeans and a jean jacket; I almost said 'Snap'. She said, 'Ooo, I expect so. Do your belt up.'

I looked back at the showroom window. Uncle George was standing with his back to the window, on his mobile. I willed him to turn round, I wanted him to see me in this classy situation. But he didn't. I said, 'What can it do nought to sixty in then?'

She said, 'Want to see?' She fiddled with the CD player and this major guitar sound came on. She revved up really hard for a few seconds, but then set off at normal speed. As we moved off I looked back at the showroom window and there was a reflection of the car, and in it my head about the size of a pea.

The reflection looked like the beginning of a film. Listening to music as we drove along was like that, too, and the city sweeping by silently outside. A film in which I became a photographer or a scientist. The Mini was highly polished. You could see the clouds reflected in the bonnet.

We whizzed over Putney Bridge. I couldn't see the river but I knew it was there. It felt exciting that it was there, although I wondered if that feeling was also to do with listening to music, the jangling of the guitars and the shish and belt of the drums. We turned right past Uncle George's block of flats. I said, 'That's where I live.'

Jennifer looked at me and smiled. 'Oh, OK,' she said. I thought, if I tidied the place up a bit and hid Uncle George's XXXX rated videos I could invite her there. We could get takeaway pizza, if she liked pizzas, from that place over the bridge. They delivered at no extra charge.

We forked left at a mini roundabout and went past a tree with lots of cards and bits and pieces stapled to it.

'Know what that was?' said Jennifer.

I said, 'No.'

She said, 'Marc Bolan?' I shook my head. 'It's a shrine to a singer called Marc Bolan. He died in a car crash right there.'

'I don't know him,' I said.

'"Ride a White Swan"? My sister was really into him. So don't you want to know where we're going?'

'OK,' I said. I didn't care where we were going. What we were doing, whizzing along like in a movie, was fine by me. And the moment would come when everything would be right and I would tell her my secret.

She said, 'We're going to see Baby Ade.'

'Baby Ade?' I said.

'Don't you want to see him?' she said.

I'd not thought about it. It was like whether I was bothered not having a baby brother or sister. I didn't think about it much but when I did I assumed the reason I didn't have one was because Mum and Dad didn't want to risk having another kid like me. 'Yeah, OK,' I said.

Jennifer said, 'You saved his life. When he grows up he'll want to meet you, shake your hand. Eh?'

'I s'pose,' I said.

'So if we do a nice photo then you'll have something to remember it by,' she said. 'You'll both be happy.'

We parked on the main road outside the hospital, right behind a people carrier. Jennifer turned off the engine. She looked at me and smiled. Underneath her jean jacket, her T-shirt had shiny reflective bits on it. It looked quite tight so you'd be able to see the outline of her bosoms if she took the jean jacket off. The driver's door of the people carrier opened and out got this really big bloke. He had on black boots with steel toecaps. The black covering on the toecaps had worn away and you could see the steel shining underneath. He looked towards us and gave a little wave. 'Who's that?' I said. I thought for a split second it was her bloke.

Jennifer said, 'That's Marlon. He's doing us a favour.' And the way she said it, I knew it wasn't her bloke. I really hoped she didn't have a bloke at all.

Marlon lifted up the hatchback of the people carrier and fiddled about in a silver box. He brought out two cameras with big lenses on them which he slung round his neck. 'Is he a photographer?' I said.

Jennifer said, 'Right, come on.' We got out of the car. Jennifer waved me round to the front of the bonnet, then she pushed me in the back towards Marlon. Marlon looked me up and down, then he stared at my hands. I couldn't believe it. 'CHECK. THESE. OUT,' he said. 'What is it?'

'Graham,' I said.

'Graham. Wow. Wow-ee. These are something else.'

I put my hands in my pockets. Jennifer said, 'Look

94

at him. Marlon is not the most subtle human being. But he takes a lovely picture, don't you, Marlon?'

Everything Jennifer and Marlon said, it was like they assumed I knew what was going on. But I didn't. Things were happening too quickly. The idea of telling Jennifer my secret suddenly seemed crazy. I should have said something, but I just got quite mardy and didn't say much. And I kept my hands in my pockets.

Jennifer said, 'We've got to be quite quick. In and out basically.'

We trotted across the road and up the drive towards the main entrance of the hospital. There were these big pillars outside the main entrance. I thought we were going to go between the pillars but just before we got there Marlon made a chopping motion in the air on his left-hand side and we veered off left. Marlon pointed at a sign.

Sir James Speke-Wilmott Wing

There was a bloke standing outside the door in a dressing gown smoking a cigarette. He hadn't shaved and his stubble was white. We went through the door and Marlon said, 'We go in. You pick up the nipper.' He looked at me. 'OK?'

Ade's room was full of flowers. You could smell it before you got there. When I looked from the doorway it took me a couple of seconds to see where Ade was.

He had a white blanket around him. He was asleep. His eyes were button holes, his mouth was open, and his hair was black and glossy. His hands were outside the blanket. Each one of my fingers was bigger than his whole hand. His tiny fingers were opening and closing and then they went still. When they were still his hands were like lovely smooth pebbles. Mine were like breeze blocks.

'Hey,' whispered Marlon. 'It's Ad-ee, Sad-ee, he's no lady, ain't that right, lickle fellah?' He said it in half a whisper, half a high girly voice. It sounded funny, this baby talk coming from such a big bloke. Marlon nodded at me. 'OK?' he said. I sat on the bed. 'Pick him up,' he said. 'Just like lean your head against his?'

I got on the bed and shuffled carefully towards Ade, who was still asleep. I leant my head against his little furry head. It felt like a peach. Marlon held this mobile-sized machine up against my face and clicked it then looked at what it said.

Jennifer was standing at the door looking outside into the corridor. She poked her head back in the room and said, 'Isn't that just lovely? Very touching that.'

Marlon stood at the end of the bed and clicked away with his cameras at me and Ade. All these lizard burps the camera made. He said to me, 'Love him up, love him up. Look like you could eat him with peas and rice, know what I mean?'

On the way out of the Sir James Speke-Wilmott Wing we got caught by a nurse. She had this big whispered row with Jennifer, who put her hand in the back pocket of her jeans and gave the nurse a twenty pound note or maybe a fifty, I couldn't quite see. I wanted to ask her what that was all about but things seemed to be moving too quickly and the moment went.

Jennifer and Marlon didn't say goodbye. He waved at her and she just nodded. Before he got in his people carrier, he made a gun out of his hand and fired at me, which I thought was a bit weird.

We drove back in silence. It felt like all the air had been sucked out of the Mini Cooper except just exactly the right amount for us to breathe. I wanted to ask Jennifer what was going on, but I didn't. I said, 'So Marlon took some photos then.'

Jennifer said, 'Yes. He's good. I'll let you have some.'

I knew she was going to leave me. Being with Jennifer was like having a really delicious meal, e.g. Chicken Jalfrezi with all the trimmings. All these tastes exploding on your tongue. Her scent and her bosoms and her eyes and her lips exploding in my head. But then when I had to say goodbye it was like someone was taking my plate away before I had finished. Before I'd even got started. I said, 'D'you want to come up to the flat? We could get a pizza.'

'I need to get on,' she said.

I knew she'd say that. She dropped me outside Uncle George's block of flats and I just stood there on the pavement, watching her Mini Cooper show me its disappearing arse, and feeling this hollow in my stomach where I wanted Jennifer to still be.

*   *   *

I thought of watching Uncle George's dirty videos but I was afraid he would be able to tell. Grandma used to put a felt tip mark on this bottle of whisky that she kept for visitors to check whether Gramps had had any when she wasn't looking. Maybe Uncle George had a way of marking the videos to see whether they had been played.

I couldn't relax.

I thought of doing some tidying so I could invite Jennifer back, plus shut Uncle George up. I got as far as dusting his John Lennon head but then I stopped doing more tidying because it didn't make me relax, it didn't stop me thinking. The phone rang a couple of times but I let it ring until Uncle George's Call Minder kicked in. I decided to go for a takeaway pizza. I could get it delivered but I fancied the walk.

I chose anchovies as one of the toppings, just to see what they were like. I'd never had them before; if they were good I could recommend them to Jennifer when she came round. I walked back across the bridge with the pizza box hot under my thumbs. I'd just got in the flat when the phone rang. As usual I let it ring until the Call Minder kicked in. I was looking for a clean plate and a clean knife that wasn't one with a bent blade that you cut grapefruit with. I recognized that grapefruit knife. Mum had given it to Uncle George with a load of other knives when he moved into the flat. It was a Christmas present. In the end I used it on the pizza and it made a wobbly line.

I was just starting to eat the pizza when the phone rang again. And again. And then I thought maybe it was

Mum or Uncle George and they were really angry because I wasn't answering so I answered it. And sure enough it was Uncle George, going ballistic at me.

He wanted to know if I'd phoned Mum. I'd forgotten all about phoning Mum. I'd forgotten what he'd said about her being not brilliant. While he was ranting and raving at me I switched my mobile on and it said I had about twelve messages from Mum and Dad, all left today.

I told Uncle George I'd call her. But first I finished the pizza. Except for the anchovies, which I left on the side of the plate. Anchovies were gross.

Chapter 10

After I'd finished the pizza I phoned Mum and Dad. I wondered who would answer. If Mum was really bad it would be Dad. Otherwise it would be Mum.

It was Dad. He was really worked up. 'Jesus, boy,' he said. 'Where've you been?' I could hear him swallowing. He was drinking whisky. There was a long silence. I thought I could hear him smoking. Then he said, 'I don't know. She's ruined herself on you.'

I said, 'Is she in bed?' Meaning with the pills and the portable TV.

'No, she's not in bed, Graham. She's in hospital, Graham. Satisfied?'

'Where are you?'

He sighed. 'I'm in the shed. I want you on that train, Graham. Your mother wants you.'

'I'll come up,' I said, 'but I've got some things to sort first.'

'Have you any idea?' he said. 'D'you want me to come down and get you? Or your mother, making a scene all over the place? D'you want that?'

'Ask Mum,' I said. 'Tell her I said it's not a good

idea. Tell her I said she'll know what I mean.'

He didn't like that at all.

Next morning I remembered what Jennifer had said about reading the papers so I bought the *Moon* at the paper shop on the other side of Putney Bridge. I flicked through it while I was waiting in World Bean Inc. for my latte. I couldn't believe it: I was in it. Page seven. The picture was big. In the top right-hand corner in very small letters it said Marlon van Nova. The picture was me with my head resting on Baby Ade's. I was smiling. It looked like Ade was smiling even though he'd been asleep. I was quite pleased with the way I looked. You couldn't see my hands, obviously, and you couldn't see how small and weedy-looking I was (I say weedy-*looking* because I wasn't weedy). Underneath the picture it said:

'THAT'S
MA BRO'
CRASH HERO'S BID TO ADOPT
Report by John Doe

Fulham Plane Crash hero Graham Sinclair yesterday made a dramatic plea to social work chiefs looking after Baby Ade: 'Make me his brother.' In a tearful bedside reunion with the miracle mite, Graham, 16, confirmed he'd asked his parents to start formal adoption proceedings . . .

I closed the paper. I was terrified someone would see it over my shoulder. I walked to the showroom wondering if I had Alzheimer's. Had I made a dramatic plea? When had I made it? I went back over the evening before, with Jennifer at the hospital. Nothing had made sense. I was always one step behind. Perhaps I was going mental, like Mum. I switched off the Discman. I thought about what was happening in my head right at this moment, looking for signs. But it was just the usual stuff, the noise and the running commentary, the noticing classy girls floating by but not showing that you've noticed. The worry about where my hands are and if anybody's looking at them. Business as usual. I was sane as rain. I was angry. I rang Jennifer on my mobile.

She answered straightaway. 'Slater?' she said. It was her cold voice.

'Have you seen the *Moon*?' I said. 'What's going on?'

'Oh, Graham, I was hoping you—I am so sorry. Marlon let me down big time, basically. I thought he was doing me a favour, doing *us* a favour. And it turned out he had other ideas. He decided he could make something out of it and he went to the papers. He's off the list as far as I'm concerned.'

'It's all mad,' I said. 'I never said those things.'

Jennifer said, 'Of course you didn't. I was there, remember. Look, I'll have a word with the reporter— what was his name?'

I looked at the paper. 'John Doe,' I said.

She said, 'John Doe, leave it to me. OK? Don't worry.

I'll email you later. Will you be at work? Oh, by the way. Are you really sixteen?'

I said, 'Yes.'

Jennifer would sort it. This thought wired me up and I turned up the volume on the Discman and got my legs working so they felt double-jointed.

There was a major scene on the streets near the show-room. A fleet of minibuses had parked up plus a load of police vans and reporters and camera crews. These foreigners were wandering around. They had narrow eyes and dinner-plate faces and they looked like they'd been in the dressing-up box. And they were freaked out, big time. You could tell by the way they shuffled, and some of them were crying. The police were there, too, walking really slowly alongside them. One woman held out her arms and started screaming at the sky and a cameraman was walking backwards in front of her sticking his camera right in her face. I couldn't work it out at first. Then I realized. They were from Uzbekistan, where Flight RF 3409 came from. They were relatives of the plane-crash victims.

I was first in the showroom. Then Mr Trainset turned up. I knew Derek had seen the *Moon* because of what he did. He shrugged at me and squashed his lips together and shook his head. Then he sat down and hit his keyboard really hard. I knew Kate hadn't seen it because she just gave me this big smile like she did every morning. Then she pointed through the window and said, 'Poor people. Did you see them?'

Derek said, 'What about our own dead?' Then he said, 'Hey, Junior Joe. What about adopting a few of them foreign kids as well what their mums got killed in the crash?'

Kate said, 'What are you on about?'

I was going to show her the article; just leave it on her desk and go in the cubicle while she read it. But Uncle George arrived. I didn't think he knew at first. He was really worked up about the Uzbeki people. His head was twitching, which it did when he was angry. 'What is going on?' he said. 'What is the matter with people? I had to park about three miles away. Don't they know people got businesses to run? Why can't they just send the bloody bodies back wherever it is they come from?'

'Uzbekistan,' said Kate. 'Because they didn't find any bodies. Just bits.'

Uncle George took off his leather jacket and started prowling about. He was like a teacher, trying to be in charge in a creepy way, coming up behind you and finding you out. 'Is the Bechstein sorted?' he said to Kate.

She said, 'Yes. It got picked up yesterday.'

He said, 'Well, unsort it,' pretending she'd done something really stupid.

She said sarcastically, 'Like really fair.' Kate was surprising sometimes. She was soft but she could be hard as well.

'Get it stopped,' he said. 'I want it going here instead.' And he slapped down a Post-It on Kate's desk. Then he said to me, 'Called your mother?'

I said, 'I spoke to my dad.'

He said, 'Was it before this?' And he got the *Moon* out of his pocket and threw it on my desk. He'd folded it up specially so he could produce it like a magician. He leaned over and flicked through the pages till he got to page seven. He hit the page with his fingernails. His nails were too long, they looked like a girl's. They made a tear in the paper.

I said, 'Yes.'

Kate said, 'What?'

Derek said, 'Junior Joe thinks he's Madonna or something. Just crap in the paper. I dunno.'

Kate picked the paper up.

'They made a mistake,' I said. 'I never said that. They made it up. As long as Mum and Dad don't find out.'

Kate put the paper down. 'Woooo,' she said.

'Your mum knows,' said Uncle George. 'Mad woman bashing my ear all the way in the car. Of course she knows. Some bint give it her in the hospital this morning. She'll be on her way down here when they unbuckle her. AND I DO NOT FANCY THAT. Who did you go with to the hospital?'

'No one,' I said.

Uncle George said, 'Oh, right. You just ended up there and someone just happened to be there with his camera, eh, Graham?' I couldn't remember the last time he'd called me Graham.

'Yeah,' I said.

Uncle George said, 'Come on, Strummer, what's the journalist's name?'

I said, 'It said John Doe. I've never met him.'

Uncle George said, 'John Doe! Do you know who John Doe is? What's the name of the journalist you went to the hospital with?'

I said, 'She's not a journalist.'

He said, 'Ah. Thank you.'

I got an email from Jennifer. It gave me the name of a bar/restaurant in the Fulham Road, and a day, and a time. The bar/restaurant was called bLING (that's how it was written), the day was today, and the time was seven o'clock. I hit return and keyed in Dear Jennifer, I will see you there, best wishes Graham.

I looked up bLING on the net. There was quite a lot of stuff about it, including a neat visual on the website. It was this dish of food and you're looking at it from above and it slowly disappears until there's just a knife and fork left in the middle of the plate. Then you're looking at this drink from the side with fruit in it and the level goes down until there's just some fruit left in the bottom. Then these words come up:

pACIFIC rIM wITH gALLIC bOTTOM

The only reason I was mucking about on the net was that Uncle George went out. Kate went out as well, to get her own copy of the *Moon*. Derek was on the phone to Sky about his Digibox. Then two things happened. One, Mum rang me. Two, I dropped a vase of flowers.

Mum was calling from the hospital. She sounded OK at first. She said, 'Are you flossing your hands?' (Flossing is what I was supposed to do now to keep my hands clean. A scrubbing brush wasn't good enough, according to Mum. But I didn't really bother.)

I said, 'Yes.'

She said, 'Are you sure? Sure sure?'

Then I realized she wasn't making sense. She said she hoped Grandma and Gramps were looking after me. She made a joke about Gramps drinking the whisky when Grandma wasn't looking. I didn't say anything because I knew what I wanted to say would sound stupid, which was: Grandma and Gramps are dead.

Then Mum said, 'Did you see the E-Type? I forgot to ask.'

Once when I was small we went to stay with Mum's parents, i.e. Grandma and Gramps, and something happened. Me and Dad and Gramps went for a ride in Gramps's car to see an E-Type Jaguar that was parked in the drive of a house. I was in the back seat. Dad and Gramps were different on their own. They saw a girl walking along the street and made comments. I remember Gramps saying, 'You don't need pacemakers.' Dad shook his head and blew out through his lips. Dad wound down the window and pulled a cigar out of his jacket pocket. When he wasn't smoking it he held it out of the window and once he drummed on the roof with the hand he held the cigar in. They had a conversation in whispers that I couldn't hear. At the end of it they both laughed and Dad said, 'Yeah, true,' like Gramps might not believe him. It was like a different person was inhabiting Dad's body.

They were worried that the E-Type might not be there but it was. It was red and had a soft black top and silver wire wheels. Gramps parked a bit away from the E-Type so people wouldn't realize what we were doing. Then we just sat there looking at it. The light reflected off the bonnet. It was the red of a perfect tomato. Dad made a comment linking the girl they'd seen walking along and the E-Type and Gramps said, 'Wouldn't it just?'

Then we drove back to Grandma and Gramps's house. On the way Dad sucked a mint.

Something had happened. Mum and Grandma had been crying. They were standing in the kitchen, one at either end. Grandma said, 'Would the menfolk require tea, by any chance?' trying to sound all jolly.

Gramps appeared in the doorway through to the lounge. There was a budgie in the lounge called Edward the Feather Man, or Eddie for short. Eddie could say 'Nuttall's Mintoes', which was the name of a sweet that was made in a factory nearby. Gramps had a better idea. He held a bottle in one hand. It was the whisky. I could hardly believe it when I saw it. Gramps and his whisky was like a fairytale that Mum told that I hadn't believed was really true. Now here it was, come to life.

I didn't know what to say to Mum's question about the E-Type. Eventually I said, 'I suppose so.'

Mum said, 'You suppose so,' and I said yes.

I asked her if she was OK and she said there was a woman gets on her nerves.

'Food's terrible,' she said. Then she giggled. She said,

'Someone knows how to get out and bring back fish and chips.' She sounded normal then.

I told her about the pizza place by Putney Bridge. I said they did takeaways if she was interested and she laughed. 'Two hundred miles on a moped,' she said. 'It'd be fit for a snowman.'

Then she said, 'You didn't have to put it in the paper, you know. About wanting a little brother. I gave you one once but it didn't work out.' Then she started crying. I was sitting at my desk holding the phone right up close to my head, turning my back right away from Derek. I told her I didn't put it in the paper. It was hard to talk. I was having to whisper. Then I said, 'When?'

'When what?' Mum said.

'When did you give me a little brother?' Talk about secrets. There are millions of them out there but you might never know them if you don't ask the right questions. What did my little brother look like? What was his name? And the main question: What were his hands like?

'You were very little, love,' Mum said.

'What was he—?' But I didn't finish because she started crying big time.

While Mum was crying somebody in the hospital must have tried to take the phone from her. I heard her shouting at them. Then she was back on the phone, just crying. While I listened I was thinking about that E-Type Jag day. I was wondering what it was between Grandma and Mum that had made them both cry. More secrets. More deep dark holes with weird stuff inside.

When Mum could speak again she said, 'Are you

coming back? When are you coming back?' She said it in a very soft voice that sounded more like a little girl's. It made me begin to cry too. And I think at that moment I was ready to say I would come back. I was ready to jack all this in in London and go back to Mum and Dad's, just to make her happy. To make up for having a kid brother who died and to make her well again. But then she switched.

She went from all soft to screaming at me in half a second, it was like a hail of bullets suddenly coming out of a flower. I couldn't understand most of it, it was just noise and vibration blasting out of the phone. And it nearly blasted my ear off because I was having to hold the receiver pressed really close so Derek couldn't hear.

When I spoke I was so quiet Mum didn't hear me at first. Then she started to go a bit quieter. I told her again that I wasn't coming back, that I was happy down here. I told her not to try to come and get me and not to send Dad to bring me back. I said, 'If you do, I'll do the thing you don't want me to do. I promise I'll do it.'

I knew Derek could probably hear this but it had to be said. Now Mum was silent.

'I don't care any more,' I whispered.

Chapter 11

The vase smashed all over the floor. Glass and flowers and about a swimming pool's worth of water going everywhere. I was taking the vase over to a piano by the window, and thinking about the phone call I'd just had with Mum, and it slipped through my fingers. It's amazing how far water spreads. It ran across the wooden floor as fast as the sea up a beach. I wasn't thinking about what happened next, I just did it. I jumped up to avoid the water. And I didn't go back down.

I hovered there, hands out, making it work. And then I realized Derek was staring. He was still on the phone to his Digibox bloke but he'd swung round in his chair to see what had happened. I was about five centimetres off the floor and Derek's mouth was open. I put my hands behind my back and let it go so I splashed back down but Derek had seen, I knew he had seen. I stood there staring back at him. I could feel water getting in the toes of my trainers. It was weird, the way Derek looked. It was like *I'd* caught *him* doing something, not the other way round. Like I'd walked in on him having a major arse scratch.

* * *

All the rest of the day I thought about dinner with Jennifer. When Derek came up to me and shouted in my ear, 'YOU'RE REALLY FOR THE INDUSTRIAL STAPLER NOW, YOU BLOODY FREAK.' When Derek sent me to Robert Dyas to buy an extra large squeegee mop. When I stopped off at World Bean Inc. on the way back to get another latte. While I mopped down the showroom floor (while Kate gave me a hand by spreading out newspapers and Derek just sat and shook his head and muttered stuff about freaks needing to be locked up). All the time, I was wondering what Jennifer would wear and what we'd talk about and I was thinking of her eyes, the way they were like the sun, and the bit of velvet on the back of her neck, and I was worrying what Pacific rim with gallic bottom meant and if there'd be something really gross I'd have to eat, like giblets or a brain, or something in a shell that might be nice if you could get into it but I wouldn't know how to crack it open in the first place and then it would scoot off the plate and all over the floor. And I got it into my head that the waiter would not like me. He'd do everything he could to make me look stupid, and Jennifer would go off me.

I thought a bit about Derek, too. Derek deserved what he had seen and I wasn't going to help him understand it.

I got to bLING at 7 o'clock and checked it out a bit. It looked very weird. The front of it was a bit like the cliffs at Lulworth Cove. It was white and knobbly and powdery. There were two windows quite high up. They were very small, like behind them you'd find a very small toilet cubicle, not a big restaurant. I wasn't sure it was bLING at first as I couldn't see any sign. But then I saw it. A little circle about the size of a lapel badge with the word on it. I decided to walk round the block to give Jennifer the chance to get there.

While I was walking round the block I realized something about bLING. I hadn't seen a door. Or at least I hadn't seen anything that looked like a door. I got very nervous, thinking about this. Probably you pressed something and it opened up like a bookcase in an old libary. Maybe you pressed the tiny sign that said bLING. It did look like a button.

When I got back to the restaurant it was ten past seven. I had no way of knowing whether Jennifer was in there. If she was she'd be getting impatient. If I went round the block again she might even get up and leave. I had to try and go in. I waited a bit, hoping someone would show up and I'd see how to do it. But nobody came. So I went and stood in front of the tiny sign. I made sure no one was looking then I pressed the sign. Nothing happened. I got the feeling someone was watching. I looked up and there was a CCTV camera pointing at me. Then something weird happened. The pavement started moving.

I thought I was imagining it at first. I thought my legs were just going to jelly like they had after the plane crash. But the pavement really was moving. It was going down. It was taking me down like a lift. This was the door to bLING. The brick wall in front of me was painted black and on it, in white letters, was written the word bLING over and over again in different sizes and sorts of writing.

bLING

bLING bLING bLING

bLING **bLING**

At the bottom was a sort of runway with lights in the floor on each side. I walked up the runway and these glass doors at the end slid open. Behind them there were men in boiler suits. There was hardly anyone in the restaurant so they all paid attention to me. They were very good. They sort of swept me along. They took my jean jacket and then I was on a bar stool, wondering what to do with my legs because my feet didn't reach down to the bit where you're supposed to put them. And I was trying to order Stella Artois, which I didn't think they'd let me do, but they were so cool they pretended they didn't notice how young I was, which meant they had to serve me booze (result!). Actually they didn't have Stella so I had something else, out of a bottle, and then everything quietened down in my head, and slowed down around me, and I felt happy. Here I was in London in a dark room with tiny glittery lights all around, feeling that first hit of better-than-Stella, and knowing that a beautiful model-type who found me interesting was on her way. And nothing else mattered. Mum and Dad and Uncle George were out the window.

Park Lane was a mile away. But in that moment I felt it was inside me, too. The funny thing was, I'd never been to Park Lane, just seen it on telly. But I knew it. All those hotels with palm trees outside and doormen in top hats and movie celebs renting whole floors and insisting on having a certain sort of room freshener that you can only get in Cincinnati or Addis Ababa so it has to be flown out specially. I really wanted Jennifer to arrive then, when I was feeling like Park Lane.

The restaurant was in the basement but the ceiling reached up to the first floor so it was huge like a shopping mall. And at ground floor level you could see through all that bit that looked like the cliffs at Lulworth Cove to the street outside. I watched people walking past. Some of them stopped and looked. They were doing what I did. They were wondering what it was, or how to get in. Some of them moved off and some stayed there till the pavement moved and they disappeared down, then re-appeared at the end of the runway. I liked seeing those people outside while I was inside. It would have been good, for instance, if Kylie Blounce suddenly came down and saw me sitting at the bar. Old Flipper. Perv. Having a drink in bLING while he waits for a beautiful classy woman to come so they can have dinner.

But then the edge came off things a bit. I felt my legs flapping about in mid-air. I ate a whole green chilli from a dish on the bar and it nearly blew my mouth off. The barman noticed and he was laughing at me. Then I felt him looking at my hands. I was used to it so I picked it up quickly when it happened. In a way it was worse than if he just stared. But he was too up himself for that. He was Mr Important, doing things behind the bar. Juggling glasses and bottles and slicing lemons really fast and then chopping some green leaves that smelt minty, and all the time just half-looking at my hands. I wanted to move them out of the way but there was nowhere for them to go, I couldn't dangle them in mid-air like I was doing with my feet. I'd look like a parachutist.

It was at this moment, with me feeling not quite so Park Lane, that Jennifer arrived. I wanted to be able to smile a proper big smile. I knew that five minutes earlier I could have. But now the smile came out weird. Or at least it felt weird, more like I was pulling a face than smiling.

Sometimes things are so good that you can't believe it. You think it's unfair on everyone else that this really nice thing happened to you. For instance, when I was nine I did this maths test at school. I'd been really bad at maths. I always came bottom or next to bottom with this fat girl who actually used to worship Kylie Blounce. She loved Kylie so much she gave her her brand new purse that her uncle had brought back from Cowboy Country in America. It was made of a cow's skin, brown and white, and had tassels on it. The girl gave it to Kylie and Kylie accepted it.

In this particular maths test, instead of coming out bottom with the fat girl, I came just below middle. Mum mentioned it to Gramps and Gramps bought me a complete Leeds United strip and the same boots David Batty wore. I couldn't believe it. I felt like Park Lane then, but that didn't last either. I didn't deserve a Premiership strip and boots for what I'd done. I hadn't done anything really. It made me really sad to think that Gramps thought I had.

I never wore the strip or the boots and then they got out of date and Mum gave them to the Cancer Research shop.

I didn't deserve Jennifer Slater, that's what I thought. Especially not the Jennifer Slater I watched coming up the runway. All that thinking about her but when I saw her I realized I'd forgotten how she really was. The way she floated. The way her top floated and rippled around her. She had on tight jeans and suede boots that came up the leg and had a fold-down bit round the top, and a loose blouse that half-stuck to different bits of her body, including her bra, as she walked and she carried a jacket that was the same colour suede as her boots and her hair was a bit roughed up and her lips were E-Type red; and her eyes. When your eyes caught her eyes, it was like they lifted you just a bit off the ground. A nice and frightening feeling.

She made herself the only thing you wanted to look at. The whole place turned and stared. Not just the few people who'd already arrived and were sitting down. Not just the men in boiler suits or the faces in the port-holes in the doors to the kitchen. It was like even the slices of lemon sitting on the little tray at the back of the bar sat up and got shinier and juicier when Jennifer walked in.

This feeling took a split second. Then I felt depressed. I didn't deserve her. The blokes in boiler suits didn't think I did either, I could tell. They watched the direction Jennifer was walking, working out where she was going. To a table? To the toilets? To that man with crinkly grey hair smoking a cigar? No. To Old Freako, dangling on his stool.

I don't remember much of what happened at the beginning. There was a kiss and a boilersuit taking her jacket, and her looking at this card with drinks on it then saying, 'Champagne' and hitting the bar and saying 'Bottle and two glasses' and me not saying much and her looking around the restaurant, turning round on her stool so I could see down her top slightly without her seeing me do it. Her scent. And then the way she turned her eyes on me so I couldn't look at them and I looked at her lips instead and they looked like red plastic. My heart thumping.

We drank champagne. She clinked my glass with hers and said, 'To amazing things.'

I tried to say 'To amazing things' back to her but the champagne caught in my throat and I just coughed and said, 'things.' I wanted to touch her lips, to see how they'd feel. I imagined the plasticness and then, underneath, squishiness. The champagne made me tingle like after a hot bath. I didn't dare tell her I'd never drunk it before. She said, 'Are you really sixteen?'

I said, 'Sure.'

A boilersuit took us to our table. He carried our champagne for us and poured another glass at the table. The chair didn't look like a chair. It looked more like a kite and it wasn't obvious how to sit in it. Jennifer showed me how. You sort of knelt on it and leaned forward. She said it was good for your back but it did my back in. Another boilersuit brought a really small thing to eat. It was in the middle of the plate and there was a thin line of sauce round the edge of the plate so the whole thing looked like a tiny kid's scribble. I said, 'What is it?'

Jennifer frowned and held up her hand. A boilersuit came over and she pointed at the thing. He said something about courgette and pigeon. When he'd gone I said, 'Pigeon?'

Jennifer said, 'Yes, pigeon. Don't worry, not your Trafalgar Square variety. Tell me, Graham, where are you from exactly?'

I looked at the thing on the plate. It was a slice of courgette but chopped differently from how we had it at school dinner. There it was in long strips and it was mushy and tasted of water and nothing else. Here it was just a little bit off the end, chopped sideways and in the middle of it was this runny brown stuff. I said, 'Yorkshire.'

She said, 'I adore the Dales.'

I said, 'Nowhere near the Dales. It's flat and there are lots of pits and stuff. Power stations. Or there were but a lot of them have closed down.'

Jennifer took her fork and used it to cut her courgette

in half. She got one half on the fork and scooped up some pigeon and put it in her mouth. Some of the pigeon stuck to her red lips. She said, 'Brothers and sisters?'

I said no and then I remembered what Mum had told me on the phone. Talk about switching. There I was very excited to be with Jennifer and the champagne really starting to work all over so my head and arms were feeling like balloons. I was feeling like a happy Balloon Man and I would squeak if I moved. And yes I was nervous about having to eat pigeon but basically I was still Park Lane. And then I remembered what Mum had said about me once having a little brother.

And then I thought of what I was really doing here with Jennifer. We weren't here because she had seen me walking along the street in my combats with my Discman plugged in and thought, He looks nice, I'll ask him out. And this made me feel sad. Because soon we would get to what Dad called the nitty-gritty and I wouldn't be able to pretend any more. Jennifer didn't like me. She wasn't interested in me. Me! Fourteen-year-old Spakky! She was just interested in what I could do, that was the truth. The be-all and end-all.

Jennifer said, 'How is it?'

And I realized that I'd started to eat the courgette and pigeon. It was disgusting. I was going to say it was fine but suddenly, just in a split second, I felt incredibly happy again. It was like being in a movie. I was that kid who came out of King's Cross station not knowing anyone in London and then I became a scientist inventing cures for Aids etc. or a photographer who goes out with

Kate Moss and here I was wining and dining another beautiful supermodel just a stone's throw from Park Lane. I knocked off a whole glass of champagne in one go to take away the taste of the pigeon. I burped into my collar and said, 'Gross.'

Jennifer laughed and reached out her hand. She said, 'Are you OK?'

I looked at her hand on the white cloth. It was the brown of cream caramel. It was smooth and it glowed as if there was a little light in there. My hands were in my lap. I thought that whatever I did it would be all right. So I lifted my right hand and I put it on the table-cloth next to hers. I didn't dare touch her hand. But there mine was, right next to hers, waiting.

We were both looking at our hands. Hers was an E-Type, mine was a campervan. No contest. It was quite dark in the restaurant. There were loads of tiny lights on the ceiling, which was about half a mile away, and then these little lights on the tables, underneath weird shades that looked like shells. The light and shadows made my hand look really old and bumpy and even more horrible than usual. But I didn't care. I was drinking more champagne and looking at my hand like it was someone else's. Like it wasn't even a hand but, say, an old football boot. One worn by David Batty in the 1994–95 season.

Jennifer moved her hand towards mine. She stuck out her little finger and looped it round my little finger. She said, 'Have your hands always been like this?'

I said, 'Yes.' No one had ever touched my hands like that before. I was even more certain, then, that Jennifer was the right person to tell.

A boilersuit came with menus. I only recognized about three words. Jennifer said, 'D'you fancy steak and chips?' I said I did and she said that one of the things on the menu was actually steak and chips except it was called something completely different. So that's what I had and she had raw fish. She said that sometimes when it arrived it was still twitching on the plate. But it didn't twitch this time because I kept clocking it just in case.

She asked about the showroom and how come I worked there and what was I doing in London etc. etc. I told her about Uncle George. I was going to say how much I disliked him but I said instead, 'They call him Mister Porky behind his back.' I said he was my mum's brother. I thought she would ask me about who knew. Who knew about the thing that she saw me do.

But she said, 'What do you want to be? Have you thought about that? What you want from life?'

I said, 'To be happy.' It felt like a very grown-up thing to say. I saw myself saying it, the serious shape my mouth made. I thought that I must look like a very wise person. And I shrugged when I said it. I had both hands out now. When I shrugged, I did this big gesture with my hands like someone making a major point in a film. After we'd finished the champagne Jennifer ordered glasses of white wine. She was laughing at me but in a nice way. I pulled faces and thought I was being quite funny. And still she didn't get down to it. And then I thought: maybe she does just like me.

But there was one thing I'd been putting off, that I had to check. I said, 'Are you a journalist?'

She looked puzzled and said, 'What, you mean—

Graham. How could you think that? Especially when I've been putting out for you. What d'you think I've been doing all day except warning them off?'

I felt terrible, like I'd really insulted her. 'It's just that Uncle George—' I said. There was another thing I remembered. I said, 'You know that nurse at the hospital, why did you give her money?'

Jennifer said, 'You don't miss much, do you? To say thank you, as a matter of fact. She'd been great to Ade and the poor little mite hasn't got anyone else looking out for him. So, you know. Call it disinterested gratitude. Next question.'

'But—' I said. There was something that still bothered me but I couldn't quite remember it. 'Oh, nothing,' I said.

There was quite a long silence. I could feel Jennifer looking at me. I couldn't look in her eyes so I kept my head down and shovelled up fries. I knew I'd said the wrong thing. I wanted to make it better but I couldn't think of what to say. Then I had an idea. 'Anyway, what *do* you do?' I said. I saw me again like I was in a film. Turning my head like a cute pooch listening at a door and looking really interested.

Jennifer went dead serious and said, 'Facilitating mutually beneficial interfaces.'

I said, 'OK. Right.'

She laughed and it was like the whole tense atmosphere burst and it was OK again. 'Introducing people to other people who can help them, and they can all help each other, basically. To put it another way, I, like, put together what you might call fighting units of

123

businessmen. And women, of course. The idea is, between them they possess all the varied resources, the ruthlessness, the ingenuity and chutzpah, required for the storming of markets. So, like, some of them are really good at dislodging opponents from slippery poles above raging rivers. I mean literally because I send them on courses to the Forest of Dean.' Etc. etc.

While she was talking, something happened. I looked up at the front of the restaurant and there was a person standing there behind the cliffs. A big bloke with a big leather jacket on. I couldn't believe it, it was Uncle George. When the pavement moved, he nearly fell over. I watched him disappear behind the brick wall. I thought of him looking at all those words saying bLING. Then he was at the end of the runway. Jennifer was still talking. She saw me looking somewhere else and said, 'I'm sorry. Yakking on.' She thought she was boring me. It made me feel good, the fact that she was worried she was boring me.

But then I was worrying about Uncle George. Was it a coincidence or did he know I was here? As he got to the end of the runway I turned my back so he couldn't see the side of my face.

Jennifer said, 'How are you feeling? More wine?'

Then my elbow got knocked off the table. My head nearly banged on the corner. I heard Jennifer make a noise and a voice said, 'It's well past your bedtime, Strummer.'

There was Uncle George, standing over me. 'Ow! That hurt,' I said.

Jennifer said, 'Excuse me.' She scraped back her chair and half stood up.

I said, 'How'd you know I was here?'

Uncle George said, 'Someone told me.'

Jennifer said, 'Who is this oaf?'

I said, 'Uncle George.'

Uncle George said to Jennifer, 'Butt out, John Doe. You should know better.'

'No one told you,' I said. 'You looked at my emails.'

Jennifer was calling a boilersuit.

'I never,' said Uncle George. 'But Derek might of. I can't be responsible for how he allots his time. But he does it usefully, as it happens. Being a case in point now. Now come on. Out of here.'

Uncle George grabbed hold of me. Jennifer said, 'No.'

A boilersuit arrived. Uncle George muscled up to him and stuck his belly towards the man. Uncle George said, 'Yes? Yes? And?' The boilersuit didn't say anything. He just stepped forward a bit till they were pressing against each other. All the pockets of Uncle George's jacket and all the buttons down the front of the man's boilersuit going head to head.

Another boilersuit came over. Uncle George switched. He stepped back and lifted his arms like a big Mafia guy who's being reasonable. 'Hey,' he said to the boiler-suits. He smiled. 'Misunderstanding, OK? I'm just here to collect my nephew who's a bit the worse for wear.' He walked between the boilersuits and round to Jennifer's side of the table. This was when he clocked her. When he really clocked her. Just by looking at his face, you could see all this stuff going on in his brain. He was thinking, she's tasty. (He never used the word classy.) He was thinking, we didn't get off to a great start but

125

the situation can be turned round. God knows how Junior Joe knows a bird like this but you don't ask which cow the milk comes from when it's in your cappuccino. Etc.

He smiled his really sickly smile that he used with women in the showroom when he knew Derek the Trainset Man was watching him. It was the sort of smile they could talk about afterwards. He said to Jennifer, 'You're John Doe, right? George Oxnard. I apologize for my family member. I'll relieve you of his company now and maybe me and you can convene at a later date to conclude these discussions.'

Jennifer said, 'Please.'

Uncle George said, 'I'm his agent too.' He was patting his pockets for his wallet.

I said, 'What?'

He got out his card and handed it to Jennifer but she didn't take it. He put it on the table. Then he clicked his heels and did a sort of half salute. He smiled at Jennifer but his head was twitching. 'Come on, Strummer,' he said to me. 'On your skateboard.'

Jennifer said, 'Graham's coming with me.'

Uncle George's head started really twitching. He couldn't even smile now. He said, 'Do you know how old Graham is?' He said the word Graham sarcastically. I thought: whoops. 'Fourteen,' he said.

I couldn't believe it: Jennifer said, 'I know.'

Uncle George said, 'He still wets the bed.'

I got really angry. I whacked the table. As I said, I was strong in my hands. I nearly broke the table. The little light jumped up and the shade fell off it. I picked up the shade and it was red hot, it burned my fingers. I could see boilersuits coming over again. I said, 'No I bloody don't. How can you say that?' Then the pain in my fingers kicked in and I said, 'Owww.'

Jennifer said to the boilersuits, 'I'm really sorry about this. Can we just have the bill?' She said to Uncle George, 'Graham is coming back to my apartment.'

Uncle George said, 'What for?'

Jennifer said, 'For under-age rumpy-pumpy, Uncle Porky. What else?'

Chapter 12

We got a taxi from the restaurant. My head was buzzing with what she'd just said to Uncle George. I was definitely Balloon Man, feeling wobbly and squeaky all over. Her scent was very heavy in the back of that taxi. It was like the taxi was a giant flower. It vibrated a lot too, which was nice. A big vibrating rose. I let the vibrations take me towards Jennifer until we were touching shoulders. She was chatting a bit about Uncle George. She asked if he was always like that, and if he was really my agent. Then she said, 'Excuse me,' and got out her mobile to check her messages. At one point she said, 'I knew it,' really quietly.

I put my hand up on the back of the seat behind Jennifer's head. My heart was thumping.

Jennifer flipped the front back on her mobile and said, 'By the way, have you got a passport?'

I moved my hand on to her neck, trying to find that velvet patch.

It was like I electrocuted her. She jumped away from me towards the door. She held my hands out in front of me. She wasn't as strong as me, I could feel it in her wrists, but I gave in anyway. I wasn't that drunk.

'Graham,' she said. 'You're fourteen. Heavens. What I said back there, that was for Uncle Porky's benefit. Understand? Now we take you back to my apartment and we give you some coffee and we have a chat. No lunging. Lunge-free zone. What is it?'

I said, 'Lunge-free zone.' Then I said, 'Actually, it's Mister Porky, not Uncle.'

She called it her apartment, not her flat. Flats were what the Uncle Georges of this world had, i.e. with mould on the floor and the *Moon* for bogpaper. Jennifer's place was like a big swanky American space that you saw in made-for-TV movies. You could start at her front door with a camcorder going and just keep walking and the whole place would roll through the viewfinder like an entire high street practically. Some of the floor had these thick, creamy carpets on it and some of it was bare wood, really smooth, and some of it was rough reddish tiles. Walking on it was really good fun if you took your shoes and socks off because you got these different feelings on the soles of your feet. That was what Jennifer showed me. First thing she did when we got through the door, she kicked off her boots and said to me, 'Are your feet stinky in those trainers?' I said no so she said, 'Take them off.' She started walking down the corridor then she turned round and said, 'Remember, what is it in here?'

I said, 'Lunge-free zone.' Then I said, 'Why did you tell Uncle George you knew I was fourteen?'

'We don't want to encourage him,' she said.

'No, we don't,' I said. 'You know he lets me drive his car? It's a Merc.'

She said, 'Really?' But I didn't think she was listening.

There was smooth wood under my feet so that I could sort of ski down the corridor. Then she opened a door at the end and it was creamy carpet. All the furniture was low and the ceiling was high. It had lots of tiny lights just below it that were connected by almost invisible wires and were like the ones in bLING. The lights were just ordinary-coloured except every now and again, depending on the angle you looked at them, they flashed a bit green or red or purple. There were big windows that reached down to the floor that didn't have curtains and were black because it was night-time outside.

Or rather not black but orange. I went to the windows and looked out and you could see London all around. Everywhere there were lights except over to the right where the river was. There there was nothing, just a lack of lights. It could have been a huge new motorway they were building that cars weren't allowed on yet, or a strip of jungle. Close to, the lights were all orange but further away they were white and they trembled like a light bulb that's just about to blow. It was like London was made up of ten million bulbs all about to ping out.

I looked back into the room and realized it was twice as big as I'd thought. The other half, the bit I hadn't seen, was a kitchen. Here there were tiles on the floor. Jennifer was at the fridge. The fridge was taller than her. She was leaning inside. It was full of bottles with silver or gold tops. I could look at her all I liked because her head was in the fridge and she couldn't see me. Her top came up above her jeans and I could see the bottom of her back. It was the browny-creamy colour of her hands and it had a little patch of tiny white hairs on it. I could also see the top of her knickers. They were green and white.

She said, 'How are your fingers?'

As soon as she said this, my fingers really hurt. I'd forgotten about them till then. I said, 'They're burning.'

She came out of the fridge holding a bottle and a tray of ice. 'Take a seat,' she said. 'By the way, you never answered my question. Have you got a passport?'

I did have one but that didn't mean I'd ever been abroad. I was going to go on a trip to Germany with Brian. He'd fixed up to stay with a family because we were learning German. So we got me a passport and then it turned out there'd been a misunderstanding or Brian had changed his mind more like and it was another boy going to Germany with Brian. So I had a passport but I'd never used it. I said yes and Jennifer said good.

She brought me a glass filled with ice cubes and said, 'Dunk your fingers in there.' She went back to the kitchen and poured herself a glass of wine. I put my fingers in the glass and it felt perfect. She saw me looking at her. 'Coffee for you,' she said. She was brilliant at operating the coffee machine. While she was doing all the bits and pieces she didn't even have to look where her hands were. She looked at me instead.

She asked me if I was going to go back to Yorkshire and I said I didn't think so, I was happy down here. She asked me if I'd been to America. I said no. I didn't tell her I hadn't been anywhere interesting except London. She poured my coffee and said, 'Milk?' and I nodded then asked for two sugars. She put the coffee down next to the glass with ice in then sat on the sofa facing the one I was on. She brought up her legs on to the sofa cushion and rested her elbow on the sofa arm with the glass of wine in her hand. I noticed she couldn't look at me. Normally her eyes were so strong they made you look away but now they were flickering about. She started talking then stopped. She said, 'Graham?' She took a drink of wine and said, 'What did you . . . ?' Then she sighed and asked how the coffee was and I said it was good, which it was.

She got up and went to the window. She looked out on the orange-blackness. Without turning her head towards me she said, 'How can I put this? OK, here goes. What did I see you do on the day of the plane crash?'

I said, 'I don't know.'

She bashed the window and said, 'You know what I mean, Graham.' She still didn't turn round.

I said, 'No I don't.'

'All right,' she said. 'Let's just talk it through.' She started to walk round the room. She wasn't even looking at me. She said, 'It's a Tuesday and I just happen to be in that part of Fulham to meet a man who has an idea about mobile phone masts. How you can combine them with conceptual art or something. Duh. Great idea, Clive. We never caught up in the end. Anyway, I'm racing along because the cab's dropped me in the wrong place and I'm late—'

'I saw you,' I said.

'I know,' Jennifer said. She stopped walking and looked at me. 'You told me.'

I said, 'You looked like you were floating. I never thought I'd end up here.'

She didn't hear what I said, she'd started walking and talking again. She said, 'And then it happens. The crash. The noise, the chaos, the dust, the people running everywhere. I thought—I didn't know what to think. I thought it was a terrorist attack. That there might be more explosions. But, anyway, I don't know what to do or where to go and then I see this very purposeful young man running down the street looking like he knows exactly where he's going and I think, I'll follow him. So I follow this purposeful young man till he comes to a dead end; there's just this great pile of rubble there that was once a block of flats and there's dust everywhere. This young man is just standing there and I'm standing there watching him because I don't know what else to do or where to go. And then something happens. I'm looking at this young man, I don't take my eyes off him because I need him to show me how to get out of this madness. I'm looking at him and I see him—do something.'

She was over in the kitchen area now. She picked up the corkscrew and fiddled with it. The corkscrew had silver arms. She moved the arms up and down so it looked like a man doing exercises. She wasn't looking at me. 'The thing is,' she said, and stopped. She poured herself more wine and had another go. 'The thing is,' she said, 'I don't know what the thing was that you did.' She turned round and looked at me. 'D'you know what I'm saying?'

I lifted my shoulders and held my hands out, like Uncle George did. Sometimes he made circles in the air with his hands and said, 'Aye aye aye.' I didn't do that this time. I didn't quite know what it meant anyway, except for something like 'You ask too many questions.' But I liked Jennifer's questions really. Being asked them was like being pinned against a wall by someone who's trying to kiss you.

You pretend to struggle but really you're dead excited about being kissed. Come on, I thought, kiss me.

Push me off the diving board.

Chapter 13

Jennifer came and sat back on the sofa facing me. 'Help me out here, Graham, for God's sake,' she said. 'I saw you do something, right? And it was so weird, it was such a-a-an amazing thing that I forgot straightaway what it was. I mean, my mind couldn't cope with what it was. So I blanked it out. That's what I think happened. Hello?' She waved at me like our sofas were on opposite sides of the street. 'Am I making any sense at all? Because I'd really like to know. Or should they be coming to cart me off?'

I said, 'No, I sort of know what you mean.'

'Oh, great,' Jennifer said. 'You *sort of* know.'

I said, 'Yeah. You know.'

'Because listen,' she said. 'I think I blanked it out. As soon as I saw you do it. It. Whatever. I couldn't handle it and my mind just brought the shutters down. But I haven't forgotten it completely. I can remember what it made me feel. It's like a dream when you can't remember what happened but you can remember what it felt like, what the mood was, the sort of taste of it. But my mind won't allow me to remember it properly because it would be like putting the wrong bulb in a light socket.

A bulb that's got too many watts and it'll blow the whole electrics. But the thing is, Graham, I can't stand this not knowing. I'd rather risk blowing my whole system than not knowing any more. So. Please. If you wouldn't mind. Just tell me. I can handle it. I think.' And she laughed.

About a second later she was crying. Then she was shivering. She said, 'There's a cardy on the end of my bed. Can you go and bring it? Second door on the left.' I didn't switch the light on in her bedroom but I could still see her bed. The duvet was turned down a bit. I imagined putting my face right into the pillow, what it would smell like. Apples and roses. The cardy was the colour of the yellow skin of a peach. While I was still in the bedroom Jennifer called out, 'There's a box of tissues on the bedside table. Can you bring that too?'

The hankies were scented: 'Pine fresh'. When I got back in the living room she said, 'Well, I didn't handle it very well, did I?' and laughed. I went up to her with the cardy. I was waiting for her to lean forward, I wanted to drape it round her shoulders, but she took it from me and held it in her lap. 'It's funny,' she said, 'I can see it all now. You've unblocked the memory.'

I just stood next to her for a bit. I thought she might touch me but she didn't so I went and sat down opposite her again. 'I can see everything that happened,' she said. 'You've plugged the lightbulb in. It was touch and go there for a second but I think the system's surviving. Phew. Ha.' She blew her nose. A really good snort. I didn't look in the hanky in case there was a gilbert there.

Just before I told her, told her my secret, it had been like there were about a hundred rock bands in my head all thrashing away. Now my head was quiet.

Jennifer knocked back her wine. She got up and went over to the fridge. On the way she said to herself, 'I don't believe this. I'm going to wake up and there'll be just this trace of a memory of a dream. Or maybe not.' She turned round to me and pinched the back of her hand, making a face then grinning. After she'd poured another glass of wine for herself she said, 'How are you doing for time?'

There was a green digital read-out of the time on her cooker. Uncle George had one too but his had got old ketchup and stuff over the top so you couldn't read it very easily. Hers said 23.40. I said, 'I'm all right. I stay up till 2 o'clock sometimes.'

'I can get you a cab later,' she said.

I said, 'I can walk.'

She said, 'Or fly, why don't you. God, listen to me. I don't think this is funny actually.' She got down another glass from the cupboard and said, 'I think you need some wine now, eh? Then you can tell me.'

This was it. I told Jennifer everything: about what happened at Lulworth Cove and what Mum said about never telling anyone. Then about Kylie Blounce and how it showed that Mum had been right about not telling anyone. 'Phew,' I said. 'You don't know what it's like.

I've been waiting to do this. Tell someone. I've been waiting all my life. I feel really happy.'

But I didn't really. I just felt numb.

Jennifer said, 'Who else knows?'

'No one,' I said.

'Uncle Porky?'

'Mister,' I said.

'Sorry, Mister Porky.'

'No way,' I said.

Jennifer went to the window again. 'Come here, look at this,' she said. I stood next to her. She had tied the arms of her cardy round her middle. The cardy hairs tickled the back of my hand, we were that close. I could smell her, her scent but also something sweet off her body. Just a little bit of sweat, like a straight glass of Stella just before you drink it. She was pointing through the window. About a mile away there were these lights pointing into the sky and moving about like searchlights in a war film. I thought of sirens going off and enemy planes overhead. She said, 'It's a club in the West End. The lights are going through the glass roof. So just your mum. And your dad too?'

I said, 'Nope.'

'Not your dad?'

'Definitely not.'

'So just your mum and Kylie Whatsit. Where's Kylie these days?'

'Nowhere. The same. She's at Roger de Coverley and she sends me to Coventry.'

Jennifer said, 'Nobody else?'

I said, 'No, that's it.'

We went and sat back down on the sofas. Jennifer was shaking her head and scratching her neck. Right on that little velvet spot. 'I'm sorry, Graham,' she said. 'You must go soon. I'm just trying to get my head round this.'

I said, 'That's OK, I'm fine.' I didn't want to go home. I just wanted to sit there looking at Jennifer. I could have done it all night. I was calm now. I saw myself in this made-for-TV movie. The scientist/photographer in his Park Lane penthouse, probably with a Jacuzzi on the roof and soon me and my glamorous assistant/supermodel girlfriend would go up there and take our clothes off and have a Jacuzzi under the stars. I could hear the music they'd use to go with it. And then they'd cut to the adverts because those sorts of made-for-TV films never went beyond a certain point.

'D'you think it'll be all right, though?' I said. 'I'm really worried. Like, if people find out it'll be a disaster.'

Jennifer said, 'Why, out of interest?'

I said, 'It's like Mum said. She was right. When I showed Kylie it was a nightmare. The world can't cope, that's what Mum said. The world couldn't cope and everything would go wrong and it would all be my fault.'

Jennifer said, 'Mmm. I've coped though, haven't I? Just about.'

I said, 'Well, yes.'

'Well then,' she said. There was a silence. I looked at the clock in the kitchen. It said 00.11. Soon I would have to go. I started to think about tomorrow. Facing Uncle George in the showroom. Having to phone Mum.

My head had been nice and empty for a while but it was filling up again. Then Jennifer said, 'Do you think I could cope again? Right now? Here?'

I said, 'What do you mean?' but I knew what she meant.

She sat forward and said, 'Give me your hands. Show me how it works. The ceiling's high enough, isn't it?'

Chapter 14

Next morning Uncle George never mentioned the restaurant or me and Jennifer. It was like it didn't happen, which meant he was thinking about it one hundred per cent. Instead he said I'd ruined the showroom floor. When I got in he was already there. He was down on his hands and knees inspecting the floor like he was inspecting his Merc for scratches. I didn't see him at first. There was no one else in yet so I assumed he was in the toilet cubicle. I thought that would give me enough time to log on and send an email to Jennifer thanking her for the night before and apologizing for knackering up the lights in her apartment.

I'd just got my jean jacket on the back of the chair and flipped off the top of my latte when I heard a squeaking noise and then I saw Uncle George's head appear between the pianos. He just said one word. Ruined. Actually he didn't use that word but that's what he meant. He got on his feet and went to his desk. 'Totalled,' he said. 'Thanks to you.'

I went and had a look at the floor myself. It didn't look so bad. Maybe a bit whiter and dried-out looking. Then I remembered that Jennifer had called Uncle George

Uncle Porky. Which meant that he knew that I'd told her his nickname was Mister Porky. I felt myself go red.

Derek came in. When he knew Uncle George wasn't looking he pointed at me and mouthed the word 'Freak', then shook his head. I just ignored him. Then Kate came in. She had new purple bits in her hair. She stopped in the middle of taking off her coat and said, 'Uh-oh,' like she could feel the bad vibe between me and Uncle George. I really wanted to email Jennifer but I got out the cleaning gear and went round dusting the pianos. I didn't look at Derek. Trainset Man was permanently sent to Coventry for calling me a freak; checking out my emails then telling Uncle George where I'd gone. I took the dead bits off the flowers and topped up the water. I didn't want to give Uncle George any more excuse to give me aggro. All the time I could feel him watching me. I knew exactly what he was thinking. He was wondering if I'd done it with Jennifer.

But it wasn't until the afternoon that he said anything about her. Or even spoke to me at all. Derek had gone off early to meet a bloke who was adjusting his satellite dish. Kate's ears were flapping, I could tell. Her ears were small even though she'd got all these silver rings in them but they picked up a lot. Uncle George said out of the blue, 'Why did that bird call me Uncle Porky, then?' I couldn't think of what to say so I didn't say anything. He said, 'Eh?'

I said, 'It's not Uncle Porky. It's Mister Porky.' I really wanted to look at Kate but I didn't dare. I knew I'd get a giggling fit and so would she.

Uncle George said, 'Oh, great. Sorry about that. Is that what you call me?'

I said, 'No.'

'Oh, who does then?'

I said, 'Derek.'

Uncle George said, 'No he doesn't.'

I said, 'Yes he does. I've heard him.'

Uncle George said, 'Kate? I know you're tuning in. Is that right? Does Derek call me Uncle Porky?'

Kate said, '*Mister* Porky.'

Uncle George said, 'Christ almighty.' Then he said to me, 'Did you boff her?'

I said, 'Pardon?' I couldn't believe he'd said this in front of Kate.

He shouted at me. 'DID YOU BOFF THAT BIRD?'

Kate did a laugh that was more like a nose explosion and I did that thing with my shoulders and hands, meaning 'too many questions'. Uncle George was really wound up but he couldn't think of anything to say until about two hours later. I put my jean jacket on and got my Discman out, ready to go home. I was going to buy a pizza on the way, strictly no anchovies. And when I got back to the flat I was going to call Jennifer. Maybe I would call Mum too if I felt like it. I wondered what Mum would say/do if she knew I'd told Jennifer. Then I thought: I didn't tell Jennifer. She was halfway there already and I just helped her along a bit. It wasn't my fault.

I was just going through the door, thinking all these things, when Uncle George said, 'What story did that journalist woman spin you, anyway?'

'She didn't spin me anything,' I said. 'She's a businesswoman.'

He said, 'Oh yeah, very good, I see. Look, Strummer, I'm looking out for you and you don't even care, do you? You haven't asked me all day about John Doe etcetera. We need to talk before that woman knackers it up.' He looked at Kate. She was concentrating really hard on her screen. Which meant she was earwigging big time. He said, 'Oi, Kate. I didn't know you were going home early. Hope it's nothing I said.'

She looked up. She moved her head so quick her earrings tinkled. She was making out she was surprised. 'I'm not going home early,' she said.

Uncle George said, 'You are now. Go on, on your skateboard.'

I just stood there while Kate got her stuff together. Nobody said anything, it was just a weird atmosphere like everyone had all these loud thoughts in their heads even though you could hear Kate's mouse clicking when she logged off and her Pumas squeaking when she walked to the door. She made a face at me as she went past. Made her eyes wide and wrinkled her nose like she was saying, 'Mister Porky's definitely off on one. But don't let him give you any shit.'

Uncle George nodded at the door after she'd gone. He said, 'She wasn't born yesterday that one.' I was still standing there like a dork holding my Discman in one hand. 'Park your arse, for Christ's sake, Strummer,' he said. I went and sat down. I didn't know whether to take my jean jacket off so I left it on. He went and stood at the window. Cars were shishing by both ways.

He opened the door for a few seconds. All this noise and engine smells came into the showroom. Yells and hot roads and someone flicking fast through radio channels.

He lifted his nose and said, 'Puts tattoos on your arse, that. See that Beemer? Plain clothes. Or anti-terrorist. You never know who you're looking at these days. The place is swarming with them. They just drive ordinary motors.' He closed the door and locked it. He dimmed the lights and went and sat at his desk. He put his hands behind his head and feet up on the desk. He had black boots on with elastic Us in the sides. I could see the soles. There were silver bits nailed to the toe and the heel. 'Oi. By the way. What've you done with my shirt?' he said.

I said, 'Oh yeah, with Honkers something on it?' I'd forgotten about that. It was in a pile somewhere on the bedroom floor.

'I got that in Florida,' he said. 'You see the cops over the States. They don't mess about. Seriously though. If you're sitting there in traffic minding your own business and some plain clothes bloke is eyeballing you in the next vehicle, getting on his mobile and whatnot, radioing for back up, oi we've got a right one here, teenage suicide bomber eleven o'clock, wilco delta bravo sort of thing, what do you do? D'you give yourself up or d'you go for it? D'you put your foot down and burn him off?'

I said, 'Burn him off.'

Uncle George was in a good mood for some reason. He was still staring out the window. He said, 'Good boy. Nothing to lose. Burn him off. Show them a fast disappearing arse. Like, your mother, what d'you think she'd do?'

It was a stupid question. Mum didn't drive. She wouldn't be sitting in a car. An anti-terrorist bod had no reason to give her a hard time. 'I don't know,' I said.

'I do,' said Uncle George.

What was he going on about? I really wanted to go. I wanted to call Jennifer. And then I'd call Mum too. But I wouldn't tell her I'd met Jennifer and she knew my secret.

'I'm not kidding though,' he said. 'Your mother would just give herself up cos that's the sort of person she is. But me and you. You're more like me, I reckon. D'you know what I mean?'

I said, 'Were you and Mum adopted?'

Uncle George didn't say anything. He was still staring out the window. Then he frowned and looked at me. 'No. Why?' he said.

I said, 'Cos you're completely different.'

He said, 'Bloody hell, you're weird sometimes, Strum.'

I looked at my Seiko. It was 17.27. I thought, if he lets me go by 17.45 then Mum will come out of hospital, I won't have to go back to Roger de Coverley, and I'll work out a way of being at school down here. Maybe even stay at Jennifer's apartment. But if he doesn't, the opposite of those things will happen.

'Have you been telling your mother what you've been getting up to down here?' he said. 'Like does she know I don't stay at the flat with you?'

'No way,' I said.

'Good lad,' he said. 'She doesn't have to know stuff in general,' he said. 'If you know what I mean.'

'Like what?' I said.

'Like for instance small matters of business I may be conducting on your behalf in the near future,' he said.

I said, 'No way. Mum's really upset already.'

He said, 'You don't get it, do you? Nothing's got to happen in real life. Nobody has to *do* anything, it's all invented by the journos. You just sit tight and the money comes in. I'll talk to her.'

There was a traffic jam outside now. A bus went by slowly in the red-coloured bus lane. Its side was vibrating like the side of a dog in the sun. A couple of classy girls floated along the pavement carrying glossy square shopping bags. Uncle George noticed me clocking them and said, 'I saw you.' Then he said, 'You know your mother told me something about you once.'

I said, 'What?' I wasn't really listening to him. I was just looking at my watch. 17.34. Eleven minutes to go.

He said, 'You tell me.'

I didn't say anything. I made out I was neatening up the papers on my desk. He said, 'Got you there, haven't I?'

I said, 'No. I don't know what you're on about.' I'd never thought that Uncle George might know. He and Mum weren't close that I knew of. But then if he knew, why hadn't he said anything till now? It didn't make sense. I said, 'What did she say then?'

He said, 'Are you sure you don't know?'

I said, 'No idea. I think I'll be off soon if you don't mind.'

He said, 'All right then. Fair do's.' He lifted up his hands and showed me the palms. 'I was just trying it on. Seeing if you came out with it.'

I said, 'Came out with what?'

He said, 'Whatever. I bet she doesn't even remember saying it now. It was years ago, you were about seven. She was a bit drunk and—' He whooshed his finger round by the side of his head. 'I didn't get it to be honest but I was thinking about it afterwards and I thought, there's something going on there with Junior Joe. I don't know what but something. Is there?'

I said, 'No.'

He said, 'Something, like, mega? No?'

'No,' I said. 'No way. I don't know what you mean.'

'It was, like, when you rescued that baby I thought, this is it. I don't know what but something to do with Junior Joe being . . . something. I can't explain. That's why I got you down here if you want to know. I told your mother I'd sort you out. I wanted to watch you, see how you get on. I wanted to find out. Like, I thought you might be a famous pianist. Just sit down and play like Mozart, all these symphonies and whatnot pouring out of you. Your first day in the showroom, I watched you. I thought there'd be a moment. You'd go up to a piano and lift the lid and sit down and just start playing and it would be straight-off "Air on a G String" bingo. But nothing happened.

'I got you driving. I thought, I don't know. Something would happen. I mean, you're an OK driver for a kid but nothing special. I couldn't put my finger on it, Strummer. But now I'm thinking, it's nothing like that. It's just you being in this place at this time. You rescue the baby, you're in the papers, the *Moon* comes along, we can clean up. We're talking about the world here, the way the world works. We just show our disappearing arse to what's happened and take this forward, right? I reckon the *Moon* will do a deal with us if—'

I said, 'Not that again.'

He said, 'This is what it's about, Joe. Listen to me. If your mother and dad pretend to adopt Baby Ade it's worth a hundred K minimum, I reckon. I mean they'd pay Britney ten times that just for flashing her Pall Mall. We get some pictures done, a journo writes the interview, boff. Thank you very much. Fifty K to me, fifty to your mum and dad, and I dare say some lube in the back pocket for Strummer here along the way. But some things have got to happen first. You've got to get rid of that woman.'

I said, 'Jennifer.'

He said, 'I'm covering my ears, right?' He held his hands over his hairy ears. You could still see the lobes dangling down from his thumbs. 'I don't want to know what happened between you. Just tell Jennifer, no deal.' He said Jennifer's name really sarcastically.

I said, 'She's a friend.'

He said, 'Strummer, you're not listening and learning. Friend! Please! Second thing. We've got to get your mother and dad down here for the photo. How's she doing, have you spoken to her today? We can't hang around on this, we need to get her out of that bin even if it's just for a day. I've thought about it and there's no way we can tell her straight cos of her mental state. So what I'm thinking is, we tell her you're in trouble with the police. Like, some incident's blown up along the lines of what happened before, if you know what I mean. Say we say you got caught in Bishop's Park doing something you didn't ought. We get her down here, and then the *Moon*'s crew get them and you to the hospital, we do the photos with Ade, one big happy family, and that's that. Stick her back on the train and she can even go back in the bin that same night if it's not too late. A nice little break for her.'

I couldn't believe what I was hearing. Plus, it was 17.36 which meant there was no way I'd get out of here by 17.45. Bad news. I said, 'Mum's having nothing to do with this adopting Baby Ade stuff. Forget it.'

He said, 'Look, let's face it, Joe. She won't have a clue what's going on. She can't even fart up a phone mast at the present moment in time.'

I said, 'She can't help it if she goes mental sometimes.'

Uncle George said, 'That's true, not with *you* around, Strum.'

I said, 'Is that why she got postnatal depression? Cos of me?'

'What you on about now?'

'Mum couldn't handle it when I was born,' I said. 'When she saw my—' I didn't say the word, I just thought of the shock Mum must have had when I popped out. Imagine little Baby Ade with these great propeller things on the ends of his arms.

'Listen,' Uncle George said. 'One hundred grand. That's what it's about. Maybe more.'

150

I had an idea. Maybe it wasn't my fault after all. 'Was Mum mental before I was born?' I said.

'One fifty K.'

'But was she?'

'Well.' He rubbed his eyes and took his feet off the desk. He rattled his shoes on the floor like he was cycling uphill.

'Well what?' I said. '*Was* she?'

'You want to know about your mother when I was a kid?' he said. 'You *really* want to know? OK, here goes.' He sighed. 'Faith's room was like a bank vault. Same as her head. You couldn't get anywhere near her or her room. Is it mad to live in a bank vault? You tell me. But I know weird things went on in there. I mean in her room and her head. You could hear noise leaking out sometimes. Our mam knew what was going on, I think, but me and the old man never got a look in.'

I looked at my watch. 17.44. I had this blinding flash. I wasn't handcuffed to the chair. I didn't have cheesewire round my ankles. I could just get up and go to the door and unbolt it. And walk out. All before 17.45. No problem.

Uncle George couldn't believe I was doing it. 'Oi,' he shouted. Then 'Oi,' again. But I carried on unbolting the door, opening the door, closing it really neatly from the other side. That's what I reckon sent him ballistic, that I did it dead calmly. Last thing I heard him say was, 'You know what? You're not like me at all. You're as bad as bloody Faith. Mad as a bag of monkeys, both of you.'

*　　*　　*

I took a bit of a detour on the way to Putney Bridge and went past a telly shop. There were loads of tellies in the windows all showing the same picture. It was a big bird flying over a green valley. The bird didn't need to flap its wings to keep up there. It just twitched the ends of them occasionally. The colours were slightly different from telly to telly. In some, the green of the valley was more like grey, in others it was the colour of lime juice, but it was exactly the same picture, the same valley. The bird was sometimes dark brown and some-times almost red. I wondered which colours were the right ones.

I thought of Mum's head being like a bank vault when she was a kid. I imagined this metre-thick steel door with a wheel on the front that you whizzed back-wards and forwards to get the right combination. And now her head was a red plastic coolbox with a lid with white trim that didn't fit properly and you could just knock off with your little finger (*my* little finger anyway). What had happened to turn a bank vault into a coolbox?

My lid wasn't fitting either, at that moment. That's why I did a runner. Because Uncle George didn't have feelings and I had too many, including new ones about my kid brother who died, and if he didn't care about anything except money, including his own sister who was my mother, then I didn't care about him, end of story.

When I got to the pizza place I suddenly didn't want to go in. I didn't want to talk to anybody, even a Mr Cheerful Italian bloke. There was a pizza box on the pavement outside with a bit of pizza in it. I was going to eat it but then I decided that was gross. Instead I waited till I got back to the flat. I found some cream crackers and a tin of sardines in Uncle George's kitchen. I spent ages picking the backbones out of the sardines. I felt better after eating.

I dialled Call Minder. I had five messages. I didn't listen to them because I knew they were from Mum and/or Dad. I'd listen to them in the morning. I kept the phone in my hand, looking at it. I called Jennifer's landline and got her Call Minder. I tried her mobile and got the Orange Answering Service. I was going to leave a message telling her about what Uncle George had said about Mum but I wasn't sure Jennifer would want to know about Mum. I already had this feeling that if they ever met they wouldn't like each other. I coughed and killed the call.

It was a cordless phone. All the time I was walking up and down, going from the hallway into the kitchen then into the bedroom then into the hallway again. I had an idea. I rootled about in the pockets of my combats until I found the bit of paper that Kate had written her numbers on. I called her landline. I don't know why except I was all wound up and just wanted to talk to someone.

Her phone rang for a long time. I thought the Call Minder was going to kick in. But then she picked it up and said, 'Yes?' She sounded sleepy.

'Hey,' I said. 'It's Graham. From work.'

She said, 'Oh. Hi.'

I said, 'How are you doing?'

153

She said, 'I'm OK. What time is it?'

'I don't know,' I said.

I went into the kitchen to look at the read-out on the cooker. I had to flick this scab of dried sauce off the digital clock. Underneath it said 19.41. I was about to tell her when she said, 'I'm not with it. I'm, like, early nighting tonight, Graham.'

I wanted to say, 'Can you really play the piano?' But I didn't in case the question made her tell a lie. Instead I said, 'Uncle George is a prat.'

Kate said, 'Can you tell me tomorrow?'

'OK yeah,' I said.

She said, 'Night then.'

I said, 'Night.'

I stood there holding the phone, just looking at it. Then my hands suddenly felt mega-filthy, like I'd been using them to shovel dead animals for a year without washing them even once. I went into the bathroom and looked in the cupboards for floss to give my fingers a good de-gunk but there wasn't any so I used Uncle George's grotty old scrubbing brush. While I was scrubbing I thought about Kate. I wondered whether she took all the rings out of her ears when she went to bed.

I wasn't ready to go to bed. With my brand new hands I wanted to go and do something.

Chapter 15

The phone woke me up really early. I lay there listening to it ringing, wondering who it was and stuffing the weirdnesses of the night before in a tightly locked box. It was probably Uncle George or Dad, so there was no way I was answering it. But it could be Mum. I wanted to ask her why her head was like a safe when she was a kid. The phone stopped ringing. Whoever it was was probably calling my mobile now and getting really mad because it was switched off. Yet again. I found Uncle George's shirt with Honkers Go Go Go on it on the floor and wore that over the top of my ordinary shirt. It had been lying on the floor so long it smelt OK, it had sort of cleaned itself but I gave myself a good spray of deodorant just in case.

My shoulders were aching. On the way over the bridge I rolled them like a boxer limbering up. I bought the *Moon* at the paper shop over the far side of the bridge. While I was standing there waiting to pay I saw this amazing thing. On the wall behind the newsagent there was a square of cardboard that had bags of pork scratchings attached to it with white bits of elastic. Across the top there was a cartoon of a happy pig and it said:

MR PORKY

I saved this up to tell Kate.

I flicked through the paper as I walked. There was something about a murder of a woman in west London that the police had just worked out was linked to other unsolved attacks and murders, which meant there was a serial killer on the loose. The headline was:

PERV WHO PREYS ON TEENS

And there was an article about terrorists having plastic surgery, and a picture of a footballer taking his clothes off in a nightclub with a black square in a certain place. There was nothing about me. I picked up a latte at World Bean Inc. I got nervous as I got near the showroom in case Uncle George was already there and still mad from last night. But he wasn't. Kate was though. Her jacket was over her chair and her bag was on the table. A magazine was poking out of it to do with classical music. A delivery had just turned up, I could hear the reversing horn honking as the truck backed down the alley at the side of the showroom. Kate was out the back in the loading bay, sorting it out. I logged on to see if I had any messages, i.e. from Jennifer, but I didn't. I called Jennifer and got Call Minder. I called her mobile and got the Orange Answering Service. I decided to try one more time and if she didn't pick up I would leave a message.

I put the phone down and it rang straightaway. It was

Dad. He said, 'It's your father,' like it was really important news, then he didn't say anything. I was about to say something sarcastic but then he said, 'Your mother's tried to kill herself.'

Wooaa. Too much information.

I saw a programme about Houdini once. He was chained up and put in a safe which was lowered into a tank of water. Suddenly I felt like Houdini: wrapped in chains, locked in a safe, sunk in a tank of water. But my hearing wasn't impaired a bit. I said, 'I'll come up.'

He said, 'Have you got enough money?'

'I'll get some off Uncle George.'

'Right then. Let me know what train.'

'OK then.'

I put the phone down. I knew it was my fault. I'd made Mum try to kill herself. It was amazing, even being all trussed up like Houdini I could still walk. I went out the back to talk to Kate. I was going to tell her about Mr Porky pork scratchings. And I was going to tell her about Mum. (But I was going to pass on what happened last night after I spoke to her. I hadn't worked that one out myself yet.) I saw the back of her. Her hair was still purple. She had it scooped up away from her neck and held in a big silver clasp that was like a claw. Her neck was really long. You could see all her earrings. She had on quite a long skirt so you couldn't see how bandy her legs were. She had a silver bracelet on one ankle and was wearing those yellow Pumas with a dark red whoosh on them. She was holding a clipboard. I said, 'Hey, guess what?'

Kate turned round. She was crying. 'Look,' she said.

She pointed at a piano standing in the loading bay. Or half standing, because one of its front legs was broken off. It still had some of the corrugated cardboard wrapped round it that I had helped put on but the cardboard was torn and the piano was all bashed and scraped about. Kate lifted the lid. Half the keys were ripped out. It looked like a bloke who opens his mouth and he's got no teeth. 'They smashed it,' she said.

It was the Bechstein boudoir grand.

Kate sat at her desk sniffing a bit. I didn't tell her about the pork scratchings or about Mum. She didn't say anything and I didn't say anything. Then I asked if she'd heard from Uncle George. She shook her head. I'd give Uncle George another hour to turn up. I needed the time anyway, just to get rid of the chains and the safe and get out of the water.

Derek came in. He inspected the Bechstein boudoir grand and came back smiling. He said, 'Godalmighty, someone *else* is for the industrial stapler now.' Derek was smiling because he knew it wasn't him for the industrial stapler. It was Kate. Which was weird because I thought he had the hots for Kate. But then I remembered that Derek was just a Nazi prat.

Derek said to me, 'Get your arse in gear, freakface, and get dusting.'

Kate said, 'How sad are you?' which was nice of her.

I'd sent him to Coventry so I didn't say anything. I waited five minutes then I got the dustpan and brush and duster and Mister Sheen out. It was good to have something to do.

Derek said, 'Where is George, anyway?'

Kate said, 'No idea. He hasn't phoned.'

She suddenly pushed back her chair, bent down and untied her trainers. She went over to the Weber upright with the rosewood finish. Her bare feet left little dull patches on the floor that vanished as you looked at them. She didn't make a noise. She sat down on the stool and opened the lid. Me and Derek were watching her. Her back was so straight it curved outward. She tilted her head back. She would have been looking at the ceiling except her eyes were closed. She shook her head a bit and the earrings made a sound. She shuffled her bum on the stool and her toes felt about on the floor for the pedals. I thought of me driving. It was unfair what Uncle George had said. For a fourteen-year-old I was very good.

Kate lifted her hands above the keys. She went very still. You could hear her breathing. Her nostrils just moved slightly when she breathed out, like a piece of paper in a breeze. Her hands looked like they were carved. She opened her eyes and brought her head down. She slowly stretched her fingers and I screwed up my eyes, waiting for the crackling sound. But it didn't come. Kate's hands didn't crackle, they were smooth and silent like fish deep in water. Her fingers went down towards the keys and I imagined the music about to come out. The music played away in my head. It wasn't anything I knew, I didn't really know piano music, or any classical music except what they used in adverts. It was just notes on a piano but each note was perfect, like a tune in itself.

It was playing away in my head but in real life there was silence. Kate had lifted her fingers off the keys. She was shuffling her bum again. She coughed and shook her head. Her earrings tinkled. And I knew it was true. Kate couldn't play the piano at all. In a second she'd just get down off the stool and go back to her desk. But it wasn't Kate's fault she couldn't play the piano. It was the world's. The world seemed terrible for that split second. It smashed people up, like someone had smashed the Bechstein up.

I thought of that time in the caravan in Lulworth Cove when I flew. I was clumsy. I banged my head. I must have looked stupid. I was thrashing about like a loony in a park. No wonder Mum never wanted me to do it again. She didn't know I could be as good as the piano music I heard in my head. I imagined Mum listening to it too. Her eyes were closed, her head was on one side, and she was smiling.

And then Kate's fingers went down on the keys. And the sound they made, her fingers, the keys, her toes, the pedals, the strings, the wood, the air, my ears, the sound all of these things made was simple and perfect, like something that happened to me once. I must have been really young because it is one of my earliest memories. Dad was coming home from work in his car. Mum said, 'Why don't you stand out the front of the house and wait for him? He'll like that.' I stood at the top of the driveway. The driveway sloped down to the road. Across the road there were more houses just like ours and then there was another street and more houses etc. etc. until you got to open fields. And after the fields there was the bypass and then there was the railway line that went down to London. Then there was the pit and then the power station that looked like mugs of steaming coffee. And in the air there were phone wires and electricity cables and the smell of coal and the whiff of something nasty that was like the inside of Grandma's shoe and that someone said was a dogfood factory where they melted down horses etc. I stood there looking at all this and thinking it and smelling it and then I noticed there was no one about in the street, just me and this world. I looked up and the sky was green; I'd never seen it that colour before. Me and the world and the green sky. Just happy.

Kate stopped playing and there was silence and in the silence I thought of something: I hadn't asked Dad how Mum had tried to kill herself.

I offered to go to World Bean Inc. and fetch Kate a coffee. She wanted a grande decaff skinny cappuccino. I didn't offer to get anything for Derek. On the way I tried Jennifer on her mobile and this time I got through. She said, 'Yes?'

Before I heard about Mum I'd really been looking forward to speaking to Jennifer. It would be the first time we'd spoken since she found out my secret, since I took off in front of her and blew her mind and made her laugh and cry and clutch her cardy in her lap. I had wanted to hear her amazement again, squeeze out more drops of it. But things were different now. I said, 'It's Graham.'

She said, 'Who?' She sounded really suspicious and bad-tempered.

'Graham,' I said. 'You know.'

Her voice changed instantly. 'Graham. Yes,' she said. 'My God. I'm still pinching myself. Did you get back all right the other night? I've tried calling you.'

'Sorry about the lights,' I said.

'Hey, listen,' she said, then she stopped. 'Are you all right?' she said. 'You sound funny.'

'I'm OK,' I said. 'Did you talk to the *Moon*?'

She said, 'I did. There's a problem. Look, can I call you back? I've got someone trying to get through. Are you sure you're OK?'

'Yep,' I said.

'OK,' she said. 'Speak in a bit.'

The line went dead. No way Jennifer loved me. How could I have been so stupid? I thought of being in the restaurant with her. I'd put one of my hands next to hers. Just left it there like it was something to be proud of. Then, in the taxi, I'd stroked the velvet patch on her neck. WITH MY FINGERS. No wonder she'd jumped away, it must have been like getting groped by a gorilla.

I wondered if Mum had taken an overdose of pills.

Jennifer called me back when I was in World Bean Inc. fitting the cardboard holders on the coffees. She didn't say hello, she launched in with, 'Yes, the thing is, Graham, the newspaper knows some things about you. Although thank God not the thing *I* know about you. They've got pictures.'

I dropped one of the coffees, just about two centimetres back on to the table. It didn't spill but where there's a

162

hole in the lid, a big bulge of froth came out. I said, 'Pictures?'

She said, 'Pictures of you driving your uncle's car.'

I said, 'So what do we do?'

She said, 'There's worse. I really can't believe this but—' She laughed. She said, 'I don't know why I'm laughing, I really don't.'

I said, 'What?'

Jennifer said, 'They say one of their snappers got shots of me and you in the back of that cab. In what they called "an intimate situation", i.e. you in full-on lunge mode. Do you know what I'm saying? They're really on your case, boy. And mine now.'

'Might they put us in the paper too?' I said. Me doing it with a gorgeous girl. All the millions of people who saw it would never know it wasn't like that. Old Spakky driving down Park Lane in a chauffeured limo with Miss World, that's what it would look like. I could live with that, as Dad used to say.

'You don't sound too put out,' she said. 'Yes, they might. They might do lots of things.'

I said, 'So what do we do?' again.

She said, 'Well there's not a lot we can do. Unless we go along with it. I can represent you, if you like. I mean, if they're going to do stuff anyway we might as well make something out of it ourselves, don't you think?'

'I don't know,' I said. 'My mum's tried to kill herself.'

There was silence. Then Jennifer said, 'Oh. Oh OK. Well, that's terrible. Is she OK?'

I didn't know. I hadn't thought of it before but maybe she wasn't. Say, for instance, she was really dead, Dad probably wouldn't tell me till I got up there so he could tell me face to face. I felt my heart flutter in my chest like Eddie the Feather Man in his cage, then heavy thu-thumping started in my ears. I said, 'I don't know. I think so.'

Jennifer said, 'What happens now then?'

I said, 'I'm going up to see her today. Then I don't know.'

She said, 'You are coming back down?' She sounded worried that I might not return.

I said, 'Yes.'

She said, 'OK, well then. I hope everything's OK. How long will you be?'

I said, 'I don't know.'

She said, 'Why don't I take your mobile number?'

'I keep it switched off,' I said. Then I realized I didn't have to do that any more. So I gave Jennifer the number and she said, 'Talk soon,' and rang off.

Uncle George's Merc was outside the showroom when I got back. My heart was thumping again when I opened the showroom door but Uncle George wasn't there, and neither was Derek. I put Kate's coffee on her desk and she said, 'Thanks. They're looking at the Bechstein.' She turned her mouth down then covered her head with her hands.

I said, 'I've got to shoot off in a bit. Go and see my mum.'

Kate took her hands off her head and looked up at me. Her eyes were very big, that really nice glass-and-toffee combo. The bits around them were pink because she'd been crying. She said, 'Is your mum all right?'

I said, 'She's all right, yeah.'

A voice said, 'Oi.' Uncle George was standing in the doorway at the back. He waggled his finger at us and said, 'Both of you,' then disappeared.

As me and Kate walked towards the loading bay she touched my elbow and said, 'Uh-oh.'

Derek was sitting down at the back of the bay on the Bechstein's stool. He had one ankle up on his knee and a grin on his face. The piano was in the middle of the concrete floor. Someone had pulled off all the cardboard padding. It was tilted over because of the missing front leg. It looked like a ship in the middle of sinking. Uncle George was looking at me and Kate then looking at the Bechstein and rubbing his hands together. He lifted his arms. There were big rings of sweat under his pits; he had the same clothes on he'd been wearing last night. You could smell him. It looked like he was going to say something to me and Kate but then he twisted right round and spoke over his shoulder to Derek. He said, 'Right, Derek?' Really sarcastic.

Derek took his ankle off his knee and sat forward. He wasn't grinning now. He said, 'What?'

Uncle George said, 'Nothing. I just said, "Right, Derek". That's OK by you, is it?'

Derek said, 'Yeah.' He shrugged. He was sulking now. Uncle George was having a go at him because he thought Derek called him Mister Porky behind his back. With a bit of luck Uncle George would never be nice to the Trainset Man again.

'OK then,' said Uncle George. 'Not a problem. Not for me anyway. Have you got a problem with it, Derek?'

'With what?' said Derek. He was looking really freaked out now. 'No,' he said. He was frowning. He was majorly pissed off.

'Glad to hear it,' said Uncle George. 'Now then.' He started tiptoeing round the Bechstein looking at it like it was a sleeping lion. He stopped right in front of it and lifted the lid. He plinked the keys a bit then turned round to me and Kate and lifted his eyebrows. He smashed the lid back down really hard and Kate made a little moan. He stepped back and put his hands on his hips. Then he lifted his right foot. He was still wearing those black boots with the elastic bits and steel tips. He did a massive swing with his leg and whacked his foot against the piano's good front leg.

He half fell over. His boots made a scuffing sound on the concrete and as he went over sideways he shoved out a hand to break his fall. The piano leg went flying off in a way that made you want to laugh even though it wasn't funny, because it was more like a cartoon than real life. As it flew across the loading bay it was also twisting in the air like a missile. It bounced off the wall and went clattering along the floor.

The piano came down on the floor. It wasn't just the sound it made, it was the feeling. It came up through my ankles. It tingled in my nose. It seemed like the air was humming for minutes afterwards. We were all standing in a sea of piano sound that wouldn't go away. Uncle George was grinning. He was shouting. He shouted, 'That's better. Why didn't they do that in the first place like I told them to?'

Uncle George said, 'Right. Strummer first. Outside in the Merc.' We went outside and I went round to the driver's side. He wagged his finger at me and said, 'Nah nah', and I carried on walking right round the Merc till I was by the passenger door. We got in. A traffic warden came up and offered him the chance to drive off but Uncle George opened the door and said, 'No, you're all right.' The traffic warden shrugged and started writing out a ticket. We just sat and watched him. I was waiting for Uncle George to explode but he wasn't even twitching. He was really whiffy and I wanted to open a window but he hadn't turned the ignition on so the electric windows wouldn't work. The traffic warden lifted up the windscreen wiper and put the parking ticket underneath. Uncle George gave him the thumbs up.

I thought he'd probably gone mad. Like his sister. Which meant one day I might go mad.

He said, 'What was that all about then? In there?'

'I don't know,' I said.

He said, 'Listen and learn is what it's about. This piano is special, right? Else why is madam in there shedding tears for a bit of wood and whatnot? So special, right, that it's like paranormal. It exists in different places at the same time, yeah? And in each of those places, because it's so special, it's insured, right? For not just the cost of a McFunny McSpecial neither, if you know what I mean. So this piano goes on a journey. It

167

goes to Switzerland and oops, some bloke in leather shorts whacks it one. By accident, of course. Then it says, "I know, I'll go to Lancashire, I hear it's nice up there, black pudding and obliging girls etcetera." So that's what it does. And oops, some ferret fancier puts a clog through it. And so it goes. Everywhere it goes it's getting duffed over. Loses a leg here, a few keys there. Meanwhile, am I going ballistic? No, I'm not. Why not? Because I'm standing here and oodles of moolah is getting fired at me from all over the shop. Geddit?' I nodded. Insurance scam. I wasn't a complete dork. 'I hope you do,' he said, 'because here endeth the lessons. For ever. Right, that's point number one. Here's point number two. Joe's out of here. Like I told you, I thought you were special and you are, Strummer, you are. But it's like Special School special and we do not need that. I've done my bit for your mother and—'

I said, 'Mum's tried to kill herself.'

Uncle George put his head in his hands and said, 'Ouch.' Then he said, 'You've got my shirt on again. You haven't washed it since last time, have you? I can smell it from here.'

I hadn't thought of that. Maybe it was me I was smelling, not Uncle George. I said, 'I'm going up to see her in a bit. Can I lend some money off you?'

Uncle George gave me fifty quid. He said he was happy to if it got rid of me but to tell Dad it was sixty. He said he'd send up any of my gear in the flat but I said there wasn't anything. I got my stuff together. Everything

I needed was in the pockets of my combats. Discman, four CDs in a holder, mobile, five tenners.

I never thought I'd be leaving for good but that's what was happening. I was just getting carried along again but I didn't feel like trying to stop it. I just wanted to see Mum. I said, 'See you, then,' without looking at anybody and I was out of the door. The last thing I heard was Mr Choppin doing his quick bit of piano playing.

I wasn't sure where the tube station was because I never used the tube normally. I walked halfway along the street then stopped. I thought I'd go into World Bean Inc. and ask in there. I turned round because it was in the other direction, and there was Kate coming along the pavement. She had to take quite small steps because her long skirt was tight. The bracelet on her ankle was bright against her skin. She said, 'Mister Porky said you're leaving, that's it.'

I said, 'I think so, yeah.'

She said, 'We never had that drink. Do you want it now? A quick one?' and I nodded.

We didn't decide where we were going, we just walked along together. Kate said, 'Mister Porky wants to see me this afternoon. About the Bechstein. I think it's like really bad? But it wasn't my fault.'

I said, 'It's not bad, it's good. It'll be OK.'

She said, 'Oh yeah, like really ace.'

I said, 'Just you see.'

She said, 'Did you ring me last night?'

I said, 'Oh yeah, sorry.'

She said, 'I woke up this morning, I'm thinking, did

Graham ring me last night or was I dreaming? Then I'm thinking, if I'm dreaming about Graham, what is going on?' Kate laughed. Then she said, 'I'll miss you, though.' We'd already walked past a pub but we didn't say anything. It was nice just walking along. She said, 'Do you remember that bloke that came in dressed as Jesus? Like fruit loop or what?'

I said, 'Yeah,' and we laughed.

'So what are you going to do then?' said Kate.

'Just see my mum first,' I said.

Kate said, 'She's OK though?'

I said, 'I think so. She tried to kill herself.'

Kate grabbed my arm. She leaned into me so I nearly overbalanced. She squeezed my arm and said, 'Graham, why didn't you tell me?'

We were walking past the tube station but I didn't say anything, I just let us keep walking. I said, 'I am telling you.'

She kept hanging on to my arm. She said, 'What happened?'

I said, 'I don't know.' Then I said, 'Hey, guess what, I went in the paper shop this morning and saw these pork scratchings and they're called Mister Porky. I couldn't believe it.'

She said, 'That's where it comes from.'

I said, 'Oh,' and she barged me with her shoulder and said, 'Duh!'

I said, 'Anyway, I really liked your piano playing. It was brill.'

Kate said, 'Was it? It wasn't.'

I said, 'It was.'

She said, 'I hope she's all right, your mum. I bet she's all right. Will you let me know? Like text me?'

'OK,' I said.

Then we didn't say anything for a bit. We were just walking along with Kate still hanging on to me. I was wondering where the next tube station was. I didn't want to get too far away but I didn't want to stop what was happening. Then Kate said, 'I know. Just shut your eyes, right. Just keep walking. Trust me.' I shut my eyes. It was weird. I was tingling all over. I thought I'd hit a supermarket trolley or a bloke skateboarding. I slowed down and Kate said, 'No, it's OK, just keep going normal.' Then she said, 'Right, OK. Listen. What does it sound like?'

A siren started going off. I said, 'An ambulance. Or cops more like. It's always cops.'

Kate said, 'Not that. In the background. What does that noise sound like that's all around you in the background?'

I heard that sound of a million cars and radios and roadworks and aeroplanes and people talking and kids crying and shoes clacking and mobiles ringing and buses braking and heavy stuff crashing in a skip. And I knew the answer. I said, 'The sea.'

Chapter 16

The train stopped somewhere and my window was right outside someone's house. I was looking down into their garden and through their windows. I could see a climbing frame and a red and yellow inflatable paddling pool. An open kitchen door and a washing machine with its window that looked like a porthole. There was a sticker for a radio station on a bedroom window. Downstairs a bloke was sat watching a telly I couldn't see. A woman in fluffy slippers came out into the garden and chucked bread out for the birds.

For the first half of the journey you think about where you've come from. For the second half you think about where you're going to. Sometimes my wisdom depressed me.

I thought about Jennifer, the look on her face when I amazed her. No bloke could ever have made her look like that before, whatever they did to her. I decided I would ask if I could stay in her apartment. It was big enough. I imagined accidentally walking in on her when she was in the bath. Then I decided she probably had two bathrooms, which meant I'd get one to myself.

I wondered if I'd see Jennifer again.

I thought about Kate. We'd walked all the way to the next tube station. She was really upset when I said, 'The sea.' She said, 'Oh no, I've done this with you before, haven't I? I don't remember it but I did, didn't I?'

I said, 'No.'

She said, 'Oh God, I'm so boring. I'm sorry, Graham.'

I said, 'No, you haven't done it before. I've thought the same thing. It was down in Dorset. The sea sounded like traffic.'

She said, 'That's it, yeah. Isn't that weird? D'you think our brains are connected?' She hit me with her shoulder again. 'I haven't been to Dorset though,' she said. 'I haven't heard the sea in England, I've never been to the seaside in England. I've heard it where my mum comes from though. We went there last winter.'

I said, 'Can I ask you a question?'

She said, 'Aks me, aks me.'

I said, 'Do you have a secret?'

She said, 'Ye-eah', like it was two words.

'Like a really major one that nobody knows?' I said.

She said, 'One that nobody knows and another one that about two people know.'

'Go on then,' I said.

'Graham!' she said.

I said, 'Are they really bad?'

She wrinkled up her nose. It was sweet, the way she did it. She said, 'One is like weird but it's not my fault and the other one is really bad but that's not my fault either.'

I said, 'Really really bad?'

Kate said, 'Oh, so bad, man.'

I said, 'Come on then.'

She laughed and said, 'No way. What about you?'

I didn't know whether what was wrong with my mum counted as a secret or not. I decided it did, just so I had two secrets like Kate. I said, 'Two really major ones.'

Kate said, 'And? They are?'

I said, 'No way.'

She said, 'You've got to say something about them.'

I said, 'Well, one quite a few people know and it's not to do with me, it's just the way somebody is. And the other only one person knows.' I remembered Kylie. And Jennifer. I said, 'Three people.'

Kate said, 'Is it bad?'

I said, 'No.'

She said, 'Why's it a secret then?'

I called Dad on my mobile. It was just when the woman came out into the garden to chuck bread for the birds. There was I telling Dad what train I was on and this woman in pink slippers was flapping a bread board up and down and all these crumbs were flying off. Dad said he'd meet me at the station and take me straight to the hospital.

I came through the ticket barrier and Dad was right there, looking at his watch. He said, 'Where's your clobber?'

I patted my pockets and said, 'So how did Mum try and kill herself?'

Somebody turned and looked at us. Dad said, 'For Christ's sake, Graham.'

We didn't talk again till we were in the car. Dad sat fiddling in his pockets trying to find the car park ticket. I said, 'She's not dead though?'

He said, 'Please.'

I said, 'Is she dead?'

He said, 'She's not dead, Graham.'

I sighed and looked out the window. Eddie the budgie was quietening down in my chest. 'So how did she do it?' I said.

He said, 'D'you do this deliberately?'

I said, 'What?'

He said, 'You know what.' He found the ticket. He said, 'Where were you all last night? I was ringing and ringing. On your mobile. In the flat.' He drove up to the barrier, wound down the window and stuck the ticket in the slot.

The barrier came up. It was jointed in the middle. It hung there like a broken wing as we drove through. Dad put his foot down and said, 'Your mother jumped off the roof of the hospital. I don't know how she survived. It's four floors. But she did. She'll be OK.'

'Chuffing hell,' I said. I watched the streets as we drove through the town. It was about five weeks since I'd been here. It looked the same and different at the same time. It was like everything had been frozen like a VCR on Pause till I came back. When I got off the train, someone pressed Play and it all started up again. Everything looked computer-generated by a bloke with no imagination. There were no tramps, no black people, no classy girls that floated, no buildings that looked like palaces or space rockets, no motorcycle couriers jumping the lights, no cars that cost a hundred thousand quid, no loonies carrying placards, no Park Lane, no jetliners coming down low, no bridges, no river, no sound of the sea.

More like the sound of a puddle.

I said, 'So she's all right?'

Dad nodded and said, 'You survived then.' I nodded. It was lecture time, I could tell. 'It's a hell of a place, London,' he said. 'Emphasis on hell. In and out is my motto. Get in, do what you have to do, get out pronto. It'll stand you in good stead, though, to say you once worked in the Smoke. Now it's sorting yourself out time, life's not a rehearsal, you know, you only get one shot at it. Your mother and I think you should retake the year at de Coverley. Keep it simple when you see her, by the way. If she's asleep let her sleep, don't go on at her. You might get a bit of a shock when you see her. Both her eyes are in a bad way but the doc says it looks worse than it is.'

I said, 'Uncle George lent me seventy quid. If you give it me I'll give it him back when I go back down to the Smoke.'

We parked in the hospital car park, which was Pay & Display. Dad got angry. It was because of what I'd just said about going back down to London but he pretended it was because the car in the next space was parked really far over and he could hardly get his door open. In the end he had to twist out of the car sideways. He inspected the ground and said, 'Look at that, right across the white line.' Then he got angry again because he didn't have the right change for the ticket machine and I had to give him fifty p. As we walked towards the hospital entrance he said, 'Get your mother some flowers,' and pointed to this shop on the left. I got some pink flowers that cost £1.50. Dad gave me the money.

Water dripped off the flowers and on to the floor of the lift. I looked at the floor because I didn't want to look at all the faces. The light was bright and I knew people would be getting a good view of my hands but there was nowhere I could put them so I looked at the floor instead so I couldn't see them looking. They probably thought I was coming in to have an operation on them, or a six-monthly check-up to make sure they hadn't got any bigger. Then just occasionally I let my eyes flick around like I was just being really casual and I didn't care about anything, I didn't care that I was just about to see my mum and she'd recently tried to commit suicide by chucking herself off the roof.

No one said anything. You could hear music coming out of this kid's earphones, squirting out like silver wires that were so thin you couldn't see them. When the lift stopped at a floor a recorded voice came out of a grille in the ceiling. It was a woman with a sexy country bumpkin accent. She sounded really happy, like she was about to burst out laughing. She said, 'Floor-r-r Two for Car-r-rdiac Unit and Oncology.'

Dad suddenly lifted his hand and moved it towards my head. I couldn't believe it, I thought he was going to hit me. I tried to dodge out of the way but he just touched my hair and brushed the front of it twice with his fingers. He said, 'Don't they have barbers in London?' and I realized he'd said it to show off to the other people in the lift. He was telling them his son had been in London, which made us both pretty serious major guys. Dad was a complete dork.

The woman in the ceiling said, 'Floor-r-r Three for Depar-r-r-tment of Psychiatry', and when the lift doors opened Dad stood behind me and pushed me out into a corridor.

The doors had to be unlocked, then locked again behind us. When we got to Mum's room Dad pushed me in there and stood back outside. I'd worked out various things to say to Mum when I saw her, but now the moment had come I couldn't say anything. She turned her head on the pillow to look at me when I went in. She had two black eyes. Plus, her nose was about twice the size it should be and it was red and purple, and she had a weird line of purple and blue right across the middle of her forehead. There was a tray on wheels by the side of the bed. On the tray there was a plate with a half-eaten bit of fish and a few grey beans on it. There were flowers in a vase on the window-sill and a copy of the *Moon* on the bed. Mum's fingers were touching it.

'Hello, love,' she said. She lifted her arms and opened them towards me and I had to nudge the tray out of the way with my knee to get near her. She held her face up so the sore bits wouldn't get hurt and hugged me really tight. She smelt quite nice and her cheek was smooth and that reminded me of other times she'd

178

pressed her cheek against mine, when I was really little. Her cheek had been like rain falling very softly. I would think, here comes the cool soft rain to soothe me to sleep.

I could hear the *Moon* crinkling where I was half sitting on it. We didn't say anything for ages. Then she said, 'Thanks for the flowers.' I'd forgotten I was still holding them. They were all squashed up behind her head. She said, 'They're dripping on the sheet.'

Dad came in the room. He said, 'Hello, love.'

Mum said, 'You found him, then.'

Dad said, 'I'll get a vase.'

Mum said, 'How was London? I don't know what you all get up to down there, I really don't.' Then she hugged me again for a long time until I thought she'd fallen asleep holding me and I tried to wriggle out of her arms but she stopped me, she gripped me really tight. Her hands were surprisingly strong; I thought she was going to break my shoulder blades. She said, 'But you're mine again now.'

In the car on the way to the house Dad said, 'It's good she's sleeping. She's calm now cos you're back. She hasn't talked about what happened. Why she did it. Do you like cottage pie? I've got in a couple of Asda's for tea.'

I said, 'Is there a pizza place anywhere?'

Dad said, 'No. Why?'

I said, 'Nothing.'

It was dark when we got back to the house. I was

pleased. I didn't want anybody seeing me get out of the car. If it was light all these people would be looking out of the kitchen windows, even though you couldn't see them. They'd be saying, 'Look, there's Graham Sinclair back from London. Just because he's been in the papers he thinks he's special but we know he's just old Perv. Plus, his mum's mental, she tried to kill herself.'

It was strange, being back. The air had a particular smell I hadn't noticed when I was here all the time. It was coal dust but it was other things. The grandma's shoe smell of the dogfood factory, the white smoke of the power station, the plastic flower smell of car shampoo, the smell of each house drifting out of open windows: the hair fix and armpit spray and quick-fry prawn sauce and DVD wrappers and toilet odorizer and old bloke's combs. I'd smelt it all before but I didn't know I was smelling it, I'd never smelt anything else. Now it was new as well as old. It was like a dream.

Dad did frozen petit pois with the cottage pie. It was OK but not as good as Chicken Jalfrezi or a Putney Bridge pizza. While we were eating in the kitchen I looked at this new kettle that they hadn't had when I left. It looked wrong, too shiny and big like a basketball made out of metal. After dinner Dad burped, which he never did when Mum was there. He picked up the plates and put them in the sink and said, 'I bet you've been drinking down there. Eh?'

I said, 'Yes. Stella and Murphy's and champagne.'

He said, 'Champagne?' like he didn't believe me.

I didn't tell him about Jennifer, I just said, 'Yes. Champagne.'

He said, 'Want to try some whisky?'

He was like a different Dad.

We went to the shed. He got out a trestle covered in paint for me to sit on, then he said, 'Go and fetch a glass for your whisky.'

When I got back from the kitchen he had out the whisky bottle and the cigar box. He unscrewed the top of the whisky. It whistled as it came off. It was all very carefully done. He put the top down next to the cigar box and sniffed the open bottle then stuck it under my nose. I coughed. I couldn't breathe. The fumes almost blew my nose off. I'd never had whisky before. He put his tin beaker and my glass together and whooshed out a slosh into each. He nodded for me to take my glass. 'Easy,' he said. 'Just a sip.' The whisky burned my lip and stung my tongue and I felt it going all the way down into my stomach, like a ball of honey round a hot spoon. I imagined it lighting a huge bonfire when it hit the bottom, but then it all flipped up to the top and my head was tingling. 'Good?' Dad said and I nodded.

Then I said, 'What was my kid brother called?'

Dad fiddled about with his cigar box. He took out a cigar and twizzled it in his fingers, then he sniffed it along its side. 'What?' he said.

'Mum said I had a brother who died. Why did he die? What was he called?' I was going to ask about my brother's hands, but I didn't. Too many questions.

'He was—it was a long time ago,' said Dad. 'He was premature. Do you know what that means?'

'Yes,' I said. 'Too early. How old was I?'

'You must have been about two, I suppose,' Dad said.

'What was he called?' I said.

'Graham, really,' Dad said. 'It doesn't matter.'

'Yes it does,' I said.

'George,' he said.

'George!' I said. I noticed scratches on the back of Dad's hand that I hadn't seen before. There were three broken lines of scabs. Where bits of scab had peeled off the skin was pink and thin-looking. 'What happened to your hand?' I said.

He said, 'It's just—When your mother has one of her turns she can be a bit of a handful sometimes.'

'She hurt your hand?' I said.

'She can be strong, you know,' Dad said.

'I know,' I said, remembering the hug she'd given me. 'What does she do then?'

'She won't be told,' he said. 'Hey, see that coat?' He pointed to the long grey coat hanging on a hook on the back of the shed door. He lit his cigar. He made popping sounds with his lips as he sucked to keep it going. The red burning line moved down the cigar and it crackled like an overhead cable in the rain. He said, 'That's an RAF greatcoat.' He could hardly speak for all the smoke coming out of his mouth. 'Belonged to an uncle who was in the air force. I used to wear it when I hitch-hiked.' And then he went on about hitch-hiking for a bit.

The white smoke and the warm brown cigar smell filled up the shed and the whisky filled up my head. 'Did you know Mum, when you hitch-hiked?' I said.

'No,' Dad said. 'It was before.'

I said, 'Where did you meet her?'

Dad said, 'Your mother? In Hendon. I was down there for three months. And I met your mother. She was a waitress.'

'Was she?' I said. I thought of her like in an old black and white film, with a white frilly thing tied on her front.

He said, 'She rented this bedsit. Her mother had thrown her out of the house.'

I said, 'What, Grandma?' I couldn't believe this.

He said, 'Drop more? So let's hear about your adventures. Did George take you out much?'

I said, 'Why did Grandma throw Mum out of the house?'

Dad blew on the end of his cigar to get it going again. It glowed like a stop light. He said, 'Oh, you know. I don't ask. They probably can't even remember now.'

I said, 'What was Mum like then? Was her head like a bank vault?'

Dad was inhaling his cigar. He kept the smoke in his mouth and screwed up his eyes as he looked at me. He blew the smoke out. For a milli-second it hung there looking like a cat's tail then it floated off into the corners of the shed. 'Like a bank vault?' Dad said. 'What do you mean?'

'It's what Uncle George said,' I said.

'Oh, Uncle George,' said Dad. 'Has he been all right to you then? Whether you like it or not it's the Uncle Georges of this world who pedal the bus.'

'I think he meant like she had major secrets,' I said. 'I suppose.'

'Not so's you'd notice,' said Dad.

183

I wanted to talk then about the day me and Dad and Gramps went to see the E- Type, what happened between Mum and Grandma when we left them behind. I wanted to talk about my little brother George, who would be twelve by now. But I didn't. Instead I talked about Uncle George. I invented all these evenings we had together in the pub. I didn't mention Jennifer or Kate, or the Bechstein boudoir grand, or Baby Ade or the plane crash. Dad wasn't interested in those things. He wanted to talk about how flat the beer was Down South.

Eventually he looked at his watch and said, 'Anyway. I suppose,' and that meant it was time for bed.

I was really sleepy. I forgot where I was, who I was with. I stretched my fingers and made the crackling sound that drove Dad nuts. 'Why d'you always have to spoil things?' he said.

My bedroom was really tidy. I opened some of the drawers. They were full of things from a million years ago like my passport that I'd never used. The picture was done in a photo booth in the Arndale Centre. My mouth was hanging open, I looked subnormal, like a real Spakky. There were clothes I'd forgotten I had, school exercise books. No way was I going back to Roger de Coverley with people like Brian setting light to my hair and Kylie sending me to Coventry.

I turned off the light. I heard Dad in the bathroom. He flushed the toilet and opened the door while it was still flushing. He closed his bedroom door. The flushing stopped. Dad's bed creaked as he got into it.

Silence. Then the sound of a single drop of water landing in the toilet bowl. Then silence. It was very quiet here.

I plugged myself into my Discman and listened to the Cooper Temple Clause. I stood looking out of the window. You could see headlights on the bypass. I paused the CD. I couldn't hear the cars. Then a train went by. It came in a clatter and a blur of lighted windows and disappeared into the night. I imagined it two hours later, arriving in King's Cross. The passengers would get off and fan out into the streets and buses and tubes and just get brushed away like dust down a grate.

I could go to school in London. I could stay in Jennifer's apartment. I thought of Mum's black eyes.

I got out my mobile and switched it on. The panel glowed green in the dark. No messages. I remembered what Kate had said. I thought of texting her but I couldn't think what to say. I willed Jennifer to ring me but she didn't.

Next morning I ran from the house to the car. I sat low down in the passenger seat. I didn't want a single person in the street to see me. Dad dropped me at the hospital on his way to work. In the car he was going on again about me going back to school. I didn't say anything. He said he would send Uncle George a cheque for seventy quid. I said not to bother, Uncle George was coming up to see Mum soon.

'Is he?' Dad said. He sounded really surprised. The only time Uncle George had been up was because he could get four grand knocked off a Merc at a car auction nearby. I don't know why I lied, except I didn't want Uncle George to get more money than he should.

Dad said I could spend as long as I liked with Mum then get a bus back home. He reached in his pocket, got his wallet out and said, 'Go on, get a taxi.' He peeled off a tenner and a fiver. Then he gave me another fiver and said, 'Dinner.' Then another fiver. He ruffled the front of my hair and said, 'Haircut. Deal?'

I said, 'Deal.'

I bought a *Moon* in the hospital paper shop and looked at it in the lift. You only had to have half a brain to know the person they were referring to was me. They'd used another of the pictures that Marlon took of me and Ade but they'd blanked me out so I was a silhouette. Underneath it said:

HERO GRILLED BY SEX CASE 'TECS
by John Doe

A young man who recently won the heart of the nation has been interviewed by a special police unit investigating attacks on girls. We understand that these investigations, dating back a number of years, refer to several different cases in different parts of the country. In the light of these revelations, the *Moon* feels a moral duty to ask whether the suspect's family should continue with its efforts to adopt a certain baby . . .

In the lift there was a cleaner with a cleaning trolley with two mops sticking up. The mops looked like thin men wearing joke wigs. I closed the paper. I was wondering what 'tecs meant. Then I worked it out: detectives. I wondered if I had been grilled by sex case detectives and just forgotten about it. Yesterday, for instance, before I got the train from King's Cross, I might have had time to pop into a cop shop and get grilled. Or had they arrested me up here and given me the quick once-over before we had the Asda cottage pies? And I'd just forgotten. In other words, was I just as mad as Mum?

Me and Mum were talking. She was propped in bed with about five pillows behind her. She kept smiling and lifting her hands to her face and saying, 'Ooo, that hurts. But I can't help smiling. You make me smile just by being here, Graham.'

She seemed normal but then she would say something that made it obvious she was a bit mad. I sat in this quite nice armchair next to the bed. I put my hands between my knees. Mum kept looking at them. I thought she was going to ask if I'd been flossing them. I really hoped she didn't because that would make me annoyed with her and then I'd feel guilty. But she never mentioned them. She said, 'What did you have for tea last night?'

Her eyes and that weird stripe across her head looked worse this morning. They were green now as well as black and blue and purple. I thought of Mum's head hitting the ground. I thought of a nurse minding her own business, dunking a chocolate chip cookie in her tea on her tea break, and suddenly this body whizzes past the window and the nurse does a double-take and rushes to have a look. And there's this crumpled body of Mum lying on the grass. Then I thought, there might not be grass there. There might be these giant metal dumpsters that people throw bin bags in, or ambulances lined up. She might have clattered on the roof of an ambulance. I wanted to ask her what had happened but I didn't. I said, 'Asda cottage pies.'

Mum said, 'Good?'

I said, 'Dad did frozen petit pois with them.'

Mum said, 'Good.'

I said, 'Remember when we had an Indian and you ate a whole chilli?' and she put her hand out. She was waiting for me to put my hand in hers but I didn't want to. Both my hands felt happy where they were, between my knees.

A nurse came in and said, 'How's Faith?'

Mum said, 'Much better.'

The nurse said, 'Life's a blast is it, Faith?' I thought she sounded a bit sarcastic.

Mum said, 'It is this morning. This is my son Graham.'

The nurse said, 'Now then.' She had big bosoms that were a bit like Uncle George's beer gut, i.e. you couldn't really tell where the bosoms stopped and the rest of her began. She wasn't like the nurse I'd just imagined, dunking a biscuit in her tea on her tea break. That nurse had looked a bit like Jennifer.

I said, 'Hello.'

The nurse gave Mum these pills in a cardboard tray. She sang, 'Swing low, sweet char-riot.' Then she said, 'D'you want some fresh water? It's not fit for a car radiator, that.'

Mum said, 'Yes please.' While the nurse was out of the room Mum said, 'The flowers you got me are nice.' I went to the window, pretending to look at the flowers, but I was really trying to look out of the window to see if I could see where Mum fell. The nurse came back in and I had to turn back before I saw anything. Mum took her pills.

While Mum was swallowing, the nurse said, 'I bet you like football.'

I said, 'Leeds.'

The nurse said, 'Oh dear.' (Yeah yeah.)

Mum said, 'He's going back to school.' I didn't say anything. She said, 'He's a remarkable young man.'

The nurse said, 'I'm sure he is.'

Mum said, 'Aren't you, Graham?'

I said, 'Not really.'

Mum opened her eyes wide and sighed. She said, 'Tell the lady, Graham.'

I said, 'Mum.'

The nurse said, 'She usually naps now. Why don't you just both sit and have some quiet time together?'

I said, 'OK.'

When the nurse had gone Mum said, 'Why didn't you tell her?'

I said, 'Tell her what?'

Mum said, 'You know what, Graham,' then she fell asleep.

I went to find a toilet. In the toilet I called Jennifer on my mobile. I didn't think she'd be there but she was. She said, 'Slater.' I'd been excited about hearing her voice but it was her cold voice. I wanted it to really warm up when she realized it was me but it only got lukewarm. She asked about Mum and I said she was OK. I asked her if she'd seen the *Moon* and she sounded a bit annoyed. She said, 'Look, I told you. I don't know what else to suggest except we regularize it. That way we have a say in what's what.'

I didn't say anything. I wasn't so much bothered by what she'd said, I was just thinking about how her voice wasn't hot enough.

She said, 'Look, I'm sorry, Graham. I've got to go now. When are you coming back? We need to do this face to face.' Then she sounded worried. 'Graham?' she said. 'Are you still there?'

I said, 'Yes.'

She said, 'You're not going to do anything stupid now, are you?'

I said, 'Like what?'

Jennifer said, 'Like talk to the wrong people.'

I didn't know what she meant. I said, 'No.'

She said, 'So when are you coming?'

I didn't know. I said, 'In a few days. I've got to get things sorted. Make sure Mum's OK and stuff.'

Jennifer said, 'And what about your passport? You won't forget that, will you? Don't forget that.'

'Don't worry,' I said. 'I'll fetch it.'

* * *

190

When Mum woke up I said, 'Why did Grandma throw you out the house?'

Mum said, 'She didn't.' She started to cry. This time I put my hands out towards her and she picked them up and put them round her shoulders and I moved them down her back and I felt her shoulder blades. Her tears were wetting my T-shirt. When she could speak again she said, 'I had to leave.'

I said, 'Why?'

She said, 'You know why.'

I said, 'No I don't,' and Mum rubbed my hair at the back of my head, meaning: Yes you do.

She said, 'Your hair's quite long.'

I said, 'Why did Uncle George say your head was like a bank vault when you were a kid?'

'He can talk,' Mum said. 'Your grandma said he came out burly and just got burlier. Burly and hairy.'

'He meant loads of stuff locked in there,' I said.

'Why?' said Mum. She'd been mumbling into my shoulder. Now she held me at arm's length and started giggling, which I didn't like. 'Did he say he peeked inside when I wasn't looking? He'd have got a shock.'

'He didn't say that,' I said. 'He said him and Gramps didn't get a look-in.'

Mum said, 'Your grandma used to say, "Don't look for what you don't want to find." *You* should know that. Eh?' She hugged me again.

I wanted to ask her about my kid brother George. I wanted to know what his hands were like. And I nearly did ask her. But then I had an idea. If his hands were normal, Mum probably thought the wrong kid had died.

191

She probably wished I'd died, not George. And I would have to ask her that and of course she would deny it even if it was the truth. And I would never know for sure. Some questions are better left unasked. So instead I said, 'Why did you jump off the roof? Why did you try and kill yourself?'

Mum said, 'I didn't.'

I said, 'You did.'

She said, 'No, Graham love.' She held me at arm's length again but this time she wasn't giggling. She looked right in my eyes. Her eyes were blue and very tired and empty looking, like she had spent two days dragging an injured person off a mountain and the person had still died. 'I was doing fine, considering,' she said. 'I just landed badly.'

His name is Graham Sinclair. This is his stupidity.

Sometimes I just switched off my brain. I knew there should have been serious noise going on in there but there was just nothingness. Mum had her hand on the back of my head. I wondered if she could feel the cold empty space under her hand. She stroked my hair and said, 'Will you have your hair cut if I give you the money?'

Our faces were ten centimetres apart but the way her voice sounded it was like I was standing at one end of a long narrow tunnel and Mum was at the other end.

'OK.'

'Look in that top drawer. There're some notes.'

Chapter 17

With the twenty quid I took off Mum I had sixty quid sixty-three p. When I left the hospital I just set off walking; I didn't know where I was going. It hadn't rained for ages and everything seemed dusty. I went past a church with scaffolding up round the spire. It looked like the sketch of a church done on graph paper. They were turning the church into a warehouse. Outside there was a sign that said:

Crazy prices on selected hover mowers

There weren't that many people about compared to London. The ones that were looked different. They were fatter or thinner, with nothing in between. They looked like either they had serious hamburger habits or they took heroin. The girls were clodhoppers and the blokes were hardnuts. They all seemed to be staring at me and I folded my arms so they couldn't see my hands. Then I heard somebody say, 'Boy hero' to his mate as he went past. Somebody called the same thing from across the street. This was what it was like outside London. London was so cool it pretended not to recognize you even if it saw you coming from a long way away but here wasn't cool like London. I felt quite glad of that. For about two seconds anyway.

I wondered whether to wave back, just a little one to say hi without being big-headed about it. A girl's voice behind me shouted, 'Oi' and this time I did wave. I turned round as well. Three kids were running round the corner where a takeaway curry shop called Captain Korma was. They were shouting and laughing. I couldn't make out what they were on about at first, then I realized. They were shouting 'Spakky' and 'Perv'.

For a milli-second it wasn't great, hearing all that again. Then I was glad it had happened because it made my mind up. Suddenly I knew where I was going: I was getting the hell out of this place, away from prats and dullness and my mad mother who had told me a terrible lie, not just once but always, her whole life. On the way to the railway station I plugged myself in and didn't look at people and tried to keep my brain in sleep mode. I watched where I scuffed up the dust and the dog ends and sent the bottle tops whizzing with the toes of my trainers.

I allowed myself to think of Kate's trainers. I fancied some Pumas myself. Then I wondered how I would afford it. After I'd got the ticket to London there wouldn't be much left of the money I had. At the station I got a kid's single to King's Cross that cost twenty-eight quid, which left me with thirty-two pounds sixty-three p. I had fourteen minutes to wait. On Platform One I called Jennifer's mobile. It answered straight away and said, 'Welcome to the Orange Answering Service.'

I said, 'It's Graham. Something really weird's happened. I'm coming back to London right now. I'm just waiting for the train. I'm getting the 14.05. It gets in at 15.53. Can I stay with you? I'll call you later. Cheers.'

It suddenly felt really hot. I could feel sweat on the back of my neck and behind my knees and in my underpants and under my arms. I lifted my arms and had a sniff. My pits were marginally whiffy.

This time I didn't look when the train went past the fields where I used to play. I was trying not to think of where I'd come from; I was concentrating on where I was going to. I was imagining me in a few months, in some new smart gear so I wouldn't have to keep wearing the same T-shirts. Me and Jennifer would go out to places together, me looking more the part. New haircut, maybe even a new accent. This Yorkshire one was a clodhopping way of speaking, aye reet enough. Ah'd get me-sen a noo'un.

That's what I was trying to think about, but then my head kept going back to Mum. What had she said? 'I was doing fine, considering. I just landed badly.' I said it over and over again in my head and felt my head filling up with stuff I remembered about me and Mum and things she'd said. Doc Morrison and Lulworth Cove and Kylie Blounce. Her standing on the landing saying she couldn't hear me. I got really hot. I was sweating all over.

Outside, the sky was like night. This cloud took up

the whole bit of the sky I could see through the train window. It was about ten kilometres long. It was black and blue, like Mum's battered eyes, except for the green. A raindrop splatted on the window right next to my head. It turned into a streak of water about two metres long on the window. Then the train turned the streak into loads of vibrating blobs. Another raindrop splatted and another and then the window was covered in rain. It wasn't soft, soothing rain.

Somewhere there would be a rainbow. The rain was still falling but there was sun too. I looked out of both sides of the carriage but I couldn't see the rainbow. Somewhere out there in England there might be a bloke standing right where the rainbow started and he would never know it. What was it Kate had said? 'Is it bad?' meaning my secret, and I had said no and she had said, 'Why's it a secret then?' It was a good question. It was a secret because Mum had told me it had to be. But it didn't have to be. If Mum had told me her secret, all those times when she could have, if she had told me her secret, then things would have been different. It would have been like seeing the rainbow and being in it at the same time.

No secret, just me.

Just me and Park Lane. This is what I thought about for the rest of the journey. I'd go to Park Lane and I'd do it. When I imagined it, it was like electric shocks were running through my body. I didn't even know what Park Lane looked like, I had just had this idea in my head. The hotels would be like cliffs. Park Lane was Lulworth Cove made out of windows. Up on the ninth floor Brad Pitt in his dressing gown was turning to a classy woman with a towel all piled up on her head and down below blokes in top hats were opening doors for men in aviator shades.

In front was a road where traffic whizzed in about five lanes and then, on the other side, a big park. I'd just go in the park at about one p.m. so there'd be people strolling about on their lunch break and I'd do it. I saw all these people half-biting into their World Bean Inc. crayfish and rocket sarnies and then looking up with their mouths full of mashed up mayonnaise. But I'd keep on the side near the hotels so people like Brad Pitt could look out of their penthouse windows and go, 'Jeez, hey, check this out.'

And then I got worried about the road. If people driving on that crazy road saw me they would probably crash. They'd be so busy looking up and around they'd shunt into the car in front and there'd be this terrible pile-up with maybe loads killed. My guts did a double-take when I thought of that. It felt like windscreen wiper fluid squirting out of my stomach and into my heart.

Jennifer would have to help me. We'd have to block off the road but not tell people what it was for. They'd just have to wait and see.

When the train got to King's Cross it felt like I'd come home. I really enjoyed just moseying (Dad's word) down the platform, listening to the announcements pinging around. I was pretending not to look at the barriers but I was giving quick clocks in that direction. I was looking

197

for Jennifer. I hoped she'd picked my message up in time. I saw us coming together in slow motion. We'd leave the station together, right into that noise of the waves. And we'd get smaller and smaller until we were just specks. We'd be walking into the future together.

But I got through the barrier and there was no Jennifer. I thought she may have gone to get a coffee or a newspaper so I decided to wait but then a voice said, 'Graham Sinclair?' and I turned round and there was a bloke in a leather jacket with this black stuff hanging out of his nostrils. I couldn't work out what it was at first. I thought it was maybe snot that had got polluted by the London air, like buildings got blackened and when you cleaned them they looked like new even though they were a hundred years old. But I had a good chance to inspect his nostrils in the next half hour because we were jammed up together in the back of a police car, and after a bit I realized it was hair, really thick hair.

When he said, 'Graham Sinclair?' I said, 'Yes,' and he said, 'Detective Inspector Somebody or Other' (I couldn't remember his name afterwards). He said, 'Can you spare us some of your time?' and I didn't say anything because it wasn't a proper question and he didn't wait for an answer. We walked out of the station. Outside was sticky and smelly like London was an opened-out crisp packet and we were right on all that greasiness that gets left on the sides. It felt like everything around me—the buses and tramps and signs for 24-hour minicabs—was vibrating a tiny amount. You wouldn't notice it in one thing, but put together it made London feel like a headache.

Nostrils had an earring in his right ear, which I thought was quite cool, but then I realized what he was. He was a sex case 'tec.

The car was parked right where only taxis are allowed; you could do that if you were a cop. It wasn't a jam sandwich, i.e. it wasn't white with those red fluorescent stripes down the side, it was a dark blue Mondeo with a big engine. But it was still a cop car. It had a walkie-talkie in the front. Nostrils opened the back door and as I got in he pushed down on my head like I was a plastic duck he was trying to hold underwater. He said, 'This is Detective Sergeant Somebody or Other,' meaning the bloke already in the back. His eyes were very light blue and the black bits in the middle were tiny but very sharp-looking, like they were very deep holes that went right through to the back of his head. His head was shaved back with a number two to dark stubble. It looked like a magnet with iron filings sticking on it. This was sex case 'tec number two. There was a driver up front who had a scar on his neck and never said anything. It was whiffy in the back of that car.

It was also dodgy. They weren't allowed to interview me without a social worker present, and I couldn't see one unless she was stuffed in the glove compartment next to some crappy old country and western CD. They could get done big time for this. They could be on the front of the *Moon* in disgrace, except the *Moon* would probably say they were heroes.

Plus Nostrils and Number Two were big guys, they must have worked out. Their arms were pressing against me from both sides. Nostrils had hair on the back of his hands. It was very straight like it had been combed. Their thighs on either side of me felt like steel. My chest was all hunched over. I had my hands down between my knees even though there wasn't really room for them there because I didn't want the sex case 'tecs to clock them and start commenting. Nostrils said, 'Do your seatbelt up, Mr Sinclair,' but I couldn't because there wasn't a seatbelt in the middle just two either side and Nostrils and his mate were sitting on them. And anyway I couldn't move.

Number Two moved his leg against mine. He said, 'You're committing an offence, riding without a belt. We could do you for that, couldn't we, detective inspector?'

Nostrils said, 'We could but we're kind.'

The driver drove off into London. I wanted them to open a window to get rid of the whiffiness but I didn't dare ask. I'd just get more sarcasm. Nobody said anything and I looked at Nostril's nostrils.

It was sometimes hard to tell when you were going up a hill in London. Everything was pressed down by the millions of tons of buildings. But before all the buildings, before the mud huts that didn't weigh much, there were hills and valleys, really steep bits and little cliffs where men with bows and arrows must have stood with their hands above their eyes, scanning the horizon, waiting for maniacs with painted faces. And you could still feel the up and downness of it if you concentrated.

The police car went up a long hill. A bloke working at a road works was digging into the hill with a pneumatic

200

drill. Maybe it was the first time that bit of the hill that was being woodpeckered into had seen the sky for thousands of years. The workman wore blue plastic ear muffs. He had his shirt off but there was no sun. Everything was grey and waiting. London was waiting for the rain that was heading down from the North.

Nostrils broke the silence. He said, 'A bit of a child prodigy, aren't we? A bit of a Mozart in our warped little way.'

I didn't know what he was on about. I said, 'Eh?'

'All right,' he said. 'D'you know what I'm talking about if I say Popsock Perv, Mr Sinclair? He likes girls' socks. And other items.'

Number Two said, 'And other items.'

Nostrils said, 'Pass it over, Kev,' and the driver took his left hand off the steering wheel and passed Nostrils something from the passenger seat in front, a blue ringbinder. I'd had one like it at school, the same colour. I did a project about the decline of cod fishing out of Grimsby in it.

I said, 'I've seen something in the paper.'

Nostrils said, 'Talking of. You're in the paper a lot, Graham. D'you like being in the paper? D'you get a kick out of it?'

I said, 'Not particularly.' I'd thought we were going to a cop shop but now I reckoned we'd just be driving around. It was mobile questioning.

Nostrils gave the ringbinder to Number Two. He opened it and said, 'Here's some other people who've been in the paper.' He put the ringbinder on my knee. He meant me to steady it with my hands but I kept them between my knees. I just went on tiptoes and lifted my knees so the ringbinder didn't slide off. There was a big photo of a girl's face. She looked weird. One side of her hair was in a sort of cone that looked like a unicorn horn, the rest was number one-ed right back to the shiny knobbly bits that were like London's hills, the bits you didn't normally see unless you took a pneumatic drill or a shaver to them. She had a tooth missing that made me think of the Bechstein. She looked weirdly familiar.

Number Two twisted his head round and up at me. His drilled eyes were in my face. He said, 'Did she put her hand in her pocket for you, *Mizz* Shelley McCabe?' He said Mizz very sarcastically. 'Alcopops on Shelley down the Bluebird Bar Grill? Or did you put your hand in your pocket for her? Was she a self-employee, no VAT? How did it work, mate?'

'I don't know what you're on about,' I said. I was doing my cool customer bit, the thing the cops hated. They couldn't hear the inside of my head, but couldn't they smell my sweat, the sweat that was coming on all over me, like street lights when it's getting dark?

Nostrils said, 'Do you think Shelley liked being in the paper?'

I said, 'I got no idea.'

Number Two said, 'What about Jade Brinkley from Orpington?' He flicked over to the next page of the ringbinder. 'She was a student of fashion, did you know that? You have to look good in that game. Shame really.'

I didn't look at the picture. I said, 'How did you know I'd be on that train?'

Nostrils said, 'There are people out there concerned for your movements.'

I said, 'George Oxnard?'

Number Two lifted the ringbinder so it was under my nose. He said, 'Is that handiwork you recognize?'

I pretended to look but kept my eyes out of focus. I just saw a blob of pink face with a blob of black hair above it.

Number Two said, 'You're quite happy looking at that then?'

I turned to Nostrils. 'Who was it?'

Nostrils said, 'You're not fazed, are you, son?'

Number Two said, 'D'you know where Bishop's Park is?'

I said, 'Yeah. Next to Fulham footie.'

Number Two said, 'Were you on July the twelfth at ten p.m. or have you ever been in Bishop's Park SW6?'

I lost it then. The noise in my head escaped. But it didn't come out as noise, it came out as more sweat. And blood. All this blood rushing into my cheeks.

I saw Number Two looking at Nostrils. They were getting the wrong end of the stick too. Number Two said, 'Cast your mind back. Bishop's Park.'

I was going to tell them. But I couldn't, they wouldn't believe me. I said, 'No.'

Number Two said, 'Excuse me.' He pushed my head forward and spoke to Nostrils over the top. He said, 'Let me ask you something, detective inspector. In a professional career spanning eighteen years of inter-viewing scumbags, have you ever heard a no that sounded more like a yes?'

Nostrils said, 'Too right. We're going to nail you, son.'

I thought they hadn't noticed my hands. But Number Two grabbed my wrists and yanked my hands out from between my knees. The ringbinder went on the floor. He turned the hands over. It made me think of Doc Morrison. Then it got weird. He kept turning them, back up then palm up, back up then palm up, and it was like when you see an ordinary word over and over again until you go a bit mad. A word like **WHAT** for instance. Even a word like WHAT looks insane after a while. My hands weren't even ordinary. They didn't stand a chance. They looked like the maddest things I'd ever seen.

Chapter 18

They dropped me on this massive interchange of dual carriageways that would look like tied shoelaces from a space satellite. We were tanking along this road that went up like Putney Bridge except there was no river underneath, just old caravans and giant bushes with purple bits waving about in the wind. Nostrils said, 'Drop him, driver.' Driver said, 'What, here?' There was no footpath, there was nowhere to stop. All these cars were whizzing up behind. We'd get shunted, is what the driver was thinking. Nostrils said to Number Two, 'Get him over,' and Number Two lifted me on his lap.

I thought of something. A photograph of me with a toy monkey on my lap. There weren't many photos of me as a kid and this was the only one you could see my hands in. I was holding the monkey to steady him on my knee. He had on a red and white stripy T-shirt and my fingers were half covering it. My fingers were creased and knobbly and they looked too big. They looked like bits of real monkey, like somehow a toy and a real monkey had got mixed up.

Now I was sitting on the knee of a hard-nut cop with hair like iron filings and we were going too fast in a revved-up Mondeo with a walkie-talkie on the dash, and I was sitting like that toy monkey but I wasn't looking at the camera, at Mum holding the camera, I was looking at the road coming up through the windscreen and the silver crash barriers whooshing by either side. And my head was empty or full, I wasn't sure which, but it wasn't working. You leave the lid off the coolbox, it doesn't work, and my lid was well and truly off. And Nostrils said, 'Do it.' He was crouched forward, getting a view of what was coming up behind in the wing mirror and he said, 'Do it.'

It wasn't like a film. They didn't bundle me out before the car had stopped; I didn't roll over and over down a grassy bank.

Car brakes screeched, major smell of burning rubber, Number Two opened the door and lifted me out. He did it gently, like he was putting a rabbit in a box. He hoiked me over the crash barrier. My feet came down together. Door slammed, car was off. Another car came up behind, flashing its brights, but it was just being macho, it had time to stop if it needed to. Which it didn't because the Mondeo disappeared like a rocket.

I was in a place where people didn't walk. I was probably the first person to walk there since the workmen who built the road. It wasn't just a road. It was a flyover. There was the crash barrier, then there was about a foot of space, and then there was a wall that you could see over. Down below there were the roofs of caravans. People lived there. A string of washing was tied between a caravan and a concrete pole. A kid pedalled a green plastic trike about between puddles.

I ran along between the wall and the crash barrier in the same direction as the traffic. It was exhausting, the noise of the cars. Every time a car zipped by, it dropped a shockwave that knocked the wind out of me and wobbled my knees. The crash barrier rattled, dust got in my mouth. Sometimes a car would parp its horn. Some of them were air horns, like big rigs have in American movies. Every time, the surprise of it was like being shot between the shoulder blades.

The gap between the wall and the barrier wasn't very wide and every so often there'd be a hubcap or an old Coke tin so I had to look down to make sure where I was putting my feet. It began to rain. Big fat splots, like eggs breaking in the dust. They made a smell that was like vanilla ice cream. I could almost dodge the rain at first. That was a joke they made about me at school (one of the OK jokes), that I was so thin I wouldn't get wet in the shower. But then the rain got heavier. It soaked through my combats till they weighed a ton. Cars put their wipers and headlights on. Rain came off the tyres and wing mirrors and spoilers and aerials and hit me in great slashing buckets along one side. My nose felt cold and clean, like a pebble on the shore. Water ran in my ears. I liked the rain, it cooled me off, except for the way my legs felt in those combats, like I was wearing glue.

And then I remembered my mobile and my Discman in my combat pockets. They must be totalled by now. I checked my cash. It didn't feel too bad. It was rolled up in a little pocket in my T-shirt. In any case, you could accidentally leave notes in a pocket in the washing machine and they'd be OK.

How long could a flyover be? I ran for ages, looking for signs. I didn't have a clue where I was. London was a monster. I was used to fiddling around between its eyes and its nostrils but I could be anywhere now, I could be heading out along its tail, or climbing the edge of a massive ear. I thought of hitchhiking. It wouldn't be easy for cars to stop but maybe there'd be a gap in the traffic. Last night in the shed Dad said he'd done it when he was a student but people didn't do it these days because there were too many nutters around. I'd asked him how he hitchhiked, what you had to do. I thought you had to get signs made and dress smart so you didn't look like a nutter or a mugger. He lifted his hand that was holding the cigar and stuck his thumb out. I said, 'That's it?'

I didn't know I'd actually be using his hitchhiking information the next day. I forgot to ask him whether you stood still and faced back towards the traffic or just carried on walking with your thumb stuck out like an indicator. First of all I turned round. I didn't stick my thumb straight up in the air because that meant 'Magic' or at least 'All right, mate'. I put an angle on it. The first car started parping from about half a mile away. He kept it going all the way, the sound getting bigger and sharper until he whooshed by me. The driver was clocking me as he went past. He ducked his head and gave me the finger.

After that I turned round and walked with my thumb half stuck out like I'd half forgotten it was there. A couple of cars went by. Nothing. Then the third one parped me again. Two long hoots, like a reversing horn. Like Jennifer's mobile. I didn't like that ring tone of Jennifer's, it was weird. Not quite clodhopping but not classy either. Like when her voice went cold or you caught her expression and it went from smile to no smile in a millisecond.

The rain eased off a bit and I gave up the hitchhiking idea. Up ahead the brake lights were slamming on. A thousand cigars being blown on. Some people coming up behind were putting on their hazards. The heavy red lights went off once they'd put their handbrakes on but the orange hazards kept blinking. Then there was another colour besides the red and orange. Blue. Flashing blue lights. It could be ambulance or fire but it was bound to be cops as well. It was always cops.

Something big was going on. It could be an accident; a multi-car pile-up in the rain. I heard a chopper. It was right above the blue lights. You could see its searchlight but it didn't get very far, the beam of light just petered out in the rain and dark. A pile-up or a roadblock. It could be a roadblock. A big operation to pick up old Freako for walking where you weren't allowed and putting drivers in danger. Somebody could have called the cops on his mobile, that bloke who gave me the finger when he saw me hitchhiking for instance. It was possible.

Then I sussed what was going on. Old Nostrils and Number Two had been playing cat and mouse with Freako here. Why would they let me go if they thought I was a pervy killer? They were just trying to soften me up and break me down. Puncture the balloon full of snot. By the time they picked me up again, at the end of the flyover, I'd be ready to spill the beans about Jade Brinkley and Shelley McCabe and the rest of them. Except I wasn't going to reach the end of the flyover.

And I had that thought I'd had in the showroom when Uncle George was interrogating me. I wasn't handcuffed or cheesewired to this flyover. I could do what I wanted. And what I wanted was to get out of this my own way, the way that only I could. Nobody could stop me now, not Mum or Dad or Kylie's dad, not the social worker, Uncle George, Derek aka Trainset Man, or the sex case 'tecs. I was going to go for it. Big time.

There were loads of reasons why it was a bad idea. I was tired for a start and I hadn't eaten. My combats and jean jacket were soaking wet and weighed a ton. I didn't have a clue where I was or where I was going. But the main reason was, I'd never gone that far before. I'd only pottered about. A few metres here and there. In front of Kylie I'd only gone about twenty metres. Then I fell like a stone and knackered my ankle on an old paint tin. And when I tried again, that was when I lost control and ran into her, knocking her over, giving her those cuts and bruises etc. When I rescued Baby Ade, it was just a straight up and down through the clouds of dust. With Jennifer the other night I hadn't done much more than lift off, like I had in the caravan in Lulworth Cove. My head got caught up with the wires on the ceiling and brought down half her little lights but she didn't seem to mind. She had other things on her mind, like why her jaw was hanging open.

And then there was Bishop's Park SW6. July the twelfth at 10 p.m.

The other night, after I'd talked to Kate on the phone and scrubbed my hands, I felt up for something. Kate had already gone to bed but no way could I go to bed at 8 p.m. I was going to go for a pizza but I'd already had the crackers and sardines. Then I remembered Bishop's Park. It was over the bridge and next to Fulham footie ground. Uncle George had taken me there when I'd just moved to London. People were walking dogs and sitting on benches reading the papers and someone had marker-penned rude bits on some statues. A sign said they locked the gates when it got dark, which gave me the idea.

So that's where I went. I walked over the bridge, climbed over the fence and checked that nobody was about, like glue sniffers or pervs and nutters. And I went for it.

Sometimes it just didn't feel right. Like sometimes you try and run and your body doesn't want to. It wants to be crashed on the sofa with the TV remote in your hand and a wheelie bin of popcorn between your knees. So it gives you the stitch and makes your legs feel like they've been hollowed out and had cement poured in them. I closed my eyes and took the breaths and felt my hands growing, but it was all too slow and bad-tempered, like my hands were complaining, saying 'Not again. Give us a break', and I was being like a pain-in-the-arse teacher making them do it.

I should have given up and gone for a pizza or whatever instead. But I made myself carry on. I managed to go about fifty metres above this kids' football pitch. I felt sick and not quite in control and I was going to come down and call it quits; I'd even planned to break my landing by swinging from the crossbar of the goalposts, when I heard a shout. It sounded like a girl's voice. I didn't know whether or not she was yelling at me, but I wasn't taking any chances. I was so freaked it gave me new energy and I managed to veer off to the right and land about ten metres up in the branches of a tree.

I hung on, getting my breath back and listening and looking around. And then I saw her. The football pitch was surrounded by trees that cast deep dark shadows but out in the centre circle the moonlight was painting the grass silver and you could see quite clearly. She was running down the pitch. I thought of David Batty tanking forward for Leeds but David Batty never screamed when he played. She had a sort of angular head, wore jeans and a jean jacket and her legs were shooting out backwards like her trainers couldn't grip properly in all the mud. She was quite old, about seventeen.

Then a bloke appeared. He ran like a crab, all low down like his bum was about where his knees should be. It was a good way to run in mud. He was gaining on her. He didn't say anything but you could hear his breathing. His breathing and her screaming, and no one to hear her. Except me.

She was heading for the goal. But then she saw the trees and bushes over to the right, just like I had. She

212

changed direction. She was running towards me. Now I could hear her sobs, the sobs that she was giving out between the screams. Her poor little arms were working overtime, trying to get her legs to go quicker. Weird hair, pulled up in a pointy shape on one side. The bloke turned to head her off. From my position they were like blobs on a radar screen. I could see that the bloke would catch up with her just as she reached the tree. The tree I was hiding in. I froze. I wished I was walking over Putney Bridge with a pizza box. I wished I was anywhere but here. The one moment I needed some Graham Sinclair wisdom and I didn't have any.

Afterwards I knew what I should have done: I should have just done it. Started yelling to get their attention, then just gone for it in front of them both. Freaked them both out so much they completely forgot what they were doing: her running away from a nutter and him being a nutter. They'd just have become two human beings united in gobsmackedness. But I didn't do that. By definition you can never do the really clever thing you thought of doing later. Yeah yeah yeah.

But I wasn't a wimp either. It wasn't my fault it went pear-shaped.

As she got closer to the tree I had to crane my neck to keep sight of her. I was flicking between her and the bloke. You couldn't see his eyes, he had his head down as if he wasn't really chasing her, he was just out for a run. His feet thumped on the ground and a milli-second later you heard his breathing. Slap, grunt, slap, grunt, closer and closer until he was so close he was just major noise in my head.

213

It happened like I thought. Just as she crashed into the bushes and I lost sight of her, he came in slightly to the side. There was a sudden silence that was probably only a milli-second but seemed like about ten minutes, then the screaming and struggling, and the muffled sounds, like he was putting his hand over her mouth. No words, just two human beings playing crocodile and giraffe right below the soles of my trainers. I was in that weird mode of panicking and being calm at the same time. My brain was like a camera, focusing down through the branches. But it also felt like that big balloon of phlegm, getting bigger and nearer to bursting the more I heard the sounds below and imagined what he was doing to her. And then, before my head exploded, I did what I did. Which wasn't brilliant but at least I tried.

It was like a ship in a bottle, a lot happened in a tiny space. I jumped straight down through the branches. I didn't know exactly where they were but by chance I landed on the bloke. I felt his head under my heel, he helped break my fall. Even about a week later I could feel the way his head felt when I accidentally kicked it: like a brick in a cushion cover. I spun off one way and he went the other. I thought he'd look like a weasel but his face was round and puddingy. He looked like a teacher's pet, not a pervy nutter, which just goes to show. And then he was screaming and scrambling in front of me and I realized a pretty weird and amazing thing, which was that he was a million times scareder of me than I was of him. He said, 'Jesus Christ', and split, crabbing backwards through the bushes and squelching off across the footie pitch.

The girl had been knocked back too. She was lying on her front with one arm up like she was in the middle of doing the crawl and I thought she was unconscious. I said, 'Are you OK?' and she twitched and screamed and started to turn round. Then she was staring at me, lying there in the bushes with her head twisted round staring up at me, and I was staring down at her and suddenly I was a camera again thinking that she looked a bit of a clodhopper, a clodhopper with very weird pointy gelled hair that was supposed to look classy but didn't, a clodhopper with a major black eye and a swollen lip and blood on her chin, and it was another one of those silences that seemed to go on for ever. Then the camera swung round and saw me, I saw myself, and I knew I must help her. I lifted my hands towards her. I was going to say, 'It's all right now, he's gone,' but she started backing away. She was shuffling back through the bushes on her bum. I lifted my hands higher and she stopped. She froze. And that was when she spoke. 'Oh. My. God,' she said. She pronounced God 'God-uh'.

I hadn't realized. My hands were big and horrible as coffins.

I put them behind my back. 'No, you don't under-stand,' I said. 'It's not me. I'm not him. He's gone.' But she was on her feet. She was tunnelling back through the bushes, pushing against them with her back, thrashing them back with her arms, sobbing and screaming. She burst out on to open grass and legged it. I followed for a bit. Every so often I'd be saying, 'No, please. Listen to me. It's OK. I scared him off for you.' But some Graham Sinclair wisdom finally kicked in and I stopped. I didn't just stop. I legged it the other way big time.

Because how would you explain stuff like this to sex case 'tecs? You wouldn't, you'd keep shtum and hope they didn't find out.

I climbed up on to the top edge of the crash barrier. I was a good balancer, I stood there no problem. A whooshing car nearly parped the arse off me but I didn't care, I was laughing. One milli-second I was a very heavy old steel safe that was about to hit the concrete world down below the flyover and sink about ten metres through the pavement. Next milli-second the safe door flew open and out floated a dandelion clock.

That night at Jennifer's—was it only three nights ago? It felt like about three years—she said to me, after my head got tangled in the wires holding her lights up, 'Do you fly in your dreams?' and I said, no, in my dreams I could never fly and she laughed, the way she laughed when I said that thing about paranoia. She thought I was making it up, it was something I'd learned to say to sound ironic, but it was true. Then she said, 'What does it feel like?'

I just said, 'It's got the grin factor.' (I heard someone say this on TV once about riding a Harley Davidson very fast along the California coast highway.) But if I'd had time to think, I could have come up with a better description than that.

When I was twelve Brian's mum took me and Brian to Sheffield Ice Rink. We'd never ice-skated before. Brian was rubbish. His legs kept zooming apart and he almost split himself. He sat on the ice and hit it with his fists. I was very good. Brian's mum said I was like a duck to water. I zipped over the ice. It was as if the skates were my feet and the ice was the place I'd always lived.

Flying was like that but better. Flying was like skating on razor blades that never cut your feet and the place I came from was air. I was lighter than Baby Ade, lighter than polystyrene. I was a zip fastener made of air. And landing was when the razor blades cut your feet and the blood appears, the heavy blood, to drag you back down. These were some of the things I thought about afterwards that I could have said to Jennifer when she said, 'What does it feel like?'

I lifted off the flyover and headed up and out over the city, through little blow-ups of wind and rain, fast and hard, feeling the power coming off my hands, knowing this wasn't the half of it. It was like I was aquaplaning the surface of an invisible sea and down on the seabed were the million lights about to ping out and the car headlights worming along like half-blind shellfish and the nine million people pushing home from work, stopping for their Stellas and curries and not one of them knowing what was up here. Superspak doing the business.

I flew high to get my bearings. I was thinking about where we'd gone in the cop car after they picked me up at King's Cross. We hadn't crossed the river, which meant the river was behind me somewhere. I tried to imagine a map of London. There was an A to Z in Uncle George's Merc. The river went right through the middle. It looped about a bit but basically it went left to right (or right to left). If only I could find the blank that was the river. I pushed on towards where the lights were brighest and densest. The scene kept disappearing through the puffs of cloud but always when it re-appeared it seemed brighter, nearer, like a hoard of ship-wrecked treasure, gold coins and a queen's diamonds, on the seabed and me a frogman flippering on down through plankton. I didn't see the river till I was prac-tically on top of it. Then there it was, like a blindfold laid out below me.

So far so good. Now more widsom was required. When I walked over Putney Bridge to go home in the evening the sun was setting to my right. Sometimes it was amazing. The whole sky above the river was lit up in orange and purple colours. And planes would be flying through the colours, going into Heathrow the way Flight RF 3409 would have gone if it hadn't crashed. On this rainy night the sky was dark orange, like the world through aviator shades, but over to one side it was still a bit light. There was a gap in the faraway clouds that was like a big tear in a sheet and through the gap there was a pale green light with little back clouds floating in front that looked like thumb smudges. If it was light over there, that must mean that Uncle George's flat was in that direction. If I could find Uncle George's flat I could find the showroom. And from the show-room I could find what I was looking for.

Now Spakky spakked it up. I flew too low over the river and got spotted by two blokes walking over a bridge. They started screaming and yelling, giving their mobiles major hammer, trying to flag down cars. I did not like that. I flew in low next to a brick wall where the blokes couldn't see me. I saw an archway, an opening, that was like a cave in a cliff face and whooshed in there. There were these stone platforms at the bottom of the archway that the river was splashing over. I tried to get my feet on them but they were sloping and slimy and I could feel it wasn't going to work. I was beginning to panic when I saw two big rusty rings hanging from the brick roof. I got right up under the highpoint of the archway and then I had about two milli-seconds to fold up my hands and get my fingers through the rings.

I hung there like a bat. My chest was heaving, I was getting knackered now. My back was up against the bricks of the roof. They were slimy. I could feel my jean jacket slipping on them. I imagined all the gunk there would be on the jacket. I was trying to listen out for the blokes but my breathing was so loud, in that brick cave, that I couldn't hear anything for about five minutes.

When my breathing had quietened down I listened really hard. Nothing. I thought I was OK, and was just about to shoot out when I saw torchlight on the water in front of the archway. An elongated circle of light was moving over the small black waves. Then I heard the chug of an engine. A boat was coming up. The chug got louder really quickly. If the boat came in the cave it was end of story for me. I imagined being in the police interview room. Yet again. What was I doing in that brick cave hanging from these rusty rings ten metres in the air above the river? How had I got there? Who had put me there? Why? Knowing me, the cops would think it was something pervy. I'd read stories in the newspaper of men who strung themselves up over girders in basements with bags over their heads and ropes round their necks and fruit in their mouths. One was a pop star and one was an MP and one was a rich bloke. There were some real weirdies out there.

Now there was a different noise. It made the brick roof vibrate, it made my head shake and my teeth rattle: a helicopter. At first I thought perhaps it was just someone going home late in his personal chopper; you saw them quite a lot, buzzing over the river like wasps. But the noise got louder and stayed loud. I had to lift my head away from the bricks, it was giving me a headache. Instead of the boat's searchlight on the water there was a floodlight from the chopper, sweeping across the river, backwards and forwards, lighting up a big semi-circle of brick inside the arch then moving off to the other side again.

Because of the helicopter I didn't hear the boat any more. But then I saw its white front coming under the archway. Its light was pointed at the water. There were two coppers in the cabin; their walkie-talkies were crackling. Now the chug of the boat engine drowned out the sound of the chopper. The searchlight lit up a green wet world of brick and slime and filthy river. Plastic Evian bottles and Iceland carrier bags and a red plastic toy the shape of an old steam train.

I waited till the chopper's searchlight was on the far side of the river. Then I let go of the rusty rings and went for it. As I flew out of the cave I heard shouts. The blokes were still there. I cut in low near the brick wall and flew parallel to that. I lifted my face. The wind was stinging my eyes. There was still a patch of green in the sky. I kept my eyes on it as I turned ninety degrees and curved out over the wide, dark river. The cold took my breath away, like the sea when it laps up around your middle. I pushed higher, feeling the power coming off my hands. The chopper was still there, somewhere in the background, but I had got away, and now I laughed, laughing to the moon which popped up on my left like a big white half-eaten peach with no visible means of support.

Further and further below, the river narrowed back into a blank strip. I climbed high, keeping the moon to my left. I soared above the bridges and nightbuses, the white lights on the bridges and the orange bulbs in the alleyways, the super-posh riverside apartments that stepped back and up like the stands at Stamford Bridge. All around, as far as I could see, the city spread like an orange stain on the night. It was so easy, up here, I felt I could go on for ever. No friction, no problem. I was tempted to turn away from the river, head out towards the edges of the stain. The roads and fields where the city stopped. On and on, till the roof of Mum's hospital was under my feet. I saw myself leaning over the edge of the roof and tap-

tapping on her window. I'd haul her out and she'd hang on round my neck and we'd take off into the night, getting smaller and smaller till we disappeared, THE END.

Chapter 19

I pressed Jennifer's number and the intercom crackled. Her voice said, 'Yes?' and I said, 'It's Graham.' I wanted her to say something, like 'Great to hear you', but she just pressed the buzzer to open the door. In the lift on the way up I suddenly thought I should have brought her flowers. That would have been nice. I left a puddle in the lift.

Standing at her door and my heart was thumping. I saw her shape getting bigger through the frosty glass panels of the door. I felt her footsteps shaking the floor. There was so much to tell her, I didn't know where to start. She was fiddling with the chain. I coughed. I was suddenly really cold. The door opened and I remembered again how her face looked. Like smooth, expensive soap before it's ever been wet. She had on a man's office-type shirt and jeans. I smiled but she didn't smile back.

Her amazement at me had gone already.

She said, 'My God. The state of you.' Then she said, 'Got your passport?'

I said, 'No.'

Jennifer said, 'I don't believe this. I called you.'

I was still standing outside the door. I said, 'Forgot. Sorry.'

She said, 'How could you do that?' She pointed at the floor. There was another puddle there. She said, 'Look at you.'

I said, 'I got wet.'

She gave me my own room with my own toilet and shower, and some clothes to change into. They were a bloke's XXL polo shirt and a dressing gown made out of towel material but no underpants, which I was pleased about. I didn't fancy wearing another bloke's kecks even if they'd been washed. I wondered how come she had a bloke's polo shirt, and where did the shirt she was wearing come from? When I'd had a shower and changed I wrapped my underpants in my T-shirt and took them and my combats to Jennifer and she put them in the washing machine. I watched them starting to go round and round then went back to the room and rubbed the Discman and my mobile with a towel and checked them out. They didn't work. Drops of water had got into the display on the mobile. I had a look round the room. It was all white with a white blind. The window looked out on an alleyway five floors below. Down in the alleyway there was a security light shining on green wheelie bins.

I went back into the main room and Jennifer asked if I'd eaten. I said no so she brought me a tin of Marks and Spencer's party snacks and a cup of tea. This upset me a little bit. Mum would have made me cheese on toast with Lea & Perrins dabbed on the toast before you put the cheese on top, followed by biscuits. I remembered the scratches on Dad's hands. They made me think of Kylie Blounce for some reason. I tried to make the connection in my brain but Jennifer's mobile kept going off and ruining my concentration. She would go into the corridor and pull the door half closed behind her to talk. I didn't manage to earwig what she said except for: 'We'll have to sort that when we come to it, basically.'

Then she said, 'Right, that's it', and switched off the mobile and sat down opposite me. She curled her feet up under her. There was no way of seeing her bra under that shirt. I'd scoffed all the peanuts and the hot chilli chips. I suddenly felt really tired. I couldn't believe what had happened in one day. Getting up this morning in my old bedroom, going to the hospital. The business with Mum that I was trying not to think about. Walking to the station, getting to King's Cross. The sex case 'tecs. The flyover. The searchlights. Spakky takes the direct route to Jennifer's apartment. It seemed more like about three weeks' worth of things had gone on.

And at the end of it all I couldn't believe I was with Jennifer. Except I was too tired to enjoy it. I was slumped right back in the sofa looking at the ceiling. She'd had the lighting fixed where I'd knocked it that night, you could just see a bit of silver tape where the repairman had been.

Jennifer said, 'So what's up?'

I said, 'When I got off the train, these cops were waiting for me. They were sex case detectives. They grilled me. Then they chucked me out on this flyover.'

Jennifer said, 'Is that what happened?'

I said, 'Yes.'

She said, 'I wouldn't bother about that if I was you. It's not important.'

'Isn't it?' I said. 'Yes it is. It's in the paper every day. I can't stand it.'

She said, 'Honestly. I know what I'm saying.'

I said, 'How d'you know?'

'I just sort of feel it, Graham, put it that way,' she said. 'How's your mother?'

I'd been planning to tell her. That was the whole point. But I couldn't do it. I felt like I was back on that flyover with all my clothes soaked through and I had to run but I couldn't. The best I could manage was slow motion. I didn't have the words to tell her about Mum. I didn't have the energy to lift the lid of the coolbox, pick out all the things, explain what they all were. I said, 'She's OK.' Then, I didn't plan it, but out of nowhere I said, 'Do you want to meet my mum?'

Jennifer looked puzzled. 'Well, at some point,' she said.

I said, 'At some point.'

'Of course,' said Jennifer. 'At some point by all means. So what was the weird thing you mentioned in your message?'

'Oh, right,' I said, and I made something up: 'Cos Mum wants me to go back to Sir Roger de Coverley and I can't handle it and we had a row.'

Jennifer said, 'So how come you're not at Uncle Porky's?'

I didn't correct her about his name this time. An idea just came into my head and I said, 'Cos he's moved back into his flat cos his girlfriend kicked him out.' All of a sudden I was lying for England for some reason. I wanted to tell her about the flying, I really did. It was a *Guinness Book of Records* effort, what I'd done. But I just reckoned she wouldn't be amazed enough, and I was too tired to cope with that.

Jennifer said, 'Ye-es' very slowly and fiddled with a button near the top of her shirt. I hoped she might undo the button but she didn't. Then she said, 'Am I harbouring a fugitive, by any chance? I'll need to square it if I am. But I can do that.'

I said, 'No.'

She said, 'Is that where your passport is, up there?'

I said, 'Yeah. What's with the passport?'

'I thought you might like to come to America with me,' she said. 'I had it sort of arranged. But I can re-arrange. If you're up for it.'

'What for?' I said.

'You know what for, in general terms,' she said.

'No I don't,' I said.

Jennifer rubbed her eyes and shook her head. She blinked at me and smiled. 'Come on,' she said, 'you do.'

Why did adults always think I understood what they meant when I didn't? I said, 'I thought of Park Lane.'

She said, 'What are you talking about?'

I said, 'Doing it next to Park Lane. The only thing I'm bothered about is the traffic. If you could help me stop the traffic so there are no pile-ups.'

Jennifer said, 'Oh, dear. Graham. You're not hearing me at all are you?'

* * *

In the night I was woken by the noise of somebody being murdered. It was bloodcurdling. Whoever it was had been stabbed with a sword and was having his guts pulled out like joined-up sausages in front of his eyes. I didn't know where I was. I didn't know my name. I was shaking. Then I realized it was cats having a fight. I told myself they were in an alleyway with green wheelie bins in it, and five floors up, I was in Jennifer's apartment sleeping in some bloke's XXL polo shirt. Etc.

I couldn't get back to sleep. I thought about Jennifer and America. She wouldn't tell me anything more about her plans. She said she'd tell me when she'd got things more sorted, which included me somehow getting hold of my passport. Before she went to bed she made me promise I wouldn't 'do anything stupid'. Which meant anything to do with the Park Lane idea.

I wondered if I would ever see Mum again. I didn't want to see her again because I hated her. But still, I wouldn't have minded keeping the option open just in case I changed my mind at some stage. I took these thoughts about Mum and locked them in a special little compartment in my head. My head carried on spinning with other stuff though. It was all whirling round and getting tangled together, like my combats, shirt, etc. in Jennifer's washing machine. Then I thought of how Mum would soothe me to sleep when I was a kid, how her cheek was like soft cool rain falling, the pitter of it on leaves.

Once in the summer when I was a kid I was down at the stream. It started to rain and I sheltered under a tree. I watched the rain falling on all this grass and weeds. When a blade of grass or a leaf was hit by a raindrop it was like it was being jerked by an invisible wire. All these invisible wires covering the ground, jerking the greenery. That's what I thought about and slowly everything got calmer and I felt myself sinking back into sleep.

Then my mobile went off. It must have got to the point where it had dried off enough, and it rang. I thought I was having a heart attack. My heart was hitting my chest, trying to get out. I jumped out of bed and felt along the wall to the chair where I'd left my Discman and mobile. The green window on the mobile was glowing, it guided me in. I wondered who could be phoning in the middle of the night, but it wasn't a new call. It was the phone telling me I had messages.

The first messsage was from Dad, who wasn't pleased to put it mildly. He said, 'Graham, are you there? I know you're there. What are you playing at? This is really serious this time. You've taken money from your mother and me under false pretences. This is a criminal offence. This is a police matter, Graham, do you know what I'm saying? If you don't get in touch we'll assume the worst and call the police. For Christ sake, boy. For Christ sake. I don't know. I really don't.'

The other five messages were from Dad too. They said the same sort of thing.

*   *   *

In the morning Jennifer poked her head round the door. She had her work face on. Make-up, and hair combed and shiny. Something black on. She said, 'Hey, listen. Chill, OK. Just hang out. I'll have some news when I get back. Around lunch time? Oh, and have a think about the best way of getting hold of your passport. OK?'

I said, 'OK.' I waited five minutes after the door closed then I went to the window and looked down into the alleyway. It had rained in the night but not enough to make puddles. A wheelie bin was tipped over. There was rubbish strewn about, shiny with rain. I recognized a big carton of Ocean Spray cranberry juice. I knew what they looked like because Kate drank miniature cartons of it. I went to Jennifer's fridge but there was no juice there, just wine and champagne. I wondered what anchovies were exactly. I looked for cereal and milk but I couldn't find those either. I went back into my room and tried the Discman. It was totalled. I made sure my mobile was switched off.

I went looking for my clothes. They were still in the washing machine, soaking wet. I looked for a tumble dryer but there wasn't one so I took my T-shirt, combats, and underpants and hung them out of the window of my room. I jammed them there with the bottom of the window.

I went into Jennifer's bedroom. I knew I shouldn't be there. She hadn't opened the curtains so it was like everything was in black and white. The air smelt of something she'd just sprayed on, plus a bit of sweat, but nice ladylike sweat. The bed was brass and the bedclothes were white. There was a chest of drawers with a small silver statue on top of a naked woman holding her arms above her head in a way that people only do in statues. I opened one of the drawers. Green knickers with a yellow stripe on the elastic waistband.

I closed the drawer. It squeaked and I pulled a face and listened. I was doing the kind of thing the Popsock Perv probably did. I imagined the sex case 'tecs jumping in on me and doing their spiel. 'You do not have to say anything but anything you do say will be taken down and may be used in evidence against you,' etc. etc. Then I had a horrible idea. I looked up into the corners of the room. I was looking for a CCTV camera but there wasn't one.

My clothes were still wet but I put them on anyway, I couldn't hang about all day inspecting knicker drawers. I wanted to go and get something to eat but Jennifer hadn't left a key. There was a little cupboard next to the front door of the apartment with the electricity meter in it. I found a key in there and tested it. It worked.

Outside, it was cloudy but warm. I jigged about a bit as I walked to try and get my clothes dry. I really missed the Discman; White Stripes would have been good to get dry to. There was a World Bean Inc. nearby. I fancied one of their All Day Breakfast sarnies containing sausage, bacon, egg, and ketchup plus a nice big full milk latte. I was feeling pretty good, considering. Considering I hated my mum and never wanted to see her again. Then I went in the paper shop.

The story took up the front of the *Moon*. It said:

HUNT FOR
MURDER SUSPECT
by John Doe
A much loved national figure is being sought
in connection with the Popsock Perv murder
inquiry. The juvenile disappeared yesterday
after being questioned . . .

It was true. I had been questioned. At least they got
that bit right. I didn't read any more. I got the gist.

In World Bean Inc. I passed on the All Day Breakfast
sarnie; I'd lost my appetite. I just got a double strength
espresso and took it to the back and sat on a high stool
facing the wall. After a bit I realized my right foot
was jigging up and down against the footrest. I stopped
it jigging but about five minutes later I noticed it had
started again. I was thinking so hard it was giving my
foot a mind of its own. What I was thinking was that
it was still true that I hated Mum, but I reckoned I
hated her a little bit less today because otherwise I
wouldn't care what she might read about me in the
papers. I pictured her in bed in hospital, with half eaten
rubber egg on a plate on a tray, the *Moon* open at the
page about me being the major suspect in a murder
inquiry. Mum looked all calm on the outside, but inside
her head it was mayhem. There was a mirror in front
of me. I saw my face going red. My foot was jigging
like a maniac, my face was red as a stoplight. I could

hardly swallow. I looked in my own eyes, my weird animal-giblet eyes, and I knew what I had to do.

I had to get the *Moon* off my back. Show John Doe he'd got the wrong end of the stick. I looked through the paper twice before I found the *Moon*'s telephone number, hidden away on the back page underneath an advert that said 'MALE PROBLEMS'. Then I went and stood outside World Bean Inc. and keyed in the number. After two rings a woman's voice said, 'Moo-oon.'

I said, 'I'd like to speak to Mr John Doe, please.'

There was a pause. Then the voice said, 'Oh, I see. Putting you through.'

The line went dead for a few seconds, then another woman's voice said, 'Newsroom.'

I said, 'I'd like to speak to Mr Doe, please.'

There was a silence. Then the voice said, 'I'm afraid John's very busy. Can I help you?'

I said, 'I need to speak to him. When is he not busy?'

The voice said, 'He's always very busy. Can I help you? What is it in connection with?'

I said, 'Is he there, though?'

The voice said, 'He's in a meeting.'

I said, 'Tell him it's Graham Sinclair.'

The voice hesitated, then the line went dead. I thought she'd cut me off. I was looking at my mobile like it had mumps, wondering what to do next, when I heard a voice coming out of it. I put the mobile to my ear but all I heard was '. . . for you?' It was a man's voice.

I said, 'I'm not the Popsock Perv.'

There was silence, then the man said, 'Well, now. That's not what the police think, is it, Mr Sinclair?'

'I can prove it,' I said. 'You know Park Lane? Be there at three o'clock.' That was before the rush hour so maybe the traffic wouldn't be so bad. My plan was that in the meantime I'd go to Park Lane and suss it out. Decide where I'd go, how high. I wouldn't do anything too big or fancy, I didn't want to really freak people out on the first go. Then I'd phone Jennifer and tell her what I was doing and she could come along too. I knew she'd told me not to do anything stupid but this was an emergency, I couldn't have this crap in the *Moon* every day and Mum reading it and sex case 'tecs giving me a hard time. God knows what they'd do to me next. It saved going to America anyway, and it saved going back up north to get my passport. And I should be able to get some money out of it, enough to stay down here and go to school and pay Mum and Dad back the money I took and pay Jennifer rent and buy her champagne and buy me a new Discman. And make Dad like me a bit more. And make Mum well.

I might try it and nothing would happen. I thought about that. Standing there, closing my eyes, taking the deep breaths, and then—nothing. Nobody even noticing. People just walking past, pushing their buggies with the awnings on the front, riding their plastic trikes, eating their Mr Whippy ice creams. Me standing there like a million other people, just another kid in the park. Except for being chief suspect in a murder inquiry. And the weird hands.

The man said, 'That sounds like a threat, Mr Sinclair. We're a responsible newspaper. We take threats very seriously. I'm not sure what you have planned exactly but

I'm afraid it's my duty to inform the police of what you've just told me.' The line went dead for real this time.

Not good enough, as Dad would say. The *Moon*'s address was next to the telephone number. It was in Canary Wharf, which was that big skyscraper-fest on an island that I'd seen on telly but I didn't really know where it was. At Fulham Broadway tube I asked the ticket bloke and he told me how to get there and sold me the ticket. I could tell he clocked that I was soaking wet but he didn't say anything. Typical London. The tube carriage smelt like a bag of dry roasted peanuts when it's just been opened. It was partly my fault. Even though I was wet I was sweating and my clothes were smelling a bit mouldy like Uncle George's washing machine. People were looking at me, probably thinking I was a weirdo. Hey, look at old Freako over there. I thought, if it rains I'll just look like I've been caught without an umbrella or a cagoule. I'll look normal again. I wished it would rain.

Nobody sat next to me until it got really crowded. Some people even stood up rather than sit next to me. One person was reading the *Moon* but he was quite far away. I watched him for a bit but he never looked at me, or he pretended not to. A girl and a woman were reading paperbacks and there were tourists wearing shorts and white Adidas socks and looking at little maps of London. Some people were English but you could tell they weren't from London because they laughed when the train swayed around or got really crammed with people.

At Canary Wharf you come up on an escalator under this big glass and steel dome. I saw me in that film, the one where I was a scientist with a supermodel girlfriend. The camera was at the top of the escalator looking down and I was getting bigger as I rode up. Then the dome above made me think of Eddie the Feather Man. Cars might crash in Park Lane and then I'd be a murderer, or at least a manslaughterer, and they might stick me in a cage. Wire me up and do tests on me. Stare at me and laugh at me. Walk away and forget I was there.

The Canary Wharf buildings were really tall. As soon as I left the tube station I felt like they were watching me all the time out of the corner of their eye. Clouds shot by behind them. It made me feel dizzy, like when I was lying on my back on the cliffs at Lulworth Cove. There were blokes in suits and classy women walking quite fast, and blokes in blue overalls carrying yellow hard hats and walking slower. A lot of them carried brown bags with coffees etc. in them from the local World Bean Inc., which made me realize I definitely wasn't hungry any more.

I didn't know where I was going. There were big doors with mirrors in them that seemed to go underground, and steps that went up to the base of the tallest and nearest tower. A weirdly dressed girl made a beeline for me. She had on a tight red swimsuit-type thing and really high heels and wore a green squishy rucksack on her back. She smiled and gave me a leaflet and I realized the green rucksack had a stalk, it was supposed to be a chilli pepper. I put the leaflet in the lower pocket of my combats.

I passed a silver Audi in a glass box, with the driver's door open. The real leather upholstery was the colour of mustard. On the road in front of the main tower there were black cabs waiting with their yellow lights on, engines running. It was hot and I wanted it to rain. Then it did rain. A big fat splot, like the day before on the flyover, landed on the concrete in front of me. It was nearly as big as a (normal-sized) hand.

I went through a revolving door and left the weather behind. Inside it was cool. I was in a space that was as big as King's Cross station. It was made of pink and grey stone with a glassy floor and it was hushed and a bit echoey but not too much; the sounds floated rather than pinged around. There was a desk with three security guards sitting behind it. I stood to one side, got the leaflet that the girl had just given me out of my pocket and pretended to be interested in it while I watched what people did.

They just kept on walking, but on the way they flashed a card at the desk and the security guards nodded. Once these people were past the security desk they wriggled off like fish towards a bank of lifts on the other side and disappeared up into the tower. But some people didn't have cards. They stood in a queue. I stood with them. I looked at the leaflet while I waited. It said:

Hot! Hot! Hot!
Please bring the bearer a free Freaking Fridge Bomb at the chilli-est joint on the Wharf

This card entitles you to a complimentary non-alcoholic cocktail at Hot! Hot! Hot!, Canary Wharf's unique food & drink venue with a Latin theme, when you spend at least £10. Offer applicable only between 9a.m.—midday and 4—6p.m. Non transferable. Rules and conditions apply.

I put the leaflet back in my combats. When my turn came I said to the security guard, 'Is this the office of the *Moon*?'

The security guard was a black African man. He had three neat scars on each cheek. He said, 'Pardon me?' He was looking me up and down. I wasn't wet enough to make a puddle but I was still pretty damp.

I said, 'The *Moon* newspaper.'

The guard laughed. His eyes opened wide and his shoulders shook. He said, 'I thought you said, "Is this the surface of the moon?" Oh dear.' When he'd stopped laughing he said I couldn't go through because I didn't have a pass. I asked how I could get one and he said I couldn't but I could leave a message. So I left a message for Mr Doe of the *Moon* newspaper saying that Graham Sinclair was waiting for him in the vestibule, that's what the security man said it was called, and that I had something really important to tell him. Then I went and sat on this black leatherette sofa to wait.

There was a glass table in front of the sofa and it had a few *Moons* on it. I didn't look at them, I didn't want to read how the story about me went on. But I did think about tomorrow's paper. I'd be in it again, but this time I'd be airborne. This time I'd want Mum to read it. I'd leave my mobile on, and if Dad didn't call me, I'd call him. I'd tell him to go and buy a copy and make sure Mum saw it too. He'd be laughing because he'd already seen it and so had Mum; they were both really happy about it. I imagined Dad shaking his head at the other end of the line.

Everything would be fitting into place in his head. All

the things in the coolbox would be tucked up nicely against each other. The lid would fit. He'd be thinking how he used to stare at my hands when I reached for the marg. How they were only good for flossing or scrubbing. How much of a dork-brain could you be? He'd remember the palaver over Kylie Blounce and the police taking me in and realize he'd got the wrong end of the stick. Everyone had got the wrong end of the stick. Big time.

Everyone except Mum, but Mum had been ill. She couldn't help what she did and said because she was sick in the head. But now she would be cured. She would see that it was OK to show the world, that there was nothing wrong with what we both could do. We could be proud of it. Old Freako and his mum could do a double act maybe, when she was better and psyched up for it. And no landing badly this time. She was just out of practice. I could teach her. We had to take it slowly. We could go back to Lulworth Cove and buzz around the cliffs. The grass was nice and springy and we could get more and more ambitious, go higher and further till we were actually going out over the sea. I saw me and Mum in the cool sea air, and Dad a tiny speck down below, clapping, with a big spiral pattern of shells next to him that he'd been making while we practised.

Jennifer came through very fast and silent. I didn't realize it was her at first. I just looked up and there was this classy woman going past. Red lips, black gear that was like a spiral winding up her from knees to neck. It was her scent that made me twig. Her scent fanned out behind her and rocked me like the wake of a ship. I half got up, I half started to say something. The African bloke gave her a full-on smile as she cruised past the security desk. On the other side she turned a corner towards the lifts. And she was gone. I couldn't believe it.

I went back to the security desk. I could still smell her. I said to the bloke, 'Who was that?' Just in case I was mad.

The bloke said, 'That, sir, was a vision of loveliness. Am I right?'

I said, 'What's her name?'

He said, 'What I do know, she not as sweet as she look. Tough cookie that one, they say.' I must have shaken my head because he said, 'Ye-eah. Oh yes. Star investigative reporter of the *Moon* newspaper. Over here, madam. Please investigate *me*. Oh yes.' And he laughed his big African laugh.

Chapter 20

All the way back to Jennifer's on the tube I was thinking about how Jennifer Slater was no better than Kylie Blounce. If it *was* Jennifer Slater. My brain was doing that awful switching thing. The tube would go one stop and I'd think, Don't worry, it was just a classy woman who looked a bit like her and wore the same perfume. When I get back Jennifer will be there in her apartment. I'll persuade her that the Park Lane idea is a good one except we'll have to choose somewhere else because John Doe will have called the cops by now and they'll be casing the joint. But that's easy enough. We'll choose somewhere else, and we'll start planning it.

Then the tube would go another stop and I'd be sure it *was* Jennifer I'd seen. Jennifer worked for the *Moon*. She'd stitched me up. Maybe she was even John Doe. Who else was involved? Derek? Uncle George? The sex case 'tecs? Mum and Dad? Who knows any more; maybe David Batty, ex-Leeds United and ex-England?

When I got in the apartment I called out her name. I went in every room and said, 'Jennifer?' I knocked on the toilet door and said, 'Anyone in there?' The apartment was empty. Then I saw the time on the cooker.

13.07. I went to my bedroom and took off my clothes. They were nearly dry now and felt really cardboardy. I hung them out of the window, jamming them there with the bottom of the frame. I put on the polo shirt and the dressing gown and went back into the living room. My head was like one big permanent explosion. I couldn't believe Jennifer didn't hear it when she came in.

I heard her key in the door. She came down the corridor saying, 'Graham? Are you up yet?' I heard her shoes clattering as she kicked them off, then she came into the living room. She said, 'Ah. You've got the right idea. It's really not nice out there. I wish it'd rain and just have done with it. Did you take your clothes out of the machine? Sorry, I forgot this morning. Which reminds me. We'll have to think about some serious clothes for you at some point. Also, we'll have to think about what you're going to say when they get microphones in front of you. People will expect personality in inverted commas so we'll have to decide what to give them. We can talk about that.'

She took off her shoulder bag and propped it against the fridge. The mobile in it started ringing, that honking sound I didn't like. She said, 'It hasn't stopped all day. You're in demand, I'm telling you. I mean, they don't know it's *you* yet. Don't worry, I haven't given you away. I mean the idea of you. I've floated the idea and it's mega.' The phone stopped ringing. She opened her eyes wide and shook her head. 'Champagne? Shall we?'

She kicked her bag away from the fridge, opened the door and took out a bottle with a gold top on it. She got two tall, thin glasses down from the cupboard then popped the cork which shot off and pinged against the ceiling wires holding up the lights. 'Get used to that sound, Graham,' she said. She concentrated on pouring the champagne. Over her shoulder she said, 'Have you got any problems doing it around tall buildings? I don't mean anthills like Canary Wharf, I mean Manhattan tall. Somebody mentioned it as a possible hazard. I'm talking wind effects.' She turned round and handed me a glass of champagne. 'You'd look nice in a Superman outfit.' She winked at me.

I didn't mean to knock the glass out of her hand. I just meant to push it away, but I was too strong. My hand was too strong. And the glass was too fast for the drink. It flew off in an arc, leaving the champagne in the air for a split second.

The glass smashed on the tiles. Jennifer said, 'Better than the carpet.'

She stared at me and I stared at her. I was wondering whether I had Alzheimer's. I didn't understand anything that was going on. There was no noise in my head, there was silence. But it wasn't a good silence. It was like when you wake up and you can't remember where you are. Or who you are. Then I remembered something, and that was when I said it: 'Where've you been then?'

Jennifer carried on staring at me. She knelt down and didn't take her eyes off me. She shuffled towards where the broken glass was and just glanced down for a split second before looking into my eyes again. She started picking up the bits of glass, except she wasn't really picking them up, she was just stirring them round on the floor with her fingers. And all the time she was looking at me. I could hear both of us breathing, it was that quiet. Eventually she said, 'Where have I *been*?' She was really sarcastic.

I said, 'Yes.'

She said, 'While you've been lolling about on your bony backside I've been out there putting myself out for *you*.' Then she said, 'Ow,' and looked down at her hand. A bead of bright red blood was coming up on her finger. She put her finger in her mouth.

I said, 'Seen any anthills lately?'

She said, 'What are you talking about?'

I said, 'You know. Canary Wharf.'

She said, 'No. I don't know. Are you going to help me pick this glass up?'

I said, 'Only I just happened to be at Canary Wharf this morning and I saw a person who looked amazingly like you. Same perfume and everything. A bit classier than you, though.'

Jennifer went and sat at the kitchen table and rummaged in her bag. She found a packet of tissues and wrapped one around her finger. Then she put her head in her hands and said, 'You're losing me here, Graham.' I could hardly hear her because she was speaking through her hair.

I said, 'Today I did not sit on my whatsit backside. I went to a certain place and saw a certain person.'

Jennifer jumped up and marched out of the room. I heard her feet thumping down the corridor, then stopping, then thumping back up. She stood in the doorway, held her hand out and said, 'Key.'

I gave her the key and she said, 'I'm not having you following me. It's not on, Graham. You do not be weird around me, OK?'

I said, 'I didn't follow you. Are you a reporter on the *Moon* newspaper?'

Jennifer shouted, 'Yes.'

There was silence. You could hear the echo of her shout. Then I couldn't help it, I started to cry.

Jennifer gave me one of her paper tissues. She sat down on the sofa next to me and sort of hugged me a bit, I could feel her bosom against my arm. Then she went and sat on the sofa opposite. I said, 'Have you been writing all those stories about me?'

She said, 'That's not how it works. You don't want to know. Gosh, people bleed.' She sucked on her finger again.

I said, 'But the *Moon*'s done all this horrible stuff about me. They think I'm a perv. Like everyone else. They're Nazi prats. Like some other people I could mention.'

She said, 'The point is, we can help you.'

I said, 'But—' I was going to say 'you' but I couldn't. I said, 'The *Moon*'s been killing me.'

She said, 'Yes. And?'

I said, 'And what?'

She said, 'And before it was killing you, what were we doing? We were loving you. Graham the plane crash hero and all that. Look, I don't expect you to get this, Graham. That's why I didn't tell you earlier. It's just to do with the way things are. Not the way we'd like them to be when we're fourteen, if you don't mind me saying so. But the way they really are, take it or leave it. We've got to give you a profile, keep your story going, we've got to get people ready for the mega-exclusive. The biggest story in the history of newspapers is what it is. In the history of the world. It'd be too much to give it to people all at once. We've got to take them there gradually. So what I'm saying is, it is working. Everything's fine. Honestly. Honestly. Mmmm?'

I didn't understand what she meant. I just nodded.

She got up and said, 'I'm going to give the champagne another try. Want some?'

I said, 'No.'

While she was pouring herself another glass she said, 'Hey, listen. Can you hear it?'

I listened but I couldn't hear anything. Except for London outside the window. That giant wave that never broke. I said, 'No.'

She said, 'Yes you do. You just don't know it yet. It's the sound of the world falling in our lap. Like fruit off a tree.' She sat back on the sofa and said, 'Hey, stop looking so tense. I'll do the worrying, that's what I'm here for. Once we've got the preliminary presentation over with we'll come up with something that does justice to what the world is about to see, this event that will change people's lives for ever—it'll all be thought through down to the finest detail. Oh yes, something else. You might not be so keen on this but we're not wild about

246

the name Graham Sinclair any more.'

I said, 'But that's my name.'

Jennifer said, 'Even Sinclair Graham is better than Graham Sinclair, frankly. So have a think. Maybe there's an old nickname we could use.'

I said, 'No way.'

Jennifer shook her head and said, 'What did your teachers make of you?'

I shouted. It was like a bloke with a really loud voice had taken over my body. 'MY NAME IS GRAHAM SINCLAIR. GRAHAM SINCLAIR IS MY NAME. NOTHING ELSE.'

There was a silence. My voice was still hanging in that room. I thought of it caught up in the ceiling wires, trying to escape but just echoing away. Jennifer got up and went to the fridge. She opened it and got out the champagne and fetched down another glass. She spoke really quietly. 'I will pour this champagne and you will drink it. If you don't want to drink it for yourself you can at least drink it for me. To say thank you for what I've done for you, and what I will be doing. OK?'

She poured it and came and sat next to me. She offered me the glass but I didn't take it.

I suddenly realized I didn't like her lips. Some of her lipstick had come off and underneath it her lip flesh was the colour of boring grey laptops. On her top lip there was a splash of blood where she'd been sucking her finger. I thought of kissing those lips and it wasn't a very nice thought. Her voice went really cold. She said, 'The world is not down to you. It's down to me. Now take the drink.'

The champagne was see-through golden, the colour of happiness. Bubbles rose through it like a million people smiling. I reached out towards the glass. I almost took it, is the truth. But at the last milli-second I switched. I swiped the glass away again but this time my hand was all wrong. It was as big and stupid and clumsy as Uncle George in that leather coat, blundering around the Piano Showroom farting. It followed through and caught Jennifer on the neck. Her head went back and she rolled off the sofa and onto the cream carpet. Her teeth made a funny noise, like a couple of mouse clicks. The glass landed on the sofa and didn't smash. There was a big dark streak on the sofa where the drink spilled.

I thought Jennifer was dead.

Chapter 21

I thought I was the Popsock Perv and I just didn't know it. I got down on the carpet next to Jennifer. Her mouth was open, her eyes were closed, and she was breathing. At least she wasn't turning blue, or choking. One leg was still half on the sofa and the way she was lying, all lolling about, it looked like she'd turned into liquid, poured off the sofa, then solidified again. I was going to shake her, make her wake up. I was kneeling down beside her when she opened one eye. Then the other one flickered open. She didn't move. She just looked at me. I froze. 'I'm sorry,' I said. 'I'm really sorry, I didn't mean—I've got to go, that's all.' I stood up. She still didn't move, except for shaking her head. 'OK?' I said. 'I'm just—'

I went into my bedroom, got my clothes from the window and put them on. They were still a bit damp. I put my mobile in a side pocket of the combats. All the time I was listening out for Jennifer, for her screams or the sound of her dialling. If she tried to stop me, I'd have to escape through the window. Five floors up shouldn't be a problem, except if someone spotted me. But Jennifer didn't make a sound.

I went back into the living room. She was in the same

position. The splash of blood on her lip looked very bright. Her eyes were following me round the room. Her eyes were frightened. It was terrible, the way her eyes were frightened 'Look,' I said, 'I'm sorry. I just didn't want the champagne.' I had an idea.

I fetched her mobile from her bag near the fridge and put it next to her on the carpet. I ran her a glass of water and put that next to her too. I thought I may as well earn some brownie points by being considerate. That was the kind of thing that was mentioned in court and got people a shorter sentence from the judge. 'Right then,' I said. 'See you then.' Jennifer didn't answer, she just shook her head again. And I ran out of her apartment.

I went back to World Bean Inc., got another espresso and sat at the back facing the wall again. I decided it was best if I carried on hating Mum. That way, I wouldn't mind when she found out for definite I was a murderer. Sitting there, I could have looked at my face in the mirror but I wasn't ready for a close-up of the Popsock Perv. I looked at my hand instead, the hand that had done it. Just below my little finger, it was growing little white hairs. I hadn't noticed them before. I felt sorry for my hand. It had just got carried away. I wondered how many other times it had got carried away. I wondered when I would stop remembering what had just happened. Because if I really was the Popsock Perv, that must be how it worked. I would do something awful, then have a sort of Alzheimer's episode and completely forget about it. People had been right about me all along. I was a Freako and a Perv. That nutter I reckoned I'd seen in Bishop's Park, I must have made him up. I'd invented an imaginary Popsock Perv to give myself a licence to kill. I was a pervy 007, I'd go out and do pervy things with girls and their socks etc. and forget about them. I waited to stop remembering but I couldn't. I saw the surprise in Jennifer's eyes. I heard her teeth clicking as she fell. I saw her terrified eyes following me around her living room. And then I thought, how would I know whether I'd stopped remembering if I couldn't remember the thing I'd stopped remembering?

About twenty minutes went past and I still remembered. And I started to feel better about things. It was an accident. I'd just meant to knock the glass away but my hand was a bit too big and strong sometimes. That bloke I'd seen in Bishop's Park, he'd been real. I could still remember what his head felt like under the heel of my trainer. And anyway, I still remembered what had happened. If I really was the Popsock Perv I'd surely remember all the other horrible things he had done, which were much worse than what I'd done to Jennifer. I wasn't a Freako or a Perv, but I was in trouble with a capital T-R etc. Big time. Because if Jennifer reported me to the cops they wouldn't believe it was an accident. They'd love it. They'd think they'd nailed me. They'd closed the case of the Popsock Perv.

I got off the stool to check all my pockets for money. Thirty-one quid forty-four p, plus I found the piece of paper with Kate's numbers on it. All washed out from the rain and the washing machine but you could still read it. And that's how come I called Kate.

*   *   *

I could have called her on the showroom number but Derek or Uncle George might have answered. When I tried her mobile, she had it switched off so I left a message asking her to call me and giving her my number. Then I switched my mobile on and set off walking in the general direction of the showroom. Every time I saw a police car with its light flashing and siren going I reckoned it was heading for Jennifer's apartment. Just in case they were on major Spak Alert, I kept well back against the walls and railings and under shop awnings and on the pavement side of bus stops.

It started to rain. They weren't big drops this time. It started off as drizzle and got harder and harder till it was making a drumming noise on the top of bus shelters. It stood on the roads and tyres made waves of it. I got soaked, which meant I needn't have bothered getting my clothes dry. My trainers were getting really scragged up. The toes on my right foot started feeling wet.

I didn't have a plan. I'd run out of plans. I just thought I'd see Kate. I thought maybe Kate would make everything OK. She'd talk to Jennifer and Mum and Dad and the cops and they'd believe her, and then, seeing as she'd got me fake ID, maybe she could find me somewhere to live and I could go to school down here and she'd play a piano concert and I'd sit in the front row and give her a standing ovation. But first I had to tell her. So that's what I was going to do. I was going to meet Kate and tell her. That was my plan, my last one.

The thing about walking in heavy rain is, you can cry

your eyes out and no one notices as long as you do it silently.

My mobile rang. I stood in the doorway of a Happy Snaps and looked at the number on the display. No way was I taking a call from Mum or Dad. I didn't recognize the number at first. Then I realized it was Kate's. I said, 'Kate.'

She was whispering. She said, 'Did you nick money off your mum and dad?'

I said, 'You can't nick money off your own mum and dad. Why?'

She said, 'Cos it's been mental round here.'

I said, 'Are you in the showroom?'

She said, 'I'm outside. Mister P's showing this bloke round what he's going to sell it to.'

I said, 'He's selling the showroom?'

She said, 'It's been weird. I think he's flipped. Plus, your dad on the phone yelling at him, the cops coming round looking for you. Have you seen the *Moon* today? Where are you? What are you doing?'

I arranged to meet her outside the World Bean Inc. near the showroom, the one they closed after the crash. I said, 'See you in a bit then.' Just as I was about to switch off I had an idea. I said, 'Hang on. You know the keys to the Merc hanging in the toilet cubicle? Can you fetch them with you?'

Kate had her Pumas on. We took ages finding the Merc. First of all we tried up in Hammersmith because that was one of his favourite places to park. Then we started working back towards the showroom. The nearer we got the jumpier I got. Kate wasn't good with cars. She kept saying, 'Over there', and when I looked it was a Lexus or a Saab and sometimes it wasn't even the right colour. It wasn't raining as hard as earlier but it was enough to get Kate wet. She turned her lower lip down and pretended to cry, saying, 'Look at my beautiful hair,' and pulling at the bits that used to be purple and had gone black with the rain. But she didn't really mind, she was laughing. She never asked me what we were doing. She trusted me.

It was me who spotted it. It was parked halfway across two disabled bays and had got a ticket. I took the ticket out from under the wiper and chucked it in a puddle. I zapped the central locking and opened the passenger door for Kate. She said, 'Most kind,' and got in. I had to adjust the driver's seat so I could reach the pedals. Kate was wriggling her bum on the seat. The leather was squeaking. She said, 'Check this out.'

I said, 'I know.'

I started driving. I didn't know where. I just felt nice and safe in the car. It was good, having Kate sat next to me. She brought her visor down and fiddled with her hair in the mirror. Then she turned to me and put her Uncle George voice on. 'So did you really boff that bird then, Strummer?'

I said, 'She's got horrible lips.'

Kate said, 'What, to kiss?'

I said, 'Euurggh. No way.'

Kate said, 'OK then. Just checking.' Then she said,

'Have you seen the paper today? Derek was wetting himself.'

'I bet,' I said. 'Did he tell the cops?'

'I think he did, yeah,' she said.

'I'm not a murderer.'

Kate said, 'I know.'

'How d'you know?'

'I can tell,' she said.

I didn't want to carry on lying, I wanted to be straight with Kate. I was going to tell her who Jennifer was and what I'd done to her, but I decided to wait. Everything could wait now. I was almost there. Instead I said, 'If Derek had been in World War Two he'd have sucked up to the Nazis.'

The wipers were in manic mode, the windows were getting all steamed up. I put on the fan really strong and loud. Kate made circles in the steam on the passenger window. It reminded me of when I was a kid and I got in trouble for doing that to the kitchen windows. I said, 'Why's Uncle George selling then?'

She said, 'Cos, I dunno, he just decided. Like this morning. And you know what he's like, he just does it. He's putting everything into the dentist's up north. He said me and Derek could go and work there but I said no way. He's given Derek a promotion but he'll be on a bit less money but Porky says that's still like a ten per cent rise cos things are cheaper up there.'

I said, 'He got four grand off this Merc in a car auction up there.' The wipers began to squeak. I turned them down to ordinary speed.

She said, 'I'm mellow anyway cos I've got this piano

audition. It's not classical but it's all right. It's the sister of a friend of my brother; she's got this band. She's kosher. Her great-uncle is Jimmy Cliff.'

'That's funny,' I said, 'cos I was having this sort of daydream earlier. You were playing a piano concert and I was in the front row and you got a standing ovation.'

'That's sweet,' she said. 'Thank you. Where are we going?'

I said, 'I don't know really. I thought we could just drive for a bit.' That was a lie, I did know. I looked at the petrol gauge. On red. But maybe the thirty odd quid would get us there.

Kate said, 'Are we going out of London? Ooo, scary. I haven't done that much. I haven't even been to the seaside. I mean, besides where Mum comes from. Her front garden was the beach. But not in England. It gives me the Herberts.'

I said, 'What's a Herbert?'

She said, 'OK, the whatevers.'

I said, 'Why?'

She said, 'Cos people stare at you.'

I said, 'Cos you're black?'

She put on an Ali G accent and said, 'Is it cos I is black?' Then she said, 'Yes. So where are we going?'

'Home,' I said, and that wasn't a lie.

We left London behind. It was like it died. One minute there were streets and people holding umbrellas and carrying brown takeaway bags that made you imagine the smell of Chicken Jalfrezi. Then there were sofa warehouses and storage units and Merc dealerships and the wipers were going like it was the beginning of a rock song and the bass would come in, followed by the shish-shish of drums. Then there were fields and sheep and cows. And if you stopped all the cars on the M1 and listened, you wouldn't hear that wave about to break any more. The wave had broken. It had died. I said, 'It's not so bad is it, being outside London?'

Kate said, 'I might turn into salt any minute. I can feel myself going.' She stretched her arms out and kicked off her Pumas and yawned.

I said, 'I like your Pumas. Do they let in water?'

She said, 'Not that I know of.'

I had a thought. Uncle George would have discovered that his car was missing by now. I didn't say anything for a bit, I was concentrating. The rain had stopped but the road was still slick and shiny. The headlights of the cars coming up behind were all blurred and bright. Kate turned round to look through the back window then said, 'Why d'you keep looking in the mirror?'

'I don't,' I said. I wasn't going to tell her I was waiting for blue flashing lights, that the cops were probably looking for me on four counts, i.e. robbery, attempted murder, suspicion of mass murder, and car theft.

Kate lifted her right hand and pinched my neck. She started to massage it, digging in quite hard with her fingers. It hurt and felt better at the same time. Her earrings tinkled as her fingers moved. She said, 'Let it go, d'you know what I'm saying?' And I switched. I was happy. I was steering with my right hand, just using thumb and forefinger. I felt I was part of the car. Even

257

if I stopped steering, it would go where I wanted it to go. I put my left hand on my left knee. My combats were still damp. They gave the car that mouldy smell. I was going to apologize for the smell but I didn't want to draw attention to it.

Kate put her right hand on top of my left hand. 'Go on,' she said.

'What?' I said.

She said, 'Didn't you play that game when you were a kid? It's not so easy with just one hand but you can still do it. Pull your hand out, that's it, and put it on top of mine.' And she put her left hand on top of my left, pulled her right one out from underneath and put it on top of her left. And so we played that game that I had avoided as a kid, building a tower of hands to the stars.

I could feel Kate looking at me. I said, 'We need to find a garage. How much money you got?'

She said, 'Nothing. I didn't know we were going on holiday. I thought you nicked a load anyway.'

I said, 'I've got about thirty quid. I'm not sure if it'll get us there.'

Kate said, 'Can we turn back? My mum'll be getting worried.'

I said, 'How old are you?'

She said, 'Seventeen.'

I was amazed. I said, 'Is that all?'

She said, 'Yes. Can we turn back?'

I saw a BP garage coming up. From a distance it looked like a giant bouncy castle. I said, 'We'll just nip in here.'

I squeezed the trigger on the pump till I'd put in a penny less than everything I had. I wanted to keep a penny for superstitious reasons. When I paid, the bloke was staring through the windows at the Merc. He said, 'Left-hand drive, is it? Get your dad to pay next time, OK?' and I said, 'OK.' When I got back in the car I said, 'You can't just turn round on a motorway. I'll have to go on a bit.' Kate didn't say anything. She put her Pumas back on.

After a bit she said, 'So what's happening? What's this about?'

I said, 'I just want you to meet somebody. Can't you phone your mum and tell her you'll be late?'

Kate said, 'Meet who?'

I said, 'My mum.'

She said, 'How much money did you take?'

I said, 'I was just borrowing it.'

She said, 'Porky said your dad said your mum was really upset about it.'

I said, 'My mum's touched up here.' I tapped myself on the head. 'I mean big time. She's in hospital.'

Kate said, 'Is that one of your secrets?'

I said, 'Yes. But it's all going to be OK. I'm going to sort it.'

Kate said, 'I'm scared to meet her.'

'Don't be,' I said. 'We're going to make her happy. What about you anyway? You've got to tell me a secret now.'

She said, 'Why is saying Herberts so funny? You laughed when I said it.'

I said, 'Stop changing the subject.'

She said, 'OK then. You know I said my brother was

259

in a young offenders' institution for robbing someone. Well, he isn't. He's in an adult jail and it's not for robbing someone.'

I said, 'Is it worse?'

She said, 'Well, it's not going to be better, is it? I'm not saying any more till you've told me your other secret.'

'Soon,' I said.

The mouldy smell had gone, there was a nice smell in the Merc now, a mixture of the leather and Kate. She'd forgotten about her mother. She was humming the tune that Mr Choppin made when you opened the show-room door. After a while the smell of the leather and of Kate and the sound of her voice all got together and knocked quietly on the door of my head, asking if they could come in. And my head let them in.

Fifteen miles to go. The petrol gauge was coming back down towards red but we'd get there. It was almost dark. The sky looked like a torn curtain again. Behind it, like a giant pale room, was a greenness. I was steering with my left hand now, still using just thumb and finger. I was happy, bursting with excitement. We were nearly there and it was all going to be OK. I stretched the fingers of my right hand. They made that rustling sound, like dry leaves.

Kate said, 'What's that noise?'

I said, 'I don't hear anything.'

Chapter 22

The Merc had been driving itself and I'd been daydreaming about Kate meeting Mum and everything slotting into place.

'Uh-o,' said Kate. 'Accident.' A wodge of blinking blue lights lit up the road ahead. The brake lights were going on on the cars in front of us. The Merc carried on driving itself: it slowed down and pulled over onto the hard shoulder. 'What are you doing?' said Kate.

'It's not an accident,' I said. 'It's a roadblock.'

'How d'you know?' she said.

'I just reckon,' I said. 'Cos it's for me.'

'*Are* you the Popsock Perv then?'

'D'you think I am?' I said.

'I told you,' she said. 'No I don't.'

'Why not? Everybody else does.'

Kate said, 'Cos Derek said it. And the *Moon* said it. Whatever the *Moon* says, the opposite is true. They said stuff about my brother. They said—but I can't tell you, not yet. That's my secret. What they said, though, was like saying stone is water, do you know what I'm saying? Kate Norley is the woman, this is her wisdom and you'd better believe it.' (Where d'you think I got the wisdom stuff from?) She unbuckled her seatbelt. 'They're after you, aren't they? What are we going to do?'

My head was very calm. Everything seemed simple. 'I'll show you,' I said.

Kate said, 'Ow, I've got my earrings caught.' She was hanging round my neck as I'd asked her to. We were standing between the Merc and the grass bank of the hard shoulder. It wasn't a place for humans to be really. Too noisy and cold. Every time a car went by it was like the air swerved. Cars began to slow because of the hold-up ahead and people were looking at us as they drove by. They weren't that interested, it was just something to do. They didn't know I was about to give them a serious gawp-fest.

It was nice having Kate's face close to mine. I said, 'Hang about,' and she laughed and said that was what she was doing. 'I mean . . .' I said, and I untwisted her earrings for her. Then I said, 'Go on, take your feet off the ground,' and then she really was just hanging there. She wasn't that heavy but it didn't feel right. 'Let's start again,' I said. 'I think you'll have to get on my back like you're a backpack.' I almost said chilli pepper.

'What is going on?' said Kate. 'It's a joke, right?'

I said, 'I assure you it's no laughing matter,' which is what Dad said to me once about something stupid I'd done. It made me laugh even more, I couldn't help it, which sent him ballistic. 'Just put your arms round my neck.' I leant forward a bit, taking her weight. 'Now just lift your feet off the ground.' I leant forward a bit more, I was taking her whole weight now. It felt better. I had no idea whether this was going to work but I had no option. I put my arms out and flexed my fingers a bit.

'There's that noise again,' said Kate. 'What I heard in the car. What is it?'

'It's my hands,' I said.

'Oh, sorry,' she said.

'No it's OK,' I said. 'Are you feeling all right?'

'Are *you*?' she said.

But I didn't reply. I'd shut my eyes. I was starting to take the deep breaths. My hands were crackling, my knees were bending. 'Whatever you do, don't let go,' I said. 'OK?' I felt Kate's head moving up and down against the back of my head. And I just went for it.

We were like the whoosh on Kate's Pumas. I took us straight up like a space rocket; I'd never done that before. I hardly knew what I was doing. It was like driving the Merc, I was on automatic pilot. Kate was shouting stuff in my ear, not words just sounds: screams and coughs. I could feel her body shaking against mine but it wasn't heavy, it was no weight at all. Kate felt as light as Baby Ade. Car horns were going off down below. The M1 looked like a bit of bacon with the white lights on one side and the red on the other. The pilot in my head pushed the joystick forward and that was a whole new feeling for Kate. We were shooting along like a bullet through little puffs of cloud. And finally she could speak proper words. She shouted in my ear.

'Huh, Graham, I don't reckon this is much of a secret.'

Then she laughed and shouted, 'No, this is just the most amazing thing that anyone has ever done since, since, *ever*.' Then she made a noise that was something like this: 'Aaaaaaaa, eeeeee, weeeeee, oooooo.' I was pretty chuffed. It proved something once and for all. It proved I wasn't the Popsock Perv. It proved I wasn't old Freako. It proved what Mum said. I was a remarkable young man.

When we landed, me and Kate couldn't speak for about ten minutes. With Kate it was because she was gob-smacked. With me, it was because my whole body felt like jelly. I'd never done it for so long, or gone so far. But you know what, having Kate round my neck didn't make it harder. It made it easier. Better than holding Baby Ade. Better than having the whole world in your hands. We were in the car park of the hospital where Mum was. I took us back into the shadows in case anyone was on the look-out for me. Kate stood bent over with her hands on her knees and her hair hanging down so I couldn't see her face properly. I got a bit worried at one point, I thought she was going do a Kylie Blounce and turn weird on me, but eventually she lifted her head up and smiled and her earrings tinkled. Then she kissed me. On the lips. 'It's a dream, though, right?' she said.

'No,' I said. 'Now it's your turn.' I was still breathing heavily.

'What?' she said.

'You know what. Your secrets. Both of them. Right now.' I held out my open hand like her secrets were coins. I laughed. 'Come on.'

'Oh all *right*,' she said, mock moaning. 'I s'pose you deserve it, just about. Come here.'

I bowed my head and she whispered in my ear for about thirty seconds. Her breath was all hot and tickly on my ear. When she had finished she stepped back and put her hands behind her back and smiled, but it was the sort of smile you do to stop yourself crying. I wanted to kiss her like she'd just done to me but I wasn't well up on that sort of stuff so I just said, 'Thanks.' Then I put what Kate had told me in a coolbox in my head marked 'Kate' so I could open it later and look at it properly, when I had more time and the world wasn't so full-on mad. Then I said, 'Are you OK? Sure? Don't move. I'll be back. Ten minutes max.'

I was feeling better already. My shoulders ached a bit and my neck was sore where Kate had held on too tight, but otherwise I felt Park Lane. More than Park Lane, more like a million Park Lanes laid end to end. I walked round to the front of the hospital and counted up five floors. It wasn't that late and most rooms still had lights on. Most of them also had vases of flowers in the windows. I could just walk in the main door and go up to the ward and ask to see my mother. It was allowed. But chances were I was a wanted man by now, even up here. Or I could just fly up to the fifth floor and cruise along outside the windows till I found which her room was. I knew the windows in the rooms were sealed, but at the end of the block were a row of frosted windows and one of the small top ones was propped open. I reckoned I was small enough to wriggle through. And if anybody inside saw me, well, it was the nuthouse wing.

No one would believe them. They wouldn't believe it themselves.

Now my superstitions were paying me back. I got her window right first time. There was Mum, propped in bed, asleep with her mouth open. Her black eyes and that horrible mark on her forehead made her head look like an old bit of fruit, which made me sad. Her hands were outside the covers. I realized I'd never looked at her hands before, I mean really looked. They were just Mum's hands, so what was the point? But now there *was* a point. I grabbed the window ledge while I clocked them. They were quite big. They were knobbly and a bit purple. But they weren't freakshow material. They didn't look like flippers or boxing gloves or campervans or David Batty's footie boots or unpleasant bits of monkey.

Which is why, as a matter of fact, Mum wasn't as good as me at flying.

I got in, just, through the frosted window and wriggled down on to a toilet. The toilet door opened into the corridor. No one was about. I counted back three doors and opened the door as quietly as I could. I was half in the room before Mum woke up. She turned round and let out this yell. 'Ssshh. It's me,' I said.

She said, 'Oh,' and covered her mouth. We both waited to see if anyone had heard. Then Mum whispered, 'They've been here. The police. They're looking for you. What have you done? Terrible things, they say, Graham.'

'It's OK,' I said.

266

Mum said, 'It's not OK, love.' And she burst into tears. She kept her hand over her face. She was trying to stop the snuffles sounding too loud. 'It's my fault, I know. I am sorry. I thought what I did was for the best. That's what your Grandma did with me. I—'

I said, 'No, it's OK. You'll see. We've got to go.'

She said, 'We can't go anywhere. Where can we go?'

I said, 'Home. To Dad's. You'll see.'

She said, 'We can't go there. They'll be looking.'

'It doesn't matter,' I said. 'Not any more.'

Mum said, 'They lock the doors here anyway.'

I said, 'So?' and I looked at the window.

Mum said, 'Graham, how did you—?' Then she said, 'Absolutely not.'

'You can just hang on to me,' I said. 'We've got to be quick.' I grabbed her hand and pulled her out of bed. She squeezed my hand and we both looked down at where our hands were all scrunched up together. She smiled. Her grip was strong.

'Oo, it's cold,' she said. 'Let me put on my special dressing gown.' I got her silk dressing gown from Singapore down from behind the door and put it round her. It was the colour of meringues. She put her slippers on and I took a couple of notes from the top drawer.

We tiptoed down the corridor to the toilet. There was hardly room for both of us in the cubicle. We giggled. Mum said, 'Is it true what George said, you stole his pride and joy?'

I said, 'He let me drive it, you know, down in London. Sometimes he *made* me even when I didn't want to.'

Mum said, 'He never.'

I said, 'He did.' I looked at the window and then at Mum.

She said, 'I'll never get through there.'

I said, 'No probs,' and wriggled through. I stood on the outside ledge and poked my head back through. 'Come on,' I said. 'It's easy.'

'I can't do it, Graham,' Mum said. She shook her head. She was crying again. 'I just can't. I'm scared.'

I put my hands through and held her under the arms. 'Yes, you can,' I said. And with a little lift from me Mum slipped through the window as smooth as honey off a hot spoon.

We stood side by side on the ledge, looking down on the roofs of two ambulances and a row of wheelie bins. Mum said, 'It's like being on a diving board.'

I said, 'I know.'

She said, 'I can't do the next bit. I've never been any good at it. These aren't really up to it.' She lifted her hands and turned them over. 'You should have seen my granda's. He died before you were born. Like dustbin lids.'

'Yes you can,' I said. 'You just don't know it. But we'll sort that later. Just hang on round my neck like a backpack, OK? Ready?'

I thought Kate had run off at first. Or maybe the cops had picked her up. I whispered, 'Kate?' No answer.

Mum said, 'What are you doing? It may look nice but there's no warmth in this dressing gown, you know.'

I said, 'I want you to meet someone. Kate!'

No answer. Then Kate came out of the shadows. Mum said, 'Oh God.'

Kate said, 'This has to be a dream, right. Or I'm going mad.'

I said, 'Mum, this is my friend Kate. You said I had to find a real girl and here she is.' I was going to say she wasn't classy and she wasn't clodhopping and that was the whole point. She was just Kate. But it wouldn't have made any sense to Mum or Kate, and anyway Kate might have been insulted, even though it was the opposite of an insult.

Mum said, 'Pleased to meet you, Kate.'

Kate said, 'Pleased to meet you, Mrs Sinclair.' They shook hands and for a milli-second I thought Kate was going to high-five Mum, which would have been really funny, but she didn't. She was on her best behaviour.

Mum said, 'I'm cold,' and Kate put her arm round Mum's shoulders.

We got a taxi outside the front of the hospital. Me and Kate distracted the driver so he couldn't get a look at Mum as she got in the back in her nightie and dressing gown and slippers. Then I got in the back with Mum and Kate got in the front. Nobody said anything for a bit. We were driving through my town. I'd done loads of things on these streets. I'd even been happy occasionally. I felt guilty for thinking it was a craphole. If London was like a very cool older brother, this town was the weirdo nipper you were ashamed of. But it wasn't its fault. Me hating it was like people calling me Spakky or Perv, i.e. unfair. It was what it was. I wound down the window to hear it better. No sound except for a knackered exhaust. No wave about to break.

'Urggh, what's that smell?' said Kate.

I said, 'Dog food factory.'

Mum said, 'It's never.'

The driver's head went up and down. He said, 'Aye, reet enough. Where d'you want dropping?'

Just before we got to our road, a police car whizzed by in the opposite direction. The taxi dropped us right outside the house. I gave the driver a tenner and didn't wait around for the change. We got Mum round the side of the house, out of sight of any neighbours that might have been looking out. I was going to go in through the side door but I saw the light was on in the shed. I whispered, 'Shed.' I knocked on the door then pushed Mum and Kate through in front of me.

Dad had these wrap-around welding glasses on. He was holding a small cylinder with a blowtorch attachment. The shed stank of cigars and whisky. Half a cigar was smoking in the ashtray. Dad's eyes looked huge behind the welding glasses. 'Hell's bells,' he said.

I said, 'Hi, Dad.'

Dad said, 'Hi, Dad? Faith, what—?'

Mum said, 'Since when did you smoke?'

Dad said, 'Since when did you know everything?' Then he noticed Kate. 'Who are you?' he said.

Mum said, 'That's Kate. She's just a real person and a real friend, so that's fine.'

Dad said, 'What is she doing here? What are you doing here?'

Kate said, 'I'm allowed.'

Dad said to me, 'Christ almighty, boy. You can't just turn up like this. It's my duty to report you. I'm sorry but the offences are really serious. The little bastard tried to kill someone, Faith. Can you believe it?'

'That's not true,' I said.

Dad said, 'You can't stop yourself, can you? We've really tried, your mother and me. It's nearly killed us, it really has. It's broken our hearts. Look at your mother, Graham. Look at your poor mother. But the time has come, boy, when you need locking up. For your own good as much as everyone else's. I'm calling the police. End of story.'

Dad put his hand on the telephone. Kate put her hand on his. 'Don't,' she said. 'Not yet. Come outside first.'

Mum said, 'Please, Vince. Listen to her. It'll just take a minute. Then you can do what you like.'

But Dad pushed Kate away and dialled 999. Kate said, 'Come on,' and we followed her out of the shed. I didn't know what to do any more. I'd run out of ideas. Kate got between me and Mum and took our hands. She pulled us out into the street. She lifted our hands and joined them together, then stepped back and looked at us like we were a wall she'd just painted. Then she opened her mouth and started screaming. It was the noises she'd made when we were flying:

'Aaaaaaaa, eeeeee, weeeeee, oooooo,' etc. etc.

Dad came rushing out of the shed. 'Has the world gone mad?' he shouted. 'Shush shush shush shush, stop it, stop it, you barmy female. Get in the house, all of

271

you, and wait there while the police come. They'll be here any minute.' But Kate just carried on screaming, and Dad had to shout to make himself heard till he was just making a huge racket too, and then the front doors started to open up and down the street. The light started to pour out of the front doors. And the people started to pour out of the light.

And it was *Close Encounters* all over again. Out there was the alcoholic and the nurse and apple-smelling Kylie and Mr Blounce and Brian with his huge feet and Brian's mum and dad and six or ten other Spakky-callers and their mums and dads. All these people who had hated me with their eyes and made Mum go mad with their eyes. But they weren't laughing, like in my dream. They were watching and waiting.

Mum squeezed my hand, she nearly broke my fingers, and smiled at me. And now I twigged what Kate was doing. I lifted my hands up. I flexed them. I felt them growing like a speeded-up film of a flower opening. I looked at Mum and nodded at her to lift her hands too. The crackling sound our four hands made was like ten firecrackers going off at once. And while the firecrackers were going off I was looking straight at Dad, straight in his eyes (he blinked first—result!). The crowd gasped, then went silent again.

Beyond all the lights from windows and doors, behind the figures of all the silently waiting people, there were blue flashes. The cops had arrived. Two big silhouettes came scrunching up the middle of the road. They pushed through the other silhouettes. They kept on coming till they turned into three dimensions and I saw that one of them was

Nostrils the sex case 'tec. Light was glinting off his earring. He shouted, 'Graham Sinclair, I'm detaining you—'

Kate said, 'Back off, OK?'

'Dad,' I said, 'just watch. That's all you have to do.'

I gave Mum's hand a squeeze. We looked at each other and closed our eyes. We stretched our arms and flexed our hands again. Mum's fingers crackled a milli-second before mine. I whispered to her, 'It's OK. You can do it. No problem.'

'Believe him, Mr Sinclair,' said Kate. She turned towards the street. 'And all you lot. You staring lot out there. You know what we say in London? We say, "Graham Sinclair is the man. This is his wisdom".'

Nigel Richardson is the author of two previous books, *Breakfast in Brighton* and *Dog Days in Soho*, and since 1992 has been deputy travel editor of the *Daily Telegraph*. He has also written several plays and a drama series for BBC Radio Four. He was born in the Midlands, grew up in Yorkshire and Sussex, and now lives in south-west London. He is a big fan of dogs and of Wolverhampton Wanderers FC. *The Wrong Hands* is his first novel for Oxford University Press.